GHOST GUN

A NOVEL

CC ECK

MIDBLOCK PRESS

For my beloved family,
none of whom know I wrote this book.

1

———

ELIJAH THOMAS-ENGEL

Everyone thought she was my nanny. That's how she tells it. Just assumed she was another Caribbean immigrant caring for another white kid whose parents were working downtown. I guess correcting people was exhausting, because after a few months she began to just go with it. Sometimes she'd even speak in a ridiculous Jamaican accent to make me laugh and to match the expectations of whatever well-intentioned but stupid-as-fuck white mother or father was trying to engage. And that's the issue, really. That's what they don't get. What you don't get. The small concessions made every day, all day, just to get through the day. The swallowing of pride. The relentless humiliation. It's just not practical to stand up to every insult and infraction. Gotta pick your battles, is what she says. My mom. And I guess that's why she's told me the story a million times. Not that she's picked many battles recently.

Even now we confuse people. Confuse you. Like when they announce "premium cabin" at the airport and we roll up with our first-class tickets. They look at me and they're cool. They look at my sister and they're cool. Then they look at our mother and there's always that flicker of a question in their eyes. Like what's with the Black lady? She a celebrity? Do I know her from some TV show, or maybe she was a professional athlete? Too skinny and young to be Oprah. Not muscular enough and too old to be Venus or Serena. And when they don't recognize her from the short list of Black celebrities in their internal Rolodex, that question is there again: who's the Black lady with the first-class ticket?

Until they see my dad straggling along behind us, probably talking on the phone, probably stabbing at the air with his pointer finger. Yeah, see, because when the family presents as a unit, the world can wrap its head around our genetic tableau, even if you don't like it. You all quickly formulate a narrative — and I'm not only talking you white folks here — that goes something like this:

The Black lady was super sexy back in the day, probably a model, and the rich white dude tasted the dark meat and liked it, and, damn, isn't it just remarkable how mixed kids are always more attractive than the sum of their parts, especially if they skew whiter in skin tone and the genetic roulette topped them off with those perfect not-too-tight, not-too-loose ringlets.

And who's to say this kinda snap origin story is wrong, or at least not partly right? But fuck 'em anyhow. Fuck all y'all. Yeah, for thinking you know so damn much all the damn time. Because no one knows the full picture, so stop fuckin' fronting.

———

But it's not the whole family this time. Dad's not flying down unless Grandpa is actually gonna die. He didn't say as much, but we all know the deal. So when "premium cabin" is called and the three of us step up, Mom gets the questioning look from the ticketing agent and every wannabe clogging the gate with their "Comfort+" tickets. I can't tell if Mom has a reaction because she's got the shades on. Maybe she doesn't even notice anymore, immune or numb. We head down the skybridge, the first ones on the plane other than some old biddy in a wheelchair.

I'm not sure if these tickets end up expensed to the Family Office, but however they're accounted for it's pretty fucked if you consider the reality we're about to step into. I googled it and a first-class round-trip ticket to Mobile is $3558. Better than the chartered jet, but not a figure I can share with our cousin, Shawna, whose mother works for the city and gets paid $36,000 a year. And they're the well-off relatives with a house and mortgage. If Grandpa knew, he'd probably break into tears. Start talking about how he wished he'd been there for Mom, how he made a mistake by leaving Grandma, how he should have fought for custody. And then he'd go on about how Grandma was white and had more money, and that her parents, my great-grandparents, were together and had more money and were white. Always circles back to skin color and how Natasha and I aren't proud or accepting of the Blackness in us, the Blackness inherited from him. And underlying it all is the tension over resources and whether Mom should be more of a redistributor of wealth from her rich white husband to her poor Black southern relatives. Grandpa likes to quote scripture about it. That one about it being easier for a camel to pass through the eye of a needle than for a rich man to enter the kingdom of God. Shit's fucked. The way everything gets scrutinized. What my sister and I wear, what car we rent, what hotel we're staying at, what stories we choose to tell about our lives up north. Less is more is what I'm learning.

"Take the headphones off, both of you."

I can read Mom's lips. I elbow my sister. We're settled in our seats, flight underway. Guess I misread the situation. I thought Mom was gonna sink into her medicated interior and I'd get to watch something from New Releases. Turns out it might be lecture hour. Off come the headphones.

"The cardiologist won't give me anything definitive, so we'll head for the hospital first. Find out what's going on. Then we'll check in at the hotel. Then probably take everyone out to eat, or at least order food for whoever's around."

My sister nods, eyes still on her book. She's old-school like that. Abandoned the e-reader at eleven. I can't remember what set her off, but she's committed. Likes "the smell and tactile feel." Also "the fact that if you turn a page wrong, you might cut your finger." It'd be fucking cliché if she didn't actually seem to have a deep and genuine love affair going with them. The books and the pages. I see her sniffing them, eyes closed. I find her asleep in bed with them. She's fifteen and reading *Anna Karenina* for the third or fourth time. Makes me wonder how it's all gonna play out. She's been told her entire life that she could be a model because of her height and "exotic" look, but her posture is going to shit because all she does is hunch over books of a thousand pages or more. Seriously, looks like some lonely heron staring down into a marsh, especially if her hair is pulled back in a bun.

Dad seems cool with the idea that Natasha will end up a writer or academic, a latitude in career paths he's never allowed me. Maybe because of gender. Or because I'm first-born. With me, it's always venture capital or law or ideally some hybrid of the two. He lobbied for me to apply early action to Yale because of their dual MBA-J.D. program, and the higher odds of admission if you attend undergrad there. Not sure where he got it, but he emailed me a breakdown of admission stats that also included average salaries for graduates — five years out, ten years, and of course the size of donations back to the beloved *alma mater*. It's the type of shit he's always handing me. He hasn't said whether he wants me to take over the Family Office but it's clear that, in his mind, the key to my future is the preservation and growth of the wealth he's preserved and grown himself. I'm supposed to "safeguard assets in uncertain times," because by safeguarding assets I'm "safeguarding us". He's always going on about ratio of cash, equities and real estate holdings vis-à-vis geopolitical variables like social and political unrest, climate change, and some "inevitable systemic shock". Which I guess is something like a dirty bomb that takes out New York or DC. Or a catastrophic earthquake that drops the entire Northwest into the ocean and sends a mega tsunami off to decimate all peoples of the Pacific Rim. Or the AI apocalypse. He hasn't told me if we already own a bunker, and how we'd get to it if the shock comes, but I know he's engaged in some serious fucking due diligence.

"Where are we staying?" asks Natasha.

"Same place," says Mom. "Downtown. Why?"

"Because if we're stuck there like last time, for hours and hours, like if you're off at the nursing home or hospital, I want to be able to go out this time. Room service sucked."

Mom shifts her weight, leans across me toward Natasha.

"Okay. And what I want is some appreciation of context. Actually, that's what I *need*. Some perspective that what's happening right now is bigger than just you."

Mom pulls off her sunglasses for the first time since we left the apartment. Glares at Natasha. Hits me with the look too. She either didn't get much sleep or was crying this morning. Maybe both.

"Understand?"

Natasha nods once and her long neck bends back toward the book that rests on the fold-out tray. Mom pulls the shades back on. Her hand finds my knee. It trembles as she taps me twice. I'm pretty sure she's upped the Celexa dosage again.

"I'm gonna need you to drive this time. I told him not to, but Dad rented a Tahoe or Escalade. Something huge. And you know I can't drive something that big."

"No problem, yeah."

She nods and taps my knee again.

———

Thumbing through the in-flight magazine, I come across an image that got heavy media rotation a few years back: a metal sculpture of a shackled slave in the foreground, and behind him up a grassy hill, a structure with hundreds of hanging sculptures suspended from two metal beams. Title of the article is: "Acknowledging Yesterday's Sins for Today's Justice." Makes no sense. I hold it up for Mom.

"Has anyone from the family been?"

She glances at the image. "Not that I know of."

"Why?"

"Guess you can ask them yourself."

"Would you want to go?" I say.

"Seriously? You're asking me that now? After what I was just telling your sister?"

"No... not like on this trip, but at some point?"

She raises the window shade, stares out at a distant storm system.

"Haven't been to Montgomery in probably fifteen years."

Typical. No one wants to talk about it. And if anyone did, Mom would have to be the one to initiate it. Because she's the one with the vocabulary, the resources, the geographic remove to talk about it. To acknowledge what happened on behalf of the family. But I guess she's never wanted to be seen as the spokesperson. Dad says several journalists, and even some author wanting to write a book, reached out to her early on in their relationship and she never even called them back. Pisses me off. Dad says it's not for him or me or Natasha or anyone to tell her how to deal. Because we can't fully comprehend what happened, why it happened, and what it means for her and those who were directly impacted. But by her not dealing with it, it becomes part of our story too. It's like Mr. Lawson described in "Intro to Film" class junior year: if a gun is intro-duced into a scene, someone better use it. The act of introduc-tion necessitates a payoff. Someone better fucking die, or at least suffer life-threatening injury. That's the genre expectation, and the genre expectation supposedly mirrors some core tenet of human behavior.

In Mom's case, I guess the "inciting incident" happened

when she was seven, and it's never been paid off like Mr. Lawson said was required by the dramatic rules written down thousands of years ago by Aristotle and regurgitated a million times by hucksters selling the "essential rules" of screenwriting. We had to read that shit. Aristotle's *Poetics* and the rules.

Or maybe Mr. Lawson and Aristotle and all the hucksters don't know shit. Maybe this isn't a story about a weapon being introduced and who's going to have to use it. Maybe this is a story about something horrible that happened and how that trauma is passed down like a hereditary disease. Instead of getting paid off in some classical three-act dramatic structure way, maybe it just morphs into family dysfunction that mutates for generations and generations, crippling and fucking up everyone in its path. Maybe every family has an Auschwitz story and this just happens to be ours. And the gas chamber's still smoking.

ZORA THOMAS

20 mg of Celexa* / day...

- Because he doesn't make me laugh anymore.
- Because of his back hair, which I never noticed until a few years ago, but now it's all I see.
- Because the higher our net worth, the more we have in our onshore and offshore accounts, the larger our real estate holdings, the less interesting his mind seems to be.
- Because I walked the runway at Paris, Milan, London and New York Fashion Week for brands like Versace, Dolce, Prada and now it's a good day if a single person, man or woman, does a double-take.
- Because that bothers me.
- Because it bothers me that that bothers me.
- Because "the former model who married the hedge fund manager" is so cliché it makes me want to vomit or weep or deny it. Or all three.
- Because at some point it seemed like the natural progression of things and not a sickening cliché.
- Because when my children were born, they were so

____

* Celexa (citalopram) is used to treat depression. It may improve your energy level and feelings of well-being. This medication works by helping to restore the balance of a certain natural substance (serotonin) in the brain. Side effects include: drowsiness, ejaculatory disorder, nausea, insomnia, and diaphoresis. Other side effects include: suicidal tendencies, agitation, diarrhea, impotence, sinusitis, anxiety, confusion, exacerbation of depression, lack of concentration, tremor, vomiting, anorexia, and xerostomia. WebMD.com

white I felt like I'd betrayed the more important half of my history, ancestry, identity.

- Because over the years, on vacations in the Caribbean and Hawaii, I encouraged them to "get some color", to lay out in the sun unprotected, so that selfishly the world would know that they belong to me. That my babies are Black too.

- Because this selfishness may make them more prone to skin cancer later in life.

- Because these are truths that I'll never be able to share with Neil. And they're really just the tip of the iceberg.

- Because of the way sweat beads on his bald forehead when he's hurrying through an airport concourse. Or when he's on top of me, pumping away with brow furrowed, desperate to maintain eye contact, desperate to see if I'm deriving any pleasure from this tired act.

- Because of the way that bead of sweat will eventually disconnect from his forehead and drop onto me, or into my mouth. Claiming me when I no longer want to be claimed.

NEIL ENGEL

Just so we're clear, I'm a white male, age 53, with a net worth that lands me and my family squarely in the 1%. Closer to the .001%, actually. Our net worth at the close of financial markets today — and it's my business to know and track this — is $213,753,223.

As you might imagine, it's not without reservation that I share this figure. It's a figure that can't be read without inspiring an avalanche of judgement and prejudice. But that would be true if the figure were $192,900, which, per the Federal Reserve, was the median net worth of an American family last year.

Just so we're clear, I'm also married to a black woman. 23 years and counting. Well, for the sake of accuracy, she's actually biracial, but identifies as Black because that's how the world has always perceived and treated her. Black was the identity forced upon her or accepted by her because who wants to constantly explain nuance. Black was and is the default identity, even though she grew up with a white hippy mother in New Mexico.

As an aside, the median net worth of an African-American family is $24,100. Another way to view this is that for every $1 of wealth a white family possesses, a Black family possesses just over twelve cents. I'll let you decide why this might be.

The reason I'm interested in these ever-shifting numbers, among many other data points, is because over the past two years I've become convinced that they are key inputs for a predictive model. A predictive model that will tell me when a family such as ours should pull the ripcord and relocate to another city or country, or even an off-the-grid bunker, to wait out what I see as an inevitable societal collapse. One that will be violent and prolonged. My proprietary algorithm says we're getting close.

Just so we're clear, my wife and I have two children. They can "pass" depending on how they choose to style their hair. One identifies as Black in most contexts because, ironically, that's the more advantageous box to check given the world we inhabit. The other, our daughter, identifies with books and the worlds she finds within their pages, and doesn't seem to care about the process of identity self-selection that seems to be part and parcel to growing up today. That may change.

Just so we're clear, I'm fine with you considering what I'm sharing here as a masturbatory thought experiment. Everything that follows. Because, really, how can I ever know how much of this approximates the truth. How can anyone know? I'm sure some will be indignant, irate even, saying this isn't my story to tell. They may be right. You may be. Perhaps what I've already shared disqualifies me as a voice that needs to be heard at this particular historical juncture. Again, I'm fine with that. Because pressing the mute or cancel button on this narrative won't impact my net worth or the preparations I'm making to protect myself and my family from what's coming. It's also not going to topple me from my privileged position. As indicated, I'm fully cognizant of all the many advantages I've been afforded due to my skin color and the time and place into which I was born. I'm aware — and I want you to acknowledge I'm aware — that I am the undeniable beneficiary of at least three hundred years of systemic advantage. Advantage that rested and still rests upon oppression, exploitation, and murder. Rape too, no doubt. But also a shitload of hard work by me and my forefathers. Just so we're clear.

NATASHA THOMAS-ENGEL

My friend AJ has these 19 words and three lines tattooed in small, neat cursive on their left ribcage:

Your absence has gone through me
Like thread through a needle.
Everything I do is stitched with its color.

If I'm being honest, I'm not actually sure AJ is a friend, per se, or ever was a friend. I read the tattoo while AJ was changing in the locker room after fencing practice. Or, more accurately, I snapped a pic without them realizing, and then zoomed in on the image to read the words, with my back turned and my phone hidden, even though I knew they wouldn't be looking at me for any reason, because I don't think I actually register in their universe. I could tell it was a new tattoo because it still had red around the edges of each letter. Of course I wanted to ask if the words were lyrics from a song, and whose handwriting it was, and, even more, what made AJ get the tattoo in the first place, because clearly love and longing and loss were involved.

Now that I've had a chance to read and reread, there really is a ton going on in only those three lines. And it's not from a song, FYI, it's a poem called "Separation" by W.S. Merwin. And there isn't anything more than that, like other stanzas that explain the who, what or where of it. That's it. Three lines and 19 words. Although, honestly, I'm not really sure what else you could even add, because it's already perfect in capturing something ephemeral that I haven't yet experienced but want to; something that literally makes my heart ache even though I know that's physically impossible. Like it's got a simple perfection to it, which might be why Merwin won the Pulitzer not once but twice. He's dead now, another DWM (dead white man), but I still wonder who he was writing about, or who he was writing to. Like who this love was that stitched his very soul, and also how many others have tattooed his perfect words on their bodies or included them in a desperate text or letter to lure back a lover who abandoned them. And, also, how many have recited these words at a funeral.

Your absence has gone through me
Like thread through a needle.
Everything I do is stitched with its color.

I'll admit I got fixated on each word because there are only 19, and because usually I'm drawn to long-form prose to describe romantic love, because all of the context and nuance helps me inch closer to understanding what seems to be the most fundamental of all human experiences, and also an experience I haven't yet had. What I like about the poem's brevity is that it forces your imagination to do the work. And when I do the work, I realize it's actually what I want, desperately, which I get is not very original for a girl my age, or maybe a girl of any age. I mean, everyone probably wants to be stitched through by love and loss and longing so that every moment of every day we're physically and mentally and spiritually connected to something beyond only ourselves. It's the word "stitched" that really drives it home for me. The idea of color going in and out and in and out through the fabric of our lives, every day, everywhere, and I realize that the issue for me right now is that there's no other thread in my life. There's no color other than my color, and honestly I'm not even sure what color that is, because doesn't color only occur or exist in relation to some other pigment that's noticeably different?

AJ's mother is an actress you would know. Everyone does. Pretty much everywhere on the planet unless you're living under a rock, and, as a result, AJ is used to carrying themselves in a way that basically says: don't ask me questions or talk to me or take pics of me or I'm liable to break your fucking nose. And the fact that at age 16 they have this new tattoo basically makes those exact points. The first point being that they've had an experience so profound that imprinting those 19 words into their skin forever feels right and expresses their truth, and another point being that they have the self-confidence to express to the world the love and loss they've experienced.

As background, AJ's been in my class since kindergarten, when they presented as a girl and went by the name Ashlyn, so the next time we were changing after fencing, I felt like maybe I'd actually earned the right to ask them one question, even if it was going to blow up in my face. I needed more details. So I waited until it was just the two of us in the row of lockers and mustered all the courage I could find, while also positioning myself on the other side of the central bench, in case they decided to lunge at me. When I asked what made them get the tattoo, they turned and looked me dead in the eyes, sort of acknowledging me in what felt like the first time since Ms. Gabriella's kindergarten class.

"Because my girlfriend moved back to Buenos Aires," they said.

I nodded and fought the urge to look away, which is one of my deficiencies.

"Or, really, her asshole parents forced her to move back even though it's a fucking shit-show down there. Like it's actually dangerous with the economy how it is."

I nodded, eyes still with them, like totally locked in. I don't know anything about economics, especially in Argentina. I'm sure my dad does.

"They totally freaked when they found out about us. Like who I am." Tears welled in AJ's eyes now and, because I'm a sympathetic crier, the water-works started for me too.

"No, fuck me! Don't start crying!" they yelled. I backed up a step.

AJ punched the locker hard and sank down on the bench, hands running through their short hair. I noticed at least one bloody knuckle.

I fought the tears as hard as I could, but the problem was this was literally the most tragic situation I'd encountered in a long time, maybe ever. I wanted to sit down next to AJ and maybe lay my hand on their shoulder as comfort. Or hug them if they wanted that. Instead, all I could do was stand there like a massive idiot with that trite Tennyson line rattling around in my head. And then I heard the unfortunate words coming out of my stupid mouth:

"Tis better to have loved and lost than never to have loved at all...?"

I said it almost like a question, and it definitely didn't help, probably because it was more about me and what I hadn't experienced than what AJ and their girlfriend had. Like it basically exposed that I was jealous that the love of my life hadn't been ripped from my arms by bigoted parents and banished to some distant country with an imploding economy.

AJ punched the locker again.

"No, fuck that, it's not over!"

Which I guess is true, or at least from what I can gather is true, because the following week AJ wasn't in school, and rumors were swirling that they had dropped out and moved to Buenos Aires under an assumed identity.

———

I recited the poem to my mother in the kitchen the morning we were leaving for Mobile to visit Grandpa. She was making her matcha and either didn't hear me or didn't want to engage. So I recited it again, and this time she stood and listened, her back to me, without moving, her hands on either side of her travel mug. She nodded when I'd finished.

"Who does your mind go to when you hear that?" I said.

She shook her head and I knew not to push. I'm sure there was someone. Maybe my father when he was younger, or the Italian photographer she dated when she was modeling in Europe. She picked up her sunglasses from the counter, pulled them on, grabbed her purse and finally turned to me.

"You didn't write that, did you?"

"I wish," I said.

"No you don't. Not yet."

"What's that supposed to mean? Yeah, I do!"

She shook her head and smiled, which felt like condescension, which is mostly what I get from her and my brother, and always have.

WILLAMITA & SHAWNA PATTERSON

Her hands have known what to do for at least eighty years. Beyond that she can't be sure. She's able to narrow it to her first decade because these earliest memories include her grandmother and both great aunts sitting around the table of the two-room shack with the dirt floors. The first home after Emancipation, built by her grandfather in a nameless sharecropper community in Pike County. It was impossible to pinpoint the first season she might have learned to hold a nutcracker and determine the brittleness of a pecan shell before squeezing with just the right amount of force so as not to damage the two halves inside. She'd been judged to have strong hands, and a matching strong will, since before she could walk or talk. She was sure her grandmother would have encouraged her to try as soon as she was physically able. Her grandfather was long dead and hunger was always knocking at the door.

Now that her eyesight was gone, cracking open pecans, extracting the two halves, and placing them on cookie sheets before roasting was an activity that connected her to these very early memories, but also demanded a connection to her neighbors in the here and now. Each neighbor on the street had at least one pecan tree in their yard and yet no one seemed to have the time or inclination to crack and roast and store the nuts that fell to the ground every November. Squandering God's bounty, is how she viewed it. She got that it was easier to just climb into your car and drive down to Government Street for fast food or out to the Walmart on Airport Blvd., but what did that connect you to? To whom did that connect you? No, she was holding onto this seasonal act because it connected her and her people — the Black people of Mobile — those alive and those long gone.

For years now, since LaVonn had been locked up at Fountain Correctional, she'd paid one of the Coleman boys $3 for every pound of nuts collected from her backyard. Or any yard. No matter that $3 could buy you a two-pound bag of pecans at Walmart. They weren't from here. They didn't carry the stories of this place. And it didn't matter that she had over 50 one-gallon Ziploc bags of pecans in the freezer in the store room, some of them probably gone bad by now. Thing is, you never know when you might need them. If folks in New Orleans had had 50 Ziploc bags during Katrina, they might not have been out looting and killing. Same goes for Biloxi. People forget, and forget quick, but fast food and Walmart aren't gonna be open when God's wrath sweeps in off the Gulf.

Willamita stood from the kitchen table. With the aid of her walker, she made it to the other side of the kitchen. She pulled on a hot mitt and opened the oven. Pulled out two sheets of pecans. Sniffed at 'em. She didn't want to admit it, but she'd overcooked this batch by a minute or two. She grabbed one, blew on it, popped it in her mouth. It was hard to take a good bite with the dentures, but the warmth, the sweet outer coating of roast, it always catapulted her back to those first memories with her grandmother and aunties. It was a taste that inspired gratitude. The Lord provided goodness and mercy even in the darkest of times. And seasonal rituals like this gave Him the opportunity to make His love and mercy tangible —

She heard keys in the front door.

"Mit-a?"

Willamita froze. She'd forgotten what day it was again.

"Auntie M, you back there?"

She'd forgotten her great-grandniece Shawna was picking her up. Of course now she realized it must be the first Tuesday of the month, because every first Tuesday of the month was the day she visited LaVonn. Now that Shawna had a license, she was the one to take her.

"Just shuttin' off the oven, baby. Gimme a moment."

She could sense Shawna already standing in the kitchen doorway. Already taking in the scene and worrying about her, questioning her physical and mental wellbeing. Only question was whether she'd report the scene to her mother. Willamita was old, forgetful at times, but she was no idiot.

"Where you hidin' at? Get on in here."

She turned toward Shawna, who moved across the kitchen and kissed her on the cheek. The old woman held Shawna's forearms, stared up at her. *Macular degeneration* is what the doctors called it, the reason she couldn't see the features of her grandniece. She reached up and ran her fingertips over Shawna's face, a delicate dance. Shawna always closed her eyes when she did this.

"Don't let no man get his hands on you, hear? 'Cause I know they lookin'. Lookin' and talking at you too."

"Yes, ma'am."

Willamita dropped her hand back to the walker.

"Now I know what you was thinkin', standing in the doorway like that. I know you was thinkin' I forgot what day it is and that you was coming. Well, gonna be honest with you, yes, Lord, I did... You right! I did forget, and I cannot lie!"

Willamita slapped the top of her walker and cackled, which launched the half-gummed pecan from her mouth in a high arc across the kitchen.

"Oh Lord! Got away from me!"

Shawna smiled and grabbed a paper towel from the counter, picked the pecan remains from the linoleum floor, and tossed them in the trash.

The girl was quiet and shy. Pretty, quiet and shy. Willamita had heard from her mother, Leticia, that Shawna was on the honor roll at the new charter school down on Seminole. She'd heard she wanted to leave Mobile and attend college out of state. Willamita couldn't argue with that. Key was that she didn't find herself a boyfriend and get pregnant between now and graduation.

———

Out of her nightgown and wearing one of her church dresses, and with Shawna's assurance that her wig was on straight and lipstick wasn't all over her cheeks, they began down the hallway from the bedroom. The house still smelled of roasted pecans. Shawna knew to let Willamita pause at the photographs on the wall just inside the front door. It had been this way since long before she lost her eyesight. Since the one-year anniversary, when she was given the framed photograph by her Bible study group. It featured the same image the newspapers had run, here in Mobile and all over the country. She knew because distant cousins had sent her clippings from as far away as Philadelphia and Chicago. Everyone knew the story.

Willamita lifted her hand from the walker. The coolness of the wall was always a relief, somehow helped her tamp down the panic. She wasn't sure why, but it helped focus her mind on what she needed to do before stepping from the house. The fingers of her right hand moved upward until they found the bottom frame, which she knew featured LaVonn in middle school. Her fingers moved over the frame like a caterpillar, continued over the glass, over the image of a boy sitting with his classmates, his smile forced and his eyes wide and fearful. The picture was taken a year before he began acting out, getting sent to the principal's office, running with the gang-bangers. Her fingertips reached the top of the frame and returned to the cool of the wall for a few inches more before finding the frame she was seeking. She took a breath and parted her lips to say what needed to be said:

"The light shines in the darkness, and the darkness has not overcome it."

John 1:5. She tapped the glass twice. That's what needed to be said and done, and now it was said and done. She'd honored her dead son, her only son, and now she could face whatever the outside world had in store for her. She tapped the glass one final time and whispered:

"We gonna go see LaVonn now. Goin' to see your baby."

———

The house was silent. Shawna stood next to the old woman, eyes on the floor, on the welcome mat, head bowed like at church. She was thinking of a website she'd visited earlier that day. Scripps College in Claremont, California. All women. It featured video clips of students — different races, styles, piercings, hair — talking about how liberated they felt by "a culture of learning free from the hegemony of the patriarchy." She had to look it up, some of the fancy words. But no matter the words, the students spoke like they meant it. There were Black students too. One talked about taking an astronomy class and doing a summer internship at NASA. Was this the type of school her cousins from up North would attend? Were already attending? She knew Elijah was about to graduate from a boarding school somewhere in New Hampshire or Vermont.

"Okay, you got my keys, baby?" said her great-aunt Willamita.

"Yes, ma'am."

"And you made sure I got my picture ID in my purse?"

"Yes, ma'am."

"Good girl."

They stepped out into the blanket of humidity. Had to be at least 95 degrees. Shawna held Willamita's elbow and guided her down the wheelchair ramp that had been installed after she broke a hip two years ago. Everyone had wanted to move her into the nursing home after that, wanted to sell the house, divide up the belongings and money, but she'd fought 'em off with cunning, guilt-slinging, and ample quotes from scripture. Such as Peter 5:5.

Likewise, you who are younger, be subject to the elders.
Clothe yourselves, all of you, with humility
For God opposes the proud but gives grace to the humble.

Without her arsenal of quotes, she'd have been shipped away and forgotten long ago. Shawna helped her into the car.

"We gonna make it in time?"

"Yes, ma'am, we fine. Momma said visiting hours are two to four."

"And what time we got now?"

"1:15."

"Uh-huh, we alright then. We good."

ELIJAH THOMAS-ENGEL

Mom's different when she's down South. The way she talks to our relatives. The way she stands in her body. It's like she's more formal, modeling a way of being she thinks others should aspire to. I know she wants to be a role model for Shawna, who she's pulled aside a bunch of times and explained that if she continues to get all As and Bs, we'll pay for college, as long as it's out-of-state. Gotta read the fine print. There are always conditions with Mom's promises.

When she walks into the hospital or nursing home, dealing with Grandpa's VA benefits, Mom plays the "you-best-not-fuck-with-this-educated-and-empowered-Black-woman" card. Always has her head thrown back a degree or two more than usual, so it's like she's looking down at whomever stands in her way, even if the person is taller. And, yeah, I did just use *whomever*. Because that's the kind of shit we're taught at the kind of school I attend. "You need to know the rules if you intend to subvert them," is what my honors English teacher is always telling us. Alan C. Baird. A fucking tool most of the time. Frustrated writer, adding the "C" to his name in a sad attempt to create intrigue and mystery that just ain't there.

Point is, Mom's got her chin in the air like it's the bow of a battleship and she's got the nervous Indian cardiologist backed against the hallway wall outside Grandpa's room at Providence Hospital. Place got a grade of "C" in the state of Alabama, which you know can't be good, but apparently it's still the best option in the area, and Grandpa refused Mom's attempts to relocate him to Emory in Atlanta.

"The issue, ma'am, is that his ejection fraction is significantly lower than we'd like," says the doctor. "Thirteen percent of what it should be. Basically the tissue damage is so extensive that the heart doesn't have the strength to pump, which leads to edema in the extremities, fluid buildup in the lungs, light-headedness, delusions."

Grandpa just wants to hold my hand. Hold Natasha's hand. He stares up at her and tears well in his eyes.

"You just so tall and pretty now," he says to her. "When was the last time y'all was down to see me? Been too long." There's spittle on his lower lip. His skin looks dry. Natasha glances over at me, then back down at him.

"Last summer. We all went down to the Beau Rivage in Biloxi, remember?"

"That's right." It's clear he doesn't.

"You won, remember? Playing the slots?" she says.

He nods, eyes on the window. His memory is shot. He thought I was Dad when we came in, and Dad's a bald white man. What's hard to determine, according to the doctors, is whether this is bona fide dementia or due to the lack of oxygen his brain is getting on account of his heart's ejection fraction being fucked.

"That hotel you stayin' at downtown, how much you say that cost again?"

Natasha shakes her head. Even if she knew, she knows better than to share the figure.

Mom wraps it up with Doc Murthy. After kisses for Grandpa and promises of imminent returns, we're back in the Escalade and heading for the hotel. Mom looks up from her phone.

"I'm going to have you and Shawna bring food over to Auntie Mita later. Ribs from J. Rodgers."

Natasha looks up from her book in the backseat.

"She still lives by herself?"

"No one's getting her out of that house alive."

"What's the relation again?"

"She's the younger sister of Grandpa's mother. My great aunt. Your great-great aunt."

Natasha doesn't know what the next question should be. I don't think Mom's ever told her anything about it. I haven't. I wouldn't know myself if I hadn't asked about the picture on Mita's wall a few years back. Not that she or Mom or anyone else told me any real details. All Auntie Mita said about the picture was: "That's my boy Elijah, your namesake. He gone and passed on now."

But the way she said it I could tell there was more. The little hitch right before she said, "passed on now." And so I Googled that shit and it was like a full-blown Pandora's box situation.

What always gets me are the newspaper descriptions of him being thrown in the trunk of the Mercury Cougar XR-7 and driven out of town. How they released him in a field, chased him, caught him again, beat him. Then let him go again. Then chased him again, caught him again, beat him again. With a baseball bat and tire iron. I guess they got those details from the eventual confessions. Just makes you wonder what was going through his head, with them just cat-and-mouse fucking with him for hours. He probably knew he was gonna die from the moment their car rolled up on him as he walked home from night school. It was just a question of how. By the time they strung him up in the camphor tree, 11 loops around the neck, I'm pretty sure he'd lost consciousness. I guess there's no way of really knowing now, but it's the fear he experienced early in the ordeal that makes me want to fucking kill someone.

When I asked Mom why she named me after him, she said she just always liked the name, and that it wasn't only his name. Apparently, Elijah is a name that's been in the family for generations, all the way back to Emancipation. The first-born son of Auntie Mita's grandparents was named Elijah, and there's been one in every generation since.

WILLAMITA & LAVONN PATTERSON

She stared at the man on the other side of the plexiglass she couldn't see. She hadn't been able to distinguish the features of his face for three years now. At first it was at the center of her vision where focus was lost, his nose and eyes. Then it was his whole face, his shoulders, the wall behind him. She came every month and every month it got worse. Like water dripping onto a still-wet watercolor painting, where all detail and color distinction got pushed to the periphery, became a muddy brown, and was ultimately lost. For her, the process continued until it was a black painting and a black frame.

But even still, because it was LaVonn, it didn't matter. Of all people — more than her dead husband, her dead son, her dead sisters and parents and grandparents — of all people, this was the person she knew best. From the outside. What went on inside she couldn't divine. She could summon his image as a five year-old, on the night the news broke. She could resurrect him again as a teen, defying her, pushing through the screen door at dusk and not looking back, not coming back. She could see him on the morning the police broke down the front door, now so many years ago. The way they threw him face-down on the floor, cuffed him, dragged him from his room wearing only the gray sweatpants he'd slept in. The gray sweatpants she'd given him for Christmas. He didn't fight back. Just looked up at her from the floor with an expression of resignation as she screamed at the police about the broken door, about the charges alleged, about how her grandson had a good heart but had been led astray. It wasn't peaceful resignation on LaVonn's face, but a resignation that spoke of inevitability. If not today, it was gonna be tomorrow. His days as a free man, or an alive man, were numbered. Three strikes, you out.

Willamita also knew what he looked like now, and it wasn't good. She was looking at a broken man, her only grandson. He was missing a front tooth. He was too skinny. He didn't bother to comb through his hair anymore. The prison had issued him prescription glasses but most of the time he couldn't be bothered to put them on because it didn't really matter if his world was in or out of focus. Talk of getting his GED in jail, talk of writing in a journal — ideas she tried to relay to him, ideas given her by their relatives from up North — it never paid off. He'd spent almost two-thirds of his life in maximum security and he'd tossed in the towel a long time ago. But she hadn't. She couldn't. She was here to tell him what she always told him. She was here to deliver the message at the heart of Proverbs 3:5; words that helped her calm her internal calculations and recalculations about what could have been, what should have been.

Trust in the Lord with all your heart, and do not lean on your own understanding.

———

LaVonn nodded as she spoke the words. Could give a fuck. He was sitting there because she was the only one who visited anymore. He knew she'd be dead in a few years, or forced into a nursing home, and then all contact with the outside world would be lost. Which is why he wondered why she couldn't bring Shawna in. He wanted to see someone young. Female. A young female, even if she was kin—

"How you doin', LaVonn?"

He nodded.

"You know I don't see no more, so you gonna have to say somethin'."

"Doin' a-ight."

"Good. That's good. You eatin'?"

He shrugged.

"Darnell's in the hospital again," she said.

"Okay."

"Shawna says they on they way down from New York now. Zora, the kids too."

"Okay."

"Wish you could meet 'em, baby. Hear what all they doin' with theyselves."

"What they doin'?"

"Way they talk about what they wanna do when they all grown."

"What they wanna do?"

"Elijah going to college, same as his daddy."

"Okay then."

The fact that they named their kid after his father, his dead father, that just never sat right with LaVonn. Did he even know? Did they tell this kid, who was basically white, anything about what actually happened? Because how the fuck were they honoring anybody by naming the kid Elijah? Or maybe they weren't trying to honor shit. Maybe they just liked the sound of the name.

He remembered meeting Zora when she visited one time as a kid. His uncle, her father, Darnell, took them fishing out on Dauphin Island. Off some rickety wooden pier that went way out into the bay. They got there at sunset and fished late into the night. She wouldn't touch the shrimp and cut-up squid they used for bait. Made him do it, or her daddy do it. But she sure liked to snatch the rod out of his hands when there was a bite. Oh yes. He'd do the nasty work and she'd get the reward. She must have been five or six years older, shrieked when they pulled out all them croakers. Trout. Catfish too. Her father brought the fish home in an Igloo, promising a fish-fry, but then he had to go back to work the next day and the fish just sat there in the cooler in the driveway all week. The ice melted and they started to stink so bad she made him do the dirty work again. Made him drag the cooler across the street and dump the fish, all swollen and eyes popping sideways, gills pink, into the woods.

Willamita had more to say.

"You know she got a store now. Furniture for your home. Online too, is what Shawna sayin'."

"Okay. That's real good."

"Magazine articles about her an' everything."

He could give a shit. That his cousin, who didn't ever live in Mobile, who had lighter skin and grew up in California or Arizona or some shit, and maybe was a model and then definitely married some rich white dude and had some kids who were also rich and white... why the fuck was she always telling him about her? He'd baited her hook, dealt with the fish stank, but he'd never see her again. And it wasn't like he was ever gonna meet the husband or kids.

"They help pay the bills?" he asked.

"Now why you askin' me that?!"

"'Cause if they ain't, they should. Claiming they kin an' all."

"They is kin! And I know they paying Darnell's doctor bills. Anything that ain't covered by the VA."

"Should pay your bills too."

"I don't got no bills I can't pay myself!"

He nodded. Every old lady he'd ever known was stubborn like this. Didn't take no shit and didn't want no hand-outs. He knew it wasn't right, but he wanted to stand up and go back to his cell. The Mexican didn't bother him anymore, not since he established that he had quick fists and didn't mind using them. The Mexican wouldn't say shit unless he was spoken to. He'd trained him good, so in the cell he didn't have to see no one or hear no one or think about no one he didn't want to. Problem now was that just by talking to her, hearing about Zora and her fair-skinned kids coming down, whatever this online store was, the fancy college, it was gonna mess with his thoughts for weeks. It would spin him out into a what-if parallel universe where maybe he didn't end up the way he was, and in the place he was. But mainly it just pissed him off that someone had reminded him that some kid who was hardly related, and didn't know shit, was walking around with the name of his murdered father. It was just another way the world wouldn't let him or his father rest. He was tired.

———

Willamita hoped nobody was bothering Shawna in the waiting room. She'd always been too pretty, and even though she couldn't see her now, she'd felt her face and knew the problem was only getting worse. Her body was probably making the boys crazy. Men too. She couldn't help but think that the guard in the waiting room was trying to talk to her right now, no matter that the guard was white. That didn't matter sixty years ago and definitely didn't matter now. She fought off the memory of the building superintendent in Chicago who'd forced her into his apartment when his wife was out shopping. Fought off the memory of his crooked bottom teeth, crooked and yellow, and the way his calloused hands scraped her thighs, leaving marks.

She leaned toward the plexiglass.

"You got anything you want me to tell anybody on the outside, LaVonn?"

"No, ma'am."

"You don't got nothing to tell Darnell?"

"That I hope he feels better real soon."

"The congestive heart is what he got."

"Uh-huh."

"Lungs fill up with fluid and it feels like you drownin', is how they explain it. Like you drownin' but you ain't even in no water."

"Uh-huh."

This wasn't going anywhere. She'd tried. Nobody could say she hadn't. The boy got dealt a tough hand. The last lynching in America is what all the papers called it. But the thing is, if it happens to you, or your father, or to anybody in your family, doesn't matter whether it's the first, the hundred and first, or the very last. LaVonn's daddy was dead. Her baby was dead. He died sometime during the night of April 15, 1983, and his spirit, which lived on through her and through LaVonn, well, he just couldn't find no peace. He wasn't ready to move on to God's Kingdom and let the mortals be, and there was really no knowing who else he was still visiting and talking to in his tormented, ghostly way.

Willamita pushed herself up on her walker. She knew the guard would be watching her and would come guide her back to the waiting room.

"You be good now, baby. Know that God loves you and there's a better place comin'. Better place for all of us. Says so right there in Isaiah: 'He gives power to the weak and strength to the powerless.' Yes, Lord."

LaVonn didn't respond. She knew he wouldn't. But she held out hope that her words touched him, somehow got under his skin and entered his bloodstream. That they filled him with her love and with God's love.

NEIL ENGEL

As a younger man traveling on business, I frequented luxury brothels in capitals all over the world. I used escort services too. Because of this, I was fortunate enough to have some of the most remarkable physical specimens a given nation had to offer up — all manner of native tongues, cultural heritages, skin tones and body shapes — step into my hotel room after a long day of deal-making. Typically, I'd preselect a girl from a password-protected website that listed their physical attributes, whether they were "natural" or "augmented", whether they allowed or specialized in CIM (cum in mouth), COF (cum on face), anilingus, golden shower, girlfriend experience, porn experience, etc. Sometimes the profiles included highly produced videos of the girls lathering their breasts and asses in the shower, rolling in slow-motion across silk sheets, groveling toward the camera on hands and knees, lips hungry and wet. Often profiles included a first-person narrative about what a given escort offered a prospective John. Enticing verbiage such as:

Hi handsome! Would you like to lose your way in my heavenly body? If your fantasy is to be with a beautiful brunette with big natural breasts, then you're in luck. As a good Latina, I know how to move my entire body very well. Enjoy a taste of my exotic Colombian roots with my soft brown skin. I will seduce you with my pronounced curves and the sensual movement of my hips. My name is Marcela and I am a luxury escort who recently arrived in town to live intense adventures of sex without commitment. Tell me your deepest fantasies and together we will make them come true. Full french? Anal? Deep throat? Rimming? Threesome or orgies? Just tell

*me. I will be waiting for you to come visit. Or, if you prefer privacy,
I can cum to your hotel or home or even office party. I'm waiting for
your call, honey!*

One of my favorite establishments is located in one of
Zurich's most upscale neighborhoods, entered through a
municipal parking garage. With a code sent to you in advance,
an elevator takes you directly to the reception floor of what
appears to be a white-shoe law firm. There you're greeted by a
receptionist dressed in conservative pantsuit and heels, the
epitome of European sophistication and grace. This particular
outfit prides itself on the fact that you'll never see another
client. Entrances and exits are choreographed with the precision of a Swiss train station. The receptionist escorts you into a
room and, if you haven't already preselected a girl from their
website, she'll inform you that she has many escorts available
and that she will now send them in, one-by-one, so you can
make your selection. The receptionist will stress that your only
task at this time is to relax and remember the name of the girl
or girls you wish to enjoy. Thus commences a parade so stunning that the first time I experienced it I literally couldn't
remember one name. In came Russians, Brazilians, Spaniards,
Thais, Nigerians, French, Filipinas, Yemenis — a literal UN
general assembly of young women, all runway-model quality.
They enter the room, kiss you on each cheek, pirouette so you
can behold their asses, breasts, napes, legs. Then they stand
above you, look you directly in the eye, powerful, and state
their name. Then another pirouette and the ass shake-shakes
its way from the room, the door closes, there's a brief pause,
and in comes the next marvel.

The economics of this interchange never ceased to amaze
me. Still amazes me. For between four hundred and a thousand
dollars you can spend an hour with the most beautiful woman
you've seen in weeks, months, perhaps ever. And although the

sex was always good, and the validation I felt as a man was always welcome and needed, it was the post-coital conversations that were most gratifying. I'm sure that sounds absurd, but it's true. I liked to lie there, both of us naked, gazing up at our reflections in the ceiling mirror, and hear whatever anecdotes about their lives they were willing to share.

The more I did this the more I realized that these women, at least at the higher-end establishments, were at their core pragmatists. They wouldn't be doing this for long. They had plans. I wish I could access statistics on their lives and career trajectories. Most of them spoke at least three languages. Many told me how they planned to return to school, get a degree, or were saving money to move to another country to realize some particular dream — fashion design in Paris, acting in LA. One, who wore vintage "librarian glasses" and whose profile said facials were her specialty, described how she planned to enroll at Trinity College, Dublin to study Yeats. Some already had businesses and real estate holdings back in their home countries. Many spoke about prior boyfriends, about the type of man they were looking for in a future spouse, about wanting to have children. This job was simply the quickest and easiest way for them to amass capital; capital that afforded them mobility, purchasing power, agency. It was the highest pay for the fewest hours worked, and at this establishment they negotiated a price for services directly with the client. Maybe some ended up as trophy wives to brutish Russian oligarchs, or junkies on the streets of Zurich, but my suspicion is that the vast majority are now settled into more conventional middle and upper-middle class lives, and elect not to talk about the stepping stone that was so pivotal in them achieving their current societal status.

Cautious by nature, I preferred to do this in countries where prostitution is legal. I just didn't want to have to make the call home explaining that I missed my flight due to being arrested. I didn't want to entangle my family or lawyers or firm.

My worst fear had me arrested and my name and likeness posted in the "Busted John" section of some local newspaper. Fortunately, prostitution is legal in much of Europe, and that's where my work took me for many years.

New York posed a challenge in this regard. The problem was that once I had a taste for the experience — both the sex and the accompanying pillow talk — I couldn't help myself. Fortunately, from a wealth perspective, New York is so stratified that I soon learned there were safe and surefire ways through which I could satisfy my evolving needs. For the past fifteen years, I've used a service recommended by someone whose money I once managed. An older man, from a prominent New England family, he'd mentioned the service as an aside. Over drinks, almost confessional, he said it was a way for him to appreciate his wife more; that fulfilling his sexual needs trans-actionally, and not through an affair that might lead to love and eventually divorce, allowed him and his wife to focus on common interests — in their case, French expressionist art and land conservation along the Connecticut River. It wasn't until my son was two, and my wife was pregnant with our daughter, that I began availing myself of the service he'd recommended.

You might think such a peccadillo would diminish or dilute my love and lust for my wife. But, as was the case with my client, you'd be wrong. The reality is I would be happy to make love to my wife every night. At least that was true until maybe five years ago. Now I'm not sure I actually have the stamina, though in my mind it's still something I desire. The body changes. At times the phallus now abandons me, limp and uninterested, when I assumed it would be willing. Rearing, in fact.

In terms of the love for my wife, it's a rich tapestry threaded through with childbirth and child rearing, shared experiences of setbacks and victories, and hopes for the years ahead. I watch Zora preparing food in the kitchen, or reading a magazine on the deck at the Amagansett house, and my heart momentarily seizes with love and longing and gratitude. Heartache also. My eyes well with tears more and more these days. Lust for her is only one thread in the tapestry, and I'm okay if it's a less visible and vibrant thread as the years march on. The tapestry expands and has depth and nuance that didn't exist even ten years ago.

———

All of this is on my mind as the helicopter lifts from Pier 6. It's on my mind because I just spent 90 minutes at The Standard with Flor. Flor from Venezuela. A remarkable twenty-three year-old. Cocoa skin, small breasts, nipples like the round black licorice children in the Netherlands love. Dubbel Zout. This isn't the first time I've selected her, and the reason why is equal parts the stories she tells of a birth country in utter shambles and her ass, which should be classified as the eighth Wonder of the World. It's large and round and so firm that when I'm fucking her from behind, grabbing each cheek, squeezing with all my middle-aged life force, it's as if the power within those two orbs could cast me off with a single sinewed twitch or twerk. I have no doubt that she could buck me across the room, sit on my face, and extinguish me with the power of those flanks. And sometimes I long for this.

Flor fled Caracas six years ago. She tells me stories of anarchy and turmoil. About the smell in the streets. Death and decay. Raw sewage. She describes the expressions on the faces of the frail and elderly, those who know their days are numbered. She's witnessed desperate, malnourished families waiting in lines five blocks long for government rations that never come. Actual starvation, and this in a nation that was the eighth largest exporter of petroleum less than twenty years ago.

Producing 2,394,020 barrels of crude per day, with the largest proven oil reserves on earth.

To me, Flor's story speaks to the resilience of certain individuals. What in her mind pushed her to the point of saying "okay, enough, I'm out"? What predictive model did she use? I've asked her. She says her father moved to Newark about a decade ago, so joining him was always an option, at least on a temporary visa. But her mother stayed on as the country came undone. She's still there and apparently has no plans to leave. Her mother is a police officer and has it good — assuming the current government doesn't collapse and the masses don't decide that all who propped up the regime should be summarily shot. I ask Flor whether she's ever discussed this possibility with her mother and she says her mother has guns, has a house, has a truck, and doesn't want to start again from scratch in a foreign land. She smiles and rolls over onto her belly, pins me with those jet-black eyes.

"Also, my mother would not have this same opportunity like me."

Flor wants to start again. She is starting again. And I see in her a survival instinct that my own children lack. An instinct that maybe I lack too. But I have to assume, like anything else, that if you factor the correct variables, if the due diligence is sufficient, then the outcomes will fall within a discernible framework. In our case, the framework being a way to survive the systemic shock that will leave millions, perhaps billions, dead.

I'm engaged in the planning work now because my wife and children are operating with limited information. Or at least a different problem set. I'm in the helicopter today to assess the viability of one particular exit strategy, should my family and I have to start again. The promotional literature says it's forty-three minutes from Manhattan, take-off to touchdown. 443 miles North-

Northwest. Other compelling selling points are that the facility sits at the center of a 1,500-acre parcel of land, already fenced, guarded, monitored. The land to the immediate North is national park, old growth forest and swamp so thick it's impossible to penetrate. To the South is national forest land currently used for timber. There are no neighbors, no structures, no access save for a single-track road built and maintained only for the construction and stocking of the facility. In two prior conference calls, the developers have made clear that their plan is to close the road once the units are sold. The fence will be sealed and fortified. The only way in or out will be via helicopter. They are marketing eight units, each with separate stairs and elevator access, separate air and water filtration systems, separate power generation systems that combine wind, solar and, as a last resort, diesel generators. Six units are half-floor, two full-floor. I'm interested in the deepest full-floor unit available, 4400 square feet, listed at $22.5 million. One has to assume the deeper the better, but that's one of my questions.

The other is, how many individuals can a unit truly protect and support, and for how long. I need to see the various supply lists and run my own numbers. The literature says the full-floor unit supports eight, which of course has me thinking about who else beyond the nuclear family gets saved. If this is about the preservation of the human race, then genetics and the ability to procreate need to be factored in. Should I include on the list my younger brother, who struggles with mental illness and addiction and scrapes by on the trust I've established in his name? Or does he get sacrificed as someone who couldn't make it in life with all the advantages, and therefore has little chance of making it — whatever that may mean — in the world that comes after the shock. I'd be lying if contemplating his death at the hands of a violent, starving mob doesn't fill me with a sense of profound guilt. And what about my mother, who we recently moved into an assisted-living community on account of dementia? Again, striving to be dispassionate, I think the answer is clear. But then we get to someone like Flor. Given her resilient mindset, youth and almost certain ability to bear healthy children, the case could be made. And the next set of questions include who would sire the children? Me? My teenage son? If this is merely about laying low for five to ten years, it's a different calculation than if we're tasked with creating a petri dish from which a new humanity will spring.

I don't have the answers yet. But I am willing to write a deposit check today if the salesperson can answer more pedestrian questions regarding food stocks, energy self-sufficiency, and what, if any, interaction we might have with the inhabitants of the other units.

9

ZORA THOMAS

40 mg of Celexa*/day…

- Because I worry about the rage inside my son. He hides it behind humor and good looks, but I see it bubbling to the surface since his Yale acceptance.
- Because I've spent seven years building a home décor / lifestyle brand and don't believe in the lifestyle I'm selling.
- Because the "taupe couch sustainably manufactured by craftspersons paid a living wage" means nothing if the asses sitting on the couch are liars and cheats.
- Because I can't shake the nagging truth that my southern family is still very much living the legacy of slavery and, because I'm lighter, and married white, I've transcended or "overcome".
- Because I feel this most acutely when visiting my hospitalized father, and am reminded that no amount of money or medical care can reverse the lifetime of damage already done.
- Because I don't tell my therapist of fifteen years any of this. Even though she's Black. Or maybe because she's Black.
- Because I've said no to my husband many, many times and we've still ended up having sex. In the shower. At his office. In an elevator. Is that rape?

---

* Citalopram hydrobromide, known under the brand name Celexa, should not be administered at doses over 40 mg per day, because it can trigger abnormal electrical activity in the heart, leading to potentially fatal heart rhythm problems (including Torsade de Pointes).

- Because some of the times I said no I ended up enjoying it.
- Because I've said yes to the life he's built for us, to the money he's "invested" in me and my company.
- Because that makes me an accomplice.
- Because naming my son Elijah was a mistake.
- Because I promised my husband of twenty-three years that I trust him enough that when he says it's time we relocate from New York to someplace "safe", I'll go.
- Because I didn't have the balls to tell him I'd rather be bludgeoned, raped, killed by the angry mobs he sees coming our way than live the rest of my life with him in some mountaintop fortress or underground bunker.

10

WILLAMITA & ELIJAH

On Tuesdays and Thursdays, she always reminded the home-care nurse to leave the television on. Those were the evenings she liked to sit in the La-Z-Boy in the den and listen to the five o'clock news. Sometimes she fell asleep and stayed in the chair all night. But tonight, she wasn't going to sleep here or anyplace because he was sitting there next to her again. He was sitting on the couch and watching too, leaning forward, elbows on knees. She first noticed him when the "Local Crime Watch" segment came on.

"What you doin' now, baby?" she said, out loud or perhaps in her head. She was never sure with their communication.

He smiled over at her. Sometimes he appeared with the purple rope burns around his neck, with his right eye swollen shut, bruised purple and blue, and the deep gash on the back of his head raw and hanging open like a dropped tomato. She wasn't sure if this was something she controlled or whether he got to decide when and how he appeared.

Either way, this time he appeared as perfect as the afternoon he stepped from the house. Khaki pants ironed just the way he liked them, creases down each leg, his baby blue polo shirt freshly laundered. He'd double-knotted the laces on the new Pumas, the ones he'd saved up for and spent almost sixty dollars on. This was how he liked to go to night class at Bishop State Community College. Maybe there was a girl there he was sweet on, he didn't say. He'd finally gotten over the breakup, and settled into a weekend schedule of seeing his son LaVonn, who was going on six at the time. And now here he was, smiling over at her, his mother, with those perfect white teeth.

Too perfect. Willamita could see mischief in his eyes and she didn't like it.

"Said what you think you doin' here tonight?"

"Well, you the one sayin' we got family visiting. And everyone knows what that means, when they come slummin'. How we gotta dress and talk all proper."

His eyes were on the TV again.

"No, uh-uh, you best be leaving 'em alone, Elijah!"

"How old you say that other Elijah be?" he said. "One living his life with my name?"

"I ain't playin'!"

There'd been times when she'd swung at him with her cane or thrown her Bible in frustration, but he was a ghost, she knew that, and she knew no hitting or swinging or throwing would make a difference. If he wanted to sit there, he'd go on and do it. If he wanted to talk to her or ignore her or lie next to her in bed touching her cheek like he did as a toddler, fingertips as soft as cotton, there was nothing she could do to stop him. What she wasn't sure about was whether he had the same power to enter the lives of others.

"You can't be steppin' into they lives, Elijah, and messing with they thoughts. That ain't right. Because they never knew you in the flesh like I knew you! Like I still be knowin' you."

"Zora knew me just fine. Took her fishin' and everything. And she didn't treat me or my boy LaVonn that good neither."

She needed to reach him. She needed to stop whatever he was thinking he might want to do. She needed to help him move on, but after all these years of trying she wasn't sure she had it in her. Pastor Fields and her sisters from Bible study kept saying it was in her power and her power only to release him. They said she brought him into this world through labor and pain and she needed to let him go the same way. She needed to say goodbye with love in her heart and simply let him move on. But despite what they said, it always seemed like he was the one with the power to come and go, to make the rules, to push her around.

"You don't remember what you was like, Elijah. Before. You was a real good boy. A good man, on your way. Getting that certificate, remember? Associate's in heating and air conditioning repair. Guaranteed job placement, is what they promised."

"Was mindin' my own business is what I was doin'," he said.

"Yes you was."

"They the ones changed it. Made my business somethin' else."

"How you mean, somethin' else?!" she said. "What business you got now? You dead, baby. Left us years ago."

"It's like when you playin' pool and break them balls. Never know where they gonna end up. Depends on how tight the rack, if you got the chalk on the cue proper, if the table is slanting one way or the other way."

"You talkin' in riddles now, Elijah."

"Talkin' about how you can't never predict who's gonna listen and who ain't. And if they listening, whether they gonna do somethin' about what they hearin' or just sit on their hands, tellin' theyselves they just having crazy thoughts. That maybe with just a lil' more prayer, it's gonna pass."

He still had that smirk on his face and Willamita didn't like it. She felt the heat rising up through her chest and around the back of her neck, which meant a headache would come next, and was a sure sign, according to her doctor, that her blood-pressure was spiking.

"You want me to understand you, Elijah, you best stop talking nonsense!"

"Fine. Only question I got for you then is if he's open to hearin' my voice, you tellin' me I shouldn't say nothin'?"

"Who?" she said.

"That boy they went and gave my name to. White kid you say is going off to that fancy college come September."

"He ain't white!"

"White enough that what happened to me would've never have happened to him. 'Cause you know they would've driven right on past white Elijah."

"You talkin' nonsense now!"

On the news, they were reporting on the weather. Hurricane season coming. Heavy rains in and around Biloxi. For a moment she focused on the voices and pretended he wasn't sitting there. But when she looked over, there he was, as real as he'd ever been. Legally blind, totally blind, it didn't matter. She could see him sitting there on the couch as clear as day.

"Why you ain't just moved on by now, baby? That's what they all say you need to do. Let go of what happened and move on into the everlasting embrace of the Lord."

"Way I see it, He didn't have my back that night, so how He supposed—"

"No, uh-uh, we don't get to speak on behalf of the Lord, or try to surmise what He might be thinking!" She pounded her fist on the arm of the La-Z-Boy and turned her body toward him.

"All I'm saying is I was in church the day before," he said. "Just like you. I was singing an' everything, feeling love in my heart. But it didn't help none. No, say what you want, but He abandoned me when I needed help, so how am I supposed to know He got plans to open His arms wide and embrace me now?"

Willamita had no appetite to debate this with him for the thousandth time. Faith had been her lifeline. Scripture had kept her head above the dark, engulfing waters. Waters that had pulled almost everyone in her life into the murky depths, drowning them one-by-one without mercy. She took a deep breath, attempting to calm herself and thereby stave off the onset of the headache. She exhaled slowly.

"How's it work anyhow?" she said. "If he hears you, then you can talk to him? If he thinks about you, then you can just walk on into his life? Like through some doorway?"

He shrugged.

"Boy, I'm talkin' to you right now! Elijah, I need to know this! You able to just infect his thoughts and mind like you do with me?"

He sat back on the couch, arms spread at his side, palms facing up, eyes on the TV.

There was a knock at the door.

"Who's that?" Willamita whispered to her dead son. "We expecting company?"

Elijah smirked, picked up the remote, changed the channel.

Another knock at the door.

"Auntie Mita, you awake? It's Shawna. Brought some ribs from J Rodgers. Got Elijah here with me too."

Willamita stared over at her son, at the smile on his face, the way he had his legs stretched out on the carpet, comfortable, confident, mischief in his eyes.

"You got the key, don't you baby?" said Willamita. "Come on in."

11

ELIJAH THOMAS-ENGEL

Shawna thought I was a girl the first time we met. That's what Mom says. My hair was long, ringlets to my shoulders, and my favorite color was purple. Apparently she thought this for the first week we were in Mobile, until one afternoon when we were thrown in the bathtub together after playing in the park. Mom says she screamed and broke into tears at seeing my little dick. She was sullen for days, refused to play, felt betrayed. Natasha was an infant at the time, so no consolation there.

Sometimes I think she's never gotten over it. Sometimes I catch her looking at me like I'm some alien. Which, I guess, I am. We are. Drop in from our universe of fancy talk, fancy clothes, always ready to slap down our matte debit cards whenever there's a bill to be paid.

When we were picking up ribs for Auntie Mita, she asked if the card I was using was my money or my parents', a question I'd never been asked before. I explained I had my own account and also had a card that draws on one of theirs. But obviously it's all theirs. Or our family's. Hard to make the distinction, assuming I don't fuck it up and piss my dad off so bad he changes the will. I mean it's a combination of earned wealth and inherited wealth that keeps compounding, building momentum, accumulating prestige and legitimacy the farther it's removed from its original sin.

Which would be what, anyhow? Hard to say. We going back to displacement of Native peoples? Trail of Tears? Maybe the original sin is that Dad's great-grandfather could get a loan from a small Pittsburgh bank to start a pharmacy and Mom's great-grandfather on the Black side was one generation from slavery and couldn't get shit other than a sharecropper's wage and a lashing or lynching if he got too uppity. Because if you lift the hood and look inside, the engine of wealth is a dirty fucking affair.

Dad's started to show me the engine. He sat me down last summer at the Amagansett house to begin what he hoped would be a series of talks about tax strategies (read: tax *avoidance* strategies), family trusts, real estate depreciation, 1031 exchanges, and snoozers like the mortgage interest deduction. He'd printed and bound a 75-page document with headings and subheadings and case studies from his career. He said if I ever had an idea for a business or creative endeavor with real "upside potential", all I needed to do was draft a business plan and submit it to him. If the idea showed "merit and promise", he'd be more than happy to invest. I know he did the same with Mom when she started her home furnishing company, Palmetto. He made her submit a plan — with ROI projections and analysis of potential competitors — because he believes with every fiber of his quant self that making her, or me, go through the exercise can only enhance prospects for success. This is the woman who gave him two children and runs the household finances, pays the gardeners and cleaning staff, the cooks and caterers, and managed the nannies and tutors and social calendar from Day One. What a fucking dick. Even though he might be right.

I could see how excited he was to share his knowledge with me. His eyes had a rare spark as he began to lift the curtain so I could get a hard-on for widget counting and widget accumulation too.

"What if my business idea is justice," I asked. "What if my idea involves recognizing and dealing with the original sin?"

He scoffed, thought my line of questioning childish. But I wasn't fucking with him. He asked what classes I was taking at school and the names of my teachers. He didn't appreciate my attitude, he said. Didn't like my posture. My literal posture at the table. He said if I wanted to focus on the family foundation, which Mom had started but hadn't done anything meaningful with, then that was fine.

"Be my guest, focus on empowering others if you don't want to empower yourself."

He was getting all fucking haughty. He stood up and sat back down. He said I didn't have the right to question the legitimacy of what his ball-busting forefathers had dedicated their lives to, or the sacrifices he himself had made, all to benefit me, my sister, and any progeny we might have.

"Wealth is a privilege," he said. "A privilege that comes with more responsibility than you can fully comprehend right now, that's what I'm seeing."

He went on and on about how it was fine to wrestle with the existential questions of why I was born into this particular family, with these resources, but ultimately it was also my duty to be clear-eyed about how best to be a steward of what was going to be passed down. When I asked why it wouldn't be just as valid to give it all away to charity, the Giving Pledge that we'd read about in school, started by Buffett and Gates, he said he'd definitely overestimated my maturity. We'd have this conversation again after my first year or two of college, after I'd studied with his econ hero, the Nobel Laureate Robert J. Shiller, and his disciples. He took back his sacred binder and stormed inside.

But back to Shawna and her question as we were picking up BBQ for Auntie Mita. She just nodded when I said there was more than one account to draw funds from, her eyes on the bag of ribs being handed our way. No follow up question or comment because, honestly, what would that even be. How'd your family make all their money? How much money do you all actually have? Why you and not me?

———

"We got the ones you like, Auntie," said Shawna. "Short ribs from J Rodgers. Elijah has 'em in a bag right here. You hungry?"

The TV was blaring and she looked distracted, wig all cock-eyed and dentures swimming unmoored in her mouth.

"No, don't see no Elijah no more," she mumbled. "Was here earlier, though."

She glared over at the couch, fierce, pissed off about something. Shawna glanced at me, concerned. Looked like senility was knocking at the door for real this time. Shawna had told me how she was always talking to herself these days. I stepped forward.

"It's me, Auntie Mita. Elijah from New York. Zora's son—"

"Yes it is!" she smiled now, snapping out of whatever vision had gripped her. "I know, baby! I know where you from and who you from."

Her hands went to her head.

"Shawna, my wig on straight?"

"Yes, ma'am."

"No it ain't! Don't be lyin' to me now!"

She cackled and rotated the wig a few degrees as pistol fire from the TV ricocheted around the room. Two cowboys crouched behind a rock, unloading lead at an oncoming sea of white actors in brownface, on horseback, playing Native Americans.

"Now don't be shy, baby. I know you gettin' more handsome every day. Come share some of that youth and goodness with your tired ol' auntie."

I moved to her, kissed her, remembering her distinct scent — roasted pecans and old-lady urine. She held me tight with one hand, while the other touched my face with fingers so soft I could barely feel them.

"Best be good to them ladies up North, now, 'cause I know you breaking hearts. Remember, you be good to them, they gonna be real good to you. Yes, Lord!" She smiled up at me, milky eyes not quite finding my face.

"Where that baby sister of yours at? Natasha here too?"

"Back at the hotel. She was tired from the flight down. But she'll come next time."

"Okay then. Everybody needs they rest. Now, you say somethin' about ribs?"

Shawna was already fixing her a plate.

"Shawna's getting you some," I said. "She's in the kitchen."

Mita leaned in, whispered. "Tell me, she sayin' anything to you?"

"Who?"

"Shawna. She tell you whether anybody be talkin' to her? Botherin' her?"

"No, she hasn't told me anything like that," I said.

"Anyone botherin' you?" I could hardly hear her over the unending TV firefight.

"Can I turn the TV down, Auntie?"

"Go on an' turn it off, baby. Seen this one too many times already!"

I turned off the TV and the house was silent, the air heavier. Mita glanced at the couch again, her lips moving silently.

"To answer your question, no one's bothering me either. Everyone's always real friendly to us down South."

"Uh-uh, no, not everybody. You watch yo-self. Just 'cause you light skinned don't mean trouble won't find you."

I sat down on the couch, reached over and took her hand. I'd seen how old folks eat this up, the physical contact. Mom is always holding hands, supporting an elbow, throwing an arm around her elderly relatives down here. Mita smiled, leaned toward me.

"Nice of you to come and see an old lady like me, baby. You a good boy. Good young man."

———

Something was bothering Shawna when we climbed back into the Escalade. I pulled out my vape pen, offered it to her.

"What's in that?"

"What d'you think?"

"For real? You flew down on an airplane with that thing?"

I nodded. I'd separated the cartridge from the battery, slipping the former into Mom's wash kit, the USB charger in my laptop case. If you're checking bags at the first class counter, no one's gonna care. Or maybe no one cares anymore anyhow. Because what are they gonna do, open and test each and every cartridge that shows up on the X-ray?

"You ain't worried it's gonna mess with your memory?"

"Got some to spare." I grinned and inhaled. Fired up the Escalade engine. "What, you never smoke?"

Shawna eyed me, nervous. But also intrigued.

"How high you score on your SATs again?" she said.

"1540."

"For real?!"

"Yeah. Just make sure you do some extra test prep and you'll do good too. Mom said she wanted to pay for that."

"Yeah, we already signed up," she said.

"Get 1450 or more and you'll get into any school in the country. From Alabama. Black. Charter school. Single mom struggling to make ends meet. Check, check, check, check. Just gotta be sure to spell that out in one of the essays so they understand the situation."

I pulled out into the street, happy Dad had rented us this beast of a vehicle, riding high above any other car, the windows tinted. Making people wonder. No doubt, in a neighborhood like this, wondering *who's the thug*? In the white part of town, they'd just assume it's another VIP car service driving another executive to or from the airport. Bottled water, breath mints, today's paper tucked in the seat-back pocket. Probably a Black driver, too.

"She ever say anything about what happened?" I asked.

"Who?"

"Auntie Mita."

Shawna watched me inhale again. Shook her head.

"Seriously? No one ever talks about it?"

One more hit and I tucked the pen back in my pocket. I'd only smoked "Your Majesty Sixteen" once before, a sativa strain a friend recommended. Worked nice. The last time I ended up fucking my girl, Liza, in her library carrel. I'd hit the pipe multiple times because the high came on slow, and in the middle of the deed, I got the giggles so bad I lost focus and slipped out. Liza wasn't amused. It wasn't that I got soft or nothing, it was just I couldn't get my limbs and torso to coordinate. Finally, just laid back on the floor and let her grind one out. Pretty sure she got off. But she was still pouty, thought I'd been laughing at her. I couldn't even say what I'd been laughing at. Might have been her, might not.

"What about you?" I said. "You ever think about it?"

"You serious?! I drive her to Fountain Correctional every month. Sit in the waiting room for like an hour while she recites scripture to LaVonn."

"Yeah, exactly—"

"You high already! What the hell you even talking about?"

"In three hundred yards, take a left on Savannah Street." I'd punched in the address on my phone and Siri was joining the convo.

"Every time I come down here, it's just like there's always that shadow. Gets longer and longer."

"No, you definitely high! Talking about shadows."

"I'm serious, though. You ever looked at the pictures? It was like a national news story."

"Elijah, I know what happened and I seen the pictures! But

that was before we were even born. Everyone's basically gone and dead. Everyone involved."

"Not LaVonn. And Mita's still with us. And they were young, but my mom was alive. Your mom too."

"Okay?"

"Okay, yeah, and so you don't think it gets passed down? That the way they are now, who they are, isn't related to what happened—"

"In fifty yards, take a left on Herndon Avenue." Siri could give a shit about me getting deep on the historical record and its ramifications for the psychology of our people.

"I ain't saying it's not related," said Shawna, getting worked up. "I mean Auntie Mita's definitely still got a hole in her heart. Still hurtin' bad. But it ain't like talking about it, or looking at them pictures, is gonna change nothin... anything."

I took the left. Loved how when we swung across the two empty lanes of the avenue it felt like it didn't matter if a car was there or not. Nothing was gonna get in the way of this beast of a vehicle.

"Where we even going?" she said.

I drove a few blocks and, heeding Siri's command, pulled to a stop at our destination. Intersection of Roper and Palmetto. Ever since I'd done the report for 11th grade history, I'd wanted to see if the tree was still standing. For some reason, almost every newspaper article mentioned it was a camphor tree, which I'd never heard of and had to look up.

"That must be it. Right there."

I pointed to a large evergreen that hung over the road. Grabbed my phone and pulled up the picture. Tried to deter-mine if the large limb above the figure in the photo — the figure being our relative, the one hanging with 11 loops of rope around his neck, feet swinging a few inches off the ground — was distinctive enough to find in the tree now. I held up the phone for Shawna.

"That look like the same tree?"

"No, take me home, please! Right now!"

She was pissed. I'd never seen her with this expression. She looked like a woman. Like how she'll look as a mom someday. Don't fuckin' mess.

I stepped out of the car into the street. This was a nice neighborhood. Homes with fresh paint jobs, lawns tight, flower boxes bursting with colorful bloom, American flags and Roll Tide banners hanging from porches. I could see several had the brass historical registry plaques beside their front doors.

"Elijah, I don't want to be here!"

She was leaning out the window, her voice a higher pitch.

I kept walking. Stood in the street looking up at the tree, trying to find the limb. Was this even it? Maybe they'd cut it down? Or maybe there was a commemorative sign somewhere, like the gold bricks we saw all over Berlin to remind Germans of all the Jews they shipped off to Buchenwald and Auschwitz. Couldn't go anywhere in that city without stepping on a reminder that they'd gassed six or seven million.

I didn't see anything. Maybe this wasn't the right spot. Or maybe I was just high and couldn't see what was there and staring back at me. A car passed in the street behind me, going slow, no doubt wondering what I was doing. I continued to stare up into the canopy above, standing on the opposite sidewalk now. It looked like the trees I'd researched. Like a camphor. The house in front of me appeared to hold within it only genteel manners, mint juleps, the two rocking chairs on the wide front porch promising neighborliness. Chin-chin. Looked like a regular mini plantation house, with three columns and everything. Beds full of petunias erupting in pinks and reds.

More lights approached from down the street. A car slowed as it approached the four-way stop. A police cruiser — muscular, southern, ready for a turbo-charged pursuit. I moved toward the car, raised a palm in greeting.

"Excuse me, Officer?"

Down came the window.

"Good evening, sir. Quick question for you: do you happen to know if this is the tree where Elijah Patterson was lynched? Back in the early 80s?"

I pointed up at the tree, the limbs and canopy now illuminated by Po-Po's headlights. Po-Po himself looked like he just came from a jelly donut convention, all fat and white, cheeks flushed. He stared up at me in disbelief.

"Son, do you know what time it is?"

"Guessing almost nine, sir." I checked my phone. "Yeah, 8:50. Why, is there a problem with me being here? I'm on the sidewalk, sir."

"Where you from, anyhow?"

I glanced back at the Escalade, couldn't see Shawna through the windshield. Had she climbed out? Run off into the shadows?

"I'm from New York, sir. My grandfather lives in Mobile and we're visiting. I read somewhere that one of the last lynchings in America happened right here, in this neighborhood. I wanted to write a report for school. Would you happen to know anything about that?"

God I loved fucking with dumb-fuck authority figures like this. I excelled at it. Almost four years of boarding school had trained me well. Key was not to break eye-contact and use plenty of "sirs" or "ma'ams" or whatever the appropriate and most respectful moniker might be.

"Listen, son, here's what I'm gonna strongly recommend: don't be walking around this neighborhood taking pictures or asking questions or whatever it is you're doing after dark. People live here. This is a real nice, real safe, real quiet neighborhood. And, no, I don't know anything about no lynching.

That history is history, and it's done with. This right here is the New South."

"Yes, sir. Absolutely. I appreciate your perspective. The New South. Thank you, sir. I'll use that in my school report, if you don't mind."

I turned, made sure to look both ways, and took my time walking back across the street to the Escalade. Climbed in, waved goodbye at Monsieur Po-Po, and fired up the beast.

Shawna was crouched on the passenger-side floor, tears in her eyes, trembling.

"Okay. Sorry. So maybe that wasn't cool."

"You know we'd have been arrested if he'd seen me in the car!"

"You can get off the floor. He's not following us."

"He sees me and you together, in this neighborhood, this car, someone's getting arrested. And it's me, hundred percent—"

"Which is exactly what I'm talking about! That shit is still in us. Around us, everywhere. The history."

"Just take me home," she said. "You make no sense."

"Although he did say we're in the New South now—"

"Take me home, Elijah!"

12

NEIL ENGEL

My old college roommate, Ben Gould, thinks life has always been this perilous. He's about to get married for the third time, to a woman nineteen years his junior. He has two sets of kids from the previous marriages, four in total, and says if the new wife wants more, he's willing. When I ask if he's worried about the future for his future children — not whether they'll get into the right private school or be "learning different" because he's old and therefore their genetics will be compromised, but whether they'll actually survive to see, say, their tenth birthday — he looks at me like I'm nuts.

"What did our parents think living through the Cold War? The Cuban Missile Crisis? You remember those drills where we had to climb under our desks? The teachers talking about radioactive clouds and reminding us to tell our parents to stock up on potassium pills?"

I remember, but this is different. More multi-pronged. Cataclysmic threats in all directions. Ben's on a roll.

"Or the Holocaust. Or AIDS in the 80s. The Bubonic Plague. Pearl Harbor. The Ming Dynasty's bloody expansion into Mongolia. Expansion of the Roman Empire. Fall of the Roman Empire. Coronavirus, for fuck's sake. Jesus, in any time I can think of there was suffering and murder, the most awful shit going on, with some subset of the population that must have been thinking: 'This is definitely the end.' I mean can you imagine being Native American or Hawaiian twenty years into the missionary era? The mid-1800s? Ninety percent of your people are dead. Leprosy. Syphilis. Flu strains they'd never encountered. Your language is dying and your people are dying. Your religion, cosmology, the deepest foundation of how you understand yourself and your world, it's all fucking dying!"

Ben's favorite drink has always been a dirty martini. Since we were tapped for the Wolf's Head Society, it's the only drink I've seen him order. He's on his third and I probably shouldn't have brought this up. He knows his history, but has always drawn alternate conclusions from the same basic facts. We're at the Yale Club. He stares across at me.

"Okay, fine, nuts and bolts. My question is this: when are you going to know exactly when it's the right time to fly off to this bunker for millionaire whack-jobs?"

He's the only person I've told about the recent purchase.

"And who's to say that when you get to the helipad there won't be an angry mob waiting to club you in the head and tie you to the back of their Mad Max truck and parade you through town, showing all their anarchist brothers and sisters that time's finally up for the profiteers and oppressors."

"Think you'll probably be behind the same truck," I say.

"No fucking kidding! You're making my point! The point is we may as well just live our lives, Neil. Be a good husband. A good father. A good citizen by giving some of your fortune away, to people who actually know what suffering is. People who are already living the suffering you're worried you might suffer in your post-apocalyptic fantasy."

Again, probably shouldn't have brought it up. He gets all high-and-mighty after the third cocktail. Loves to dole out advice even though he's one big walking contradiction.

"Elijah got accepted at Yale. Early action."

"I heard. Congrats."

"How much you think is legacy?"

"No idea. Isn't he a good student?"

He is a good student. But, heeding the advice of his counselor, in one of the supplemental essays he definitely let them know his mom is Black and has southern roots. Also, I called the dean and reminded her I donated $250,000 last year.

"What's he plan to study?"

"Hopefully econ."

"Okay, what's he *want* to study?"

"He talks about justice. Or injustice. Apparently, sees it everywhere."

"Who doesn't? Except maybe you."

———

We were mercenaries, one side of the family. Descendants of Heinrich Engelbert, a twenty-three year old Hessian soldier whose prince, Landgraf Friedrich II, rented his conscripted army to the British during the Revolutionary War. In December 1776, after fighting in the battle of Trenton, apparently Heinrich deserted, eventually making his way to Pittsburgh. He didn't leave a journal and no one in the family left an account of events until about a hundred years later. What we do know is he opened a dry goods business and married the daughter of a Scottish immigrant, Mary MacDonald. Somewhere along the way the name Engelbert got shortened to Engel, and their son Peter opened an apothecary and started a line of health remedies which, over the next generation, grew into the fifth largest pharmaceutical company in the U.S. In 1928, the company was purchased in a cash and stock deal by Eli Lilly. Some descendants elected to sell their stock and, by and large, have lost what could have been a fortune. My grandfather and father held on to their shares, and built upon the industriousness of our mercenary ancestor. I've done the same.

I look at this legacy, and the broader sweep of history, and know Ben's assessment is wrong. I know it intellectually, know it mathematically. Silo thinking will kill us.

An example. To the more astute observer, the war in Syria

stems from years of drought, which displaced several agrarian communities with distinct religious and cultural norms. Their displacement, in turn, destabilized numerous urban communities, and threatened the Assad family's grip on power. So civil war breaks out and you get refugees on the move — millions and millions of them, many heading for Europe. This mass exodus from the Middle East — with poor, non-English and non-German speaking immigrants showing up in cities across the Continent — not surprisingly creates a populist backlash, which fuels the narrative that the Judeo-Christian West is under siege by Muslim infidels. This undermines the *Pax Americana*, the trans-Atlantic alliance that has brought wealth, democracy and stability to much of the world for over 80 years. It seeds nationalist backlashes across Europe. You get Brexit. In the US, you get the Muslim travel ban and the backlash against immigrants at the Southern border. The fabric of Western societies shows stresses and, more and more, the stresses are becoming tears that will prove irreparable. So a drought in the Middle East has a very long tail.

And the scientific consensus is clear. Rapid climate change will continue to spawn 1,000-year storms and droughts, food shortages, refugee crises, xenophobia, protectionism and war. On a global scale. When you factor all this together, it's enough to come to the conclusion that humanity is at a tipping point. Additionally, the nuclear threat we had during the Cold War remains, though it's even more acute now. We have North Korea. Iran. Russia with its unsecured uranium. The odds of a dirty bomb being detonated have never been higher.

Maybe Ben doesn't see this because he's suffering a second midlife crisis. Maybe he's blinded by the optimism of youth, by a 31 year-old fiancée whose morning blowjobs make him feel virile and relevant. We all want to feel that. It's not that I don't question what my predictive model is beginning to tell me. I can walk into my office, smile at my receptionist, listen to the reports of my young staff members with their projections and charts and, on some level, of course, I don't want to think these people aren't connecting all the datapoints, and therefore will be dead within 12-18 months. Some part of me wants to ostrich my neck deep into the sands of ignorance and denial too.

But within the month, I expect to shutter the Family Office and liquidate most assets. I'm getting out of the market and selling the investment properties. I haven't finalized it yet, but the new asset ratios will be something like this:

- 75% gold & silver, in bricks and coins of various denominations
- 10% US currency
- 2% euros
- 2% yuan
- 1% crypto
- 10% in real estate, including the 4500-square-foot ResoluteX bunker upstate, the NY apartment and the Amagansett house (because I'm not without sentimentality and, on some level, of course hope I'm wrong about all this).

13

NATASHA THOMAS-ENGEL

The thing about the way it's described in the book is that it's definitely going to happen. They're going to fall for each other, and there's no other possible outcome in the history of the world. Like it's fated. Like it's definitely their destiny. Not that there aren't lots of obstacles, like the fact that she's married and has a kid and their families and the entire upper class of Russia is against it. But still, you know it's going to happen, and you also know it's probably not going to end well. And you still want it to happen. The reader does. Because you really want them to have those pure moments of love, like the fateful rendezvous at the railway station, or the stolen kisses, because you sort of know that these might be the most important moments of their entire lives. Like that's maybe why they were even born to begin with, to experience those moments, even though those same moments are going to be ruined as a result of the fact that they are allowing the moments to happen in the first place.

I mean it's way better than the movie *Titanic* with Kate Winslet and DiCaprio which, don't get me wrong, I adored, and watched probably like 11 times, and cried to the point that it was embarrassing even to myself. It's really way better than all other love stories I've seen in films or read in books. And I get that maybe me wondering whether it's realistic or possible is useless or even stupid. But it's stood the test of time, which has to mean something. Like thousands and thousands or maybe millions of people have read it, in probably a hundred different languages, so there must be some actual truth about love in there. Like it touches something that we're all born with, which I guess is an idea of what romance or love is, or should be. And obviously there are different kinds of love, but this is the romantic kind between a man and a woman, which is the kind I'm most attracted to, even though at camp last summer I did kiss a girl named Larissa who was a year older and definitely seemed to be attracted exclusively to girls. It felt good, even when her hands went under my shirt and down my pants, and even though I definitely wasn't expecting that. And I'd probably do it again because it all happened so easily and felt kind of familiar, like her fingers and lips were almost an extension of my own fingers and lips. I've thought about it a lot even though I haven't talked to anyone about it, not even Larissa, who I guess is from Colorado, and texted me a few times, but then we both got busy with our normal lives away from camp. She probably has a real girlfriend back home, or maybe more than one. She's really confident like that. Anyway, that wasn't love.

The love in this book is the kind of love that when you meet it, it totally makes you change the course of your life, and makes you willing to sacrifice everything else or at least all the material things, and your sanity, and also makes you willing to hurt other family members or even spouses if you have them. I've never experienced that. And, really, I'm not sure I've seen it in my own life, like around me. Or maybe you can't really see it from the outside because it's something that lives in your heart and mind, and I guess also your actual body if we're talking about the urges you feel for other people. I mean I don't see it in my parents, but I guess it had to have been there at one time because I've heard them tell other people about how they met and they definitely weren't the most likely two people to get together, so you have to assume that there was something in each of them that sort of sparked inside. I mean my mother is gorgeous, so you can easily see what my father saw in her, like on the outside. But if you look at their wedding pictures and video, you actually see something in their expressions, in both of their eyes, that isn't there anymore. I've looked for it and I don't see it. But in the wedding video there's this one clip where my mom reaches for his hand, and just the way she does that, and takes his hand, and sort of leans into him, it's definitely what I'm talking about in terms of the soft and gentle feeling that's described in the book so well. Maybe it's trusting someone. Or feeling like you totally know them. But the way she does that, leaning into him, and his body is there and holds her up, almost unconsciously, it's something I don't think I've seen in real life. Like since I've started paying attention to what happens or doesn't happen between them. So I guess the question is whether whatever that was, let's call it the spark of love, is gone forever, or whether it's just sort of underneath layers and layers of ordinary life. Like work and dealing with us and money issues and the fact that our grandfather is dying.

What I witness now is pretty much her avoiding him. Not that she's totally disgusted by him, but more like he doesn't provide anything that she wants or needs anymore. She doesn't need or want to reach for his hand and lean into him anymore, as if that kind of support is no longer needed or desired. He still surprises her with flowers and gifts, and she thanks him, but that unspoken thing is absent, that electricity. Sometimes it looks like he wants that, the way he looks at her, but it's like her eyes don't really recognize what's in his eyes and it just falls flat. Like the spark hangs there waiting for the other electrode to accept the current but it doesn't, and so it hangs there and hangs there and finally turns back and gives up.

But maybe it's more complicated than that. I mean it must be. Just like in AK, where Old Man Tolstoy is all over the place in talking about it. For example, he says: "If it is true that there are as many minds as there are heads, then there are as many kinds of love as there are hearts." Which would be over eight billion. So maybe it's still genuine love from my dad, and that counts for something, and whatever is in her is just shrunken down to something so small that I can't recognize it, and maybe he can't either. Like a flower bulb that actually could bloom again if the weather and water and sun create the right conditions. Or the lungs of a deep-sea diver, crushed to the size of a walnut at 100 meters, but able to expand again if the diver makes it back to the surface. I really don't know.

Maybe for Mom it's more like what Anna says: "Respect was invented to cover the empty place where love should be." Except even the word "respect" might be too much to describe what I see in her. It's probably more distant than respect, because there is also some kind of hurt there, which I'm not sure if it's a betrayal of some kind or pain from something else. All I know is I hope someday someone will look at me, or we'll interact and there will be a recognition that there's something between us that existed before we met, maybe even before we were born, and by meeting, that recognition has the chance to blossom, and that if we both recognize it for what it is, the blossoming, then that means it's something real and should be cherished in whatever way you're supposed to cherish these things, which is still a mystery to me, and that maybe there's even something eternal about the connection.

I know I'm inexperienced and naive. My brother tells me all the time. Maybe I'm being stupid about all this, thinking that Russian words published in a book in 1877 somehow relate to me now. But everything I've read and heard says this book is held up as something timeless and true, and so I want what Dolly says: "I've always loved you, and when you love someone, you love the whole person, just as he or she is, and not as you would like them to be." I really want that to be true. I also love how poetic it sounds when he writes: "Every heart has its own skeletons." I'm not sure exactly what that means, but it's beautiful. That an organ without any bones has a skeleton. That each love has its own protective structure that allows it to survive but that it's also flexible enough to sort of meld with someone else's.

And then of course this one: "The law of loving others could not be discovered by reason, because it is unreasonable." Which maybe hints at the experience my mother had or is having, and definitely what my friend AJ must have experienced before they got that tattoo on their ribcage and left high school and New York for whatever they're now experiencing in Buenos Aires. I'm willing to be unreasonable.

14

———

ELIJAH THOMAS-ENGEL

Monsters exist, but they are too few in number to be truly danger-
ous. More dangerous are the common men, the functionaries ready
to believe and to act without asking questions
    — Primo Levi

My girlfriend is Jewish and she likes to fuck. Not like my last two girlfriends. Liza likes to fuck in a fierce way. Knows what she wants and what gets her off. Sometimes it feels like she's using me. Not that she's not happy if I nut too, not at all, but she isn't cool with the idea that there's not gonna be some kind of orgasm parity (yeah, SAT word, that last one). Freaked me out at first, the look in her eyes, and the way she clenches her jaw when she gets all focused on getting where she needs to get. Made me wonder where that self-confidence comes from, because it's a fierceness that seems like it's rooted in some deep survival instinct. Something way deeper than just her mom and dad telling her it's a new era and she can be whomever she wants and accomplish whatever she wants.

It all made more sense when I went to visit her family over break. Both her parents are professors at Washington U in St. Louis. Smart as fuck. Nice old house near the Botanical Gardens. We walked around that garden and talked about what happens after graduation. She's pretty clear it's not realistic that we're gonna stay together. She's doing an internship in D.C. over the summer, then we'll be separated by like three thou-sand miles. And I know she's got the urge, that animal need. She knows I got it too. We talked about all of it in the Garden, fired up the vape, and I got a little emotional. She owns part of my heart even though that's not really how it started. We both caught feelings, as they say. I told her that, about her and my heart, and she blew me in this little Japanese hut that's on the edge of one of several ponds. I promised I'd give her tongue lashings later — lashings like I mean it — and she punched me hard in the arm. But I know she wants it.

———

Was cool, that trip. I was there for a Seder dinner. My first. Her dad told the whole story of how the Jewish people were persecuted and fled Egypt. He read it from the Haggadah, and then talked about how Jews have been enslaved, oppressed, and rootless throughout history.

Later, Liza and I fucked until my dick was sore in the pool house and, after that, while lying there, I asked Liza if she ever looks at blond, blue-eyed Teutonic types and wants to smash their heads in on account of the Holocaust and the pogroms before that. Like the exchange student from Munich who looks like he stepped off the cover of Aryan Youth Monthly. Joachim Müller. Chiseled as fuck, this kid, with the jawline and everything. Always smiling and fist-bumping, especially anyone who's Black or Brown. Liza says she likes him fine, especially the way he talks about global poverty and "mitigating climate change with simple, everyday solutions." WTF? I guess his family owns a company that installs green roofs and solar, so he knows some practical shit and knows the jargon. And so I guess that's a no in terms of wanting to smash his head in for the sins of his forefathers. 'Course then I had to ask if she'd fuck him. She laughed, smacked me, said that yeah she would if she wasn't so happy fucking me right now.

So I'm wondering if I'm supposed to be cool, theoretically speaking, with fucking the granddaughter of some Klansman? Because that's basically the analogue here. When I think about it, I'm not sure I could even get it up. Or maybe I could if it was going to be some real angry sex, with ass-slapping, nutting on her face, blinding her with the goo goo from my darkish cock. Real demeaning shit. But I don't think so. Don't think I could make the separation and distinction between generations that Liza apparently can.

———

Her dad told me that he had a great-aunt who died in the Holocaust. This was after the Seder dinner, when Liza was talking to her mom in the kitchen. He showed me a picture on the mantel in the living room. A couple stood there, in their best dress clothes, I guess in some old-time photo studio. Real stern faces from Eastern Europe with wide eyes, like maybe they weren't getting enough to eat. He said they were from Poland. That's where the picture was taken. Their eyes looked like they could see what was coming down the tracks and that they were almost resigned to it. It was like they saw their murder as inevitable, but something in their eyes also demanded revenge from their descendants. Like they needed to be avenged even though they hadn't died yet. Maybe they'd already lived through a pogrom or two and knew that the odds of getting out before some mob beat them to death, or they got shipped to the gas chamber, was virtually nil. The picture was like a coded message to their ancestors: don't forget us, and the best way not to forget us is to work to dominate the fucking oppressors at some future time by prioritizing education, amassing wealth, and skewing politics in your favor. It just made me think about how at some level it's just a straight-up win or lose situation. Like the zero-sum games Mrs. Stanfield made us play in Global Ethics class. Dominate or be dominated. Very little room, if any, for compromise or middle ground.

I tried to describe what I saw in the photograph to Mr. Salzman, and he told me for like the fifteenth time to call him Ira. Then he said that if all we're capable of is tit-for-tat, Old Testament eye-for-an-eye, then we're lost. Humanity is lost. All we'll have is a vicious cycle of hatred and death and injustice. I could tell he wanted to throw his arm around my shoulder or maybe hug me or something, but I'm probably six inches taller than him and this was our first time meeting.

"I don't know that much about you, Elijah. And even if you married Liza and we spent the next fifty years talking, I still wouldn't know everything. We never can. Know the nuance and complexity of another person's inner life. Our thoughts and fears and longings. But I'm sure there are acts of bravery and love and compassion in your family history, as well as horror and pain and suffering inflicted upon your ancestors, and also by your ancestors upon others. So what do we do with that?"

I nodded, my eyes still on the photograph and those haunted expressions. I wasn't sure if I was expected to attempt an answer. Fortunately, the good professor had more to his lecture.

"I mean, of course I can be angry at all the many people who have oppressed the Jews. Those who persecuted and killed us, or kept us from certain professions or schools. But on some level, I know we're not the Chosen People. We're the same people, all of us, capable of the same things. Beautiful, selfless acts and also horrific, barbaric ones. Personally, I try to be kind, and use what power I have to better the world in small ways — teaching, hopefully inspiring my students, working with my patients — but ultimately I don't really know."

I thought of my father and whether he ever talked this way with anyone. Like maybe some young employee who was questioning the why of it all. He definitely didn't talk to me this way.

Dr. Salzman still wasn't done. "I also try to be vigilant, my eyes always open to what we're capable of. Reminding myself that I need to recognize the violence within me, within each of us, and also the capacity we each have for goodness and love. And from that, hopefully, we build societies and norms that maximize the best living conditions for the most people. Some semblance of universal justice. Obviously we're screwing it up pretty royally right now."

No wonder Liza fucks the way she does. And no wonder she looks at me the way she does when we lie there afterwards. She's had this Yoda talking to her her whole life. Wise words and complicated ideas and love and death and somehow some capacity to hold it all together in one being or mind or heart. Dad would probably like this guy, but would also probably say he's lost in the weeds. Blinded by too much compassion and not enough clear-eyed analysis and due diligence.

But what about those eyes staring out from that photograph on the mantel? Those are eyes of people who got fucked and no one really made it okay for them to rest in peace. Less than a hundred years later and what, Jews have moved to the US and have reached the highest levels of society? Okay, yeah, I guess. They have a nation state of their own in Israel. But are they safe? Are any of us safe? If we could listen to the silenced voices of our ancestors, I'm pretty sure what they'd tell us is more along the lines of: "No, fuck those people who raped, killed and stole what we'd worked so damn hard to make ours. They need to pay, for at least a few generations." I mean, why should Germany be a dominant economy after what they did to the Jews? Why should Fortune 500 companies like Aetna, Lehman Brothers, Brown Brothers — where my dad worked for a moment — companies that started out benefitting from slave labor still be making the ancestors of their founders billions? Real justice has not been served. No trials. No jail time. No restitution.

Or how about the Rothschild Bank of London? I read the guy who founded it made huge profits by using slaves as collateral in some of his deals. We're talking about a Jewish guy here.

You know he knew about the mistreatment of his people at the time — probably why he was in banking and not in some other career — but that didn't keep him from leveraging and enriching himself by mistreating a group that was even more disadvantaged. Dog eat dog, baby.

————

Liza doesn't want to talk about it later that night when she slips into the downstairs guest room wearing her flannel pajamas. She climbs into the single bed and just stares at me.

"What?"

She smiles, reaches down, pulls off her pajama bottoms.

"If I'm remembering right, you made a promise earlier," she says.

I could almost cry again, the way she just stares at me, right into me.

"Guess I've come to give you the opportunity to do the right thing. To make good on that promise."

She nods. I nod. And below deck I go.

Thank you. Thank you, Liza Salzman, and your once-oppressed people. No longer oppressed, at least not here in this nice ass house in St. Louis. Possibly oppressed again. We'll see. But right now you are fierce and you tell me what to do and how to be and I might love you. So thank you.

Less talk, more action. Tongue lashing time.

15

WILLAMITA PATTERSON

She'd known some of the women at Bible study for over forty years. Doloris and Henrietta had been at her side when she was called to identify the body. They'd stared down into the unzipped body bag at the same swollen, brutalized form. They'd felt the chill of the morgue with her, and inhaled the scent of fear and decomposing flesh with her. And because it wasn't their son in the body bag, they'd had the fortitude to lift her from the floor where she'd collapsed. They'd lifted her and held her.

Seven years before that, they'd kept her from succumbing to a heartache so profound she thought she'd never leave her bedroom again. Never leave her bed. They'd marched up her front walk with casseroles in hand, forced themselves inside, bathed and dressed her, and made sure she got to and from Bible study on Tuesday evenings, and services on Sundays. And they'd reminded her, over and over, that her husband Alfred abandoning her for Cleveland and a woman fifteen years younger was something everyone had expected to happen years ago. He'd always had wandering eyes and wandering hands. The issue was Willamita had been in denial.

They'd also flanked her in the courthouse when her grandson LaVonn was sentenced to life in prison, their trembling hands encircling her trembling hands. Yes, they'd been her guardrails, over and over and over. Guardrails that nudged her toward the center of the road when she veered toward a ditch from which she'd never re-emerge, or a cliff she'd never survive.

Not that they always provided sound advice. And not that they hadn't suffered plenty themselves. Stillbirths. Teenage sons shot dead in the streets. Daughters lost to drugs. Stunted educational opportunities and demeaning careers. But they were always there, steadfast. And, as had been true for so many years now, they could not abide her talking about her interactions with Elijah's ghost.

"If you accept him in, talk to him like he's right there beside you, then you make him real. But that's on you! That's you lettin' Satan and his deceitful ways walk right on through the front door." Henrietta stared at Willamita through thick glasses, her dog-eared Bible resting in her lap. Doloris nodded in agreement.

"But this ain't like everybody else who's gone and passed on," said Willamita. "Not like my Momma. Grandmomma. Not like Cloretta. The boy's got powers they just don't got."

"Except that ain't your boy!" Doloris was getting mad again. "That's your mind gettin' twisted inside out because your heart's still broken. That's the Devil preying on weakness!"

Others in the circle nodded and muttered in agreement.

Henrietta found the passage she was looking for.

"Says right here in Ephesians 6:11. Put on the full armor of God, so that you are able to stand firm against the schemes of the Devil."

"That's right, armor is what you need!" Doloris had her eyes closed and her head bowed in prayer. "We all be needin' your armor, Lord."

Finding her stride, Henrietta had another passage locked and loaded.

"For the living know that they will die, but the dead know nothing; they have no further reward, and even their name is forgotten. Their love, their hate and their jealousy have long since vanished; never again will they have a part in anything that happens under the sun."

More nodding and amens. Henrietta held up her Bible. "Ecclesiastes 9:5-6."

Doloris jumped in. "Which means that what you experiencin', that ain't your boy Elijah! He long gone, and in a better place now!" The other ladies yes-Lorded in agreement.

Taking them to the mountaintop, Henrietta found her final passage, and fixed Willamita with unwavering eyes. No matter that Mita couldn't see anything. This was a performance for the entire group, and also an entreaty to a higher power.

"Submit yourselves, then, to God. Resist the devil, and he will flee from you!"

Willamita stared down at the floor, into her darkness, and imagined her circle of friends surrounding her. Imagined their feet on the wooden floor. She knew the passage. James 4:7. She knew all these passages. As the "amens" of her friends rained down over and around her, she knew they were right. But she also knew that for so many years she'd lost her battles with Ghost Elijah, or perhaps Satan himself, and that expecting these same passages to make any difference was as futile as petitioning the courts for LaVonn's early release. There were three immutable truths in her life:

1. Her eyes would never allow her to see again;
2. LaVonn would die in jail;
3. Ghost Elijah would be with her until her final breath.

———

And sure enough, not three hours later, when she climbed into bed, pulled up the covers, and rolled over toward the center, there he was, lying on top of the bedspread, hands folded across his chest, wearing the pressed khakis and polo shirt. Willamita rolled away, willing him to be gone.

"Put on the full armor of God, so that you are able to stand firm against the schemes of the Devil." She wasn't sure if she said it out loud, or recited it in her mind, but she was sure he was smiling at her.

"Now why you smilin'?" she said.

"Remember how last time you was asking if I can visit other people?"

She shook her head.

"Yes, you was. You was asking if I could visit others, or only you. But what you was meaning was if I can visit my namesake, Elijah. That's what you was really asking—"

"Didn't ask you nothing of the kind!"

"Well, what I can tell you is he be thinkin' about me plenty, which is only natural. Other'n you, sometimes he the only one thinkin' about me."

She couldn't help it. He was talking and she couldn't help but roll over to watch him talk. Especially because he looked so clean, the way he looked when he left the house that final afternoon, still believing in a future that might include a better job, new romance, a chance for him to be the father he never experienced in his own father.

"So if he thinks about you, is that what lets you enter into his mind and heart?" she said.

He shrugged.

"Because even if you can, Elijah, don't mean you should! You been haunting us too long! Ladies in Bible study say I need—"

"You think I don't know what they be sayin'?! Been sayin' the same tired words since the very beginning. Reading them same Bible passages like some broken record."

Willamita shrugged. Figured if he could drop in unannounced here, he could probably listen in on whatever she was talking about with her friends. Or maybe he had access to everything in her mind, like some little implant from Satan that kept metastasizing and rewiring her brain and her heart. He smiled.

"See now, that white Elijah, he got his own ideas. Don't need nothin' from me. Because he sees the truth all by his self. Knows what needs to happen too—"

"Ain't nothing need to happen! Other than you need to remember that man's dust will go back to the earth, returning to what it was, and the spirit will return to the God who gave it. For the righteous will go into the eternal life."

Ghost Elijah smiled up at the ceiling.

"Why you smilin'?!"

"Because you keep tryin' these same ol' words on me, which I know by heart and really don't need to hear no more—"

"Yes you do! Because if you the work of Satan, me seeing and hearing you like this, then that's my armor!"

He rolled over toward his mother. Reached over and touched her cheek, gentle, loving.

"Uh-uh, no, I don't got any need for all them words no more, Momma. We long past scripture with this."

She let herself be lured in by his touch. His proximity. By his smile. Her breathing slowed. She was on the threshold of sleep, but then noticed that his smile wasn't what she'd first seen. It had transformed and was no longer merciful or empathetic. No, she'd let herself be tricked once again, because this was a mischievous smile. A secretive smile. A smile that meant there was some plan or series of events he wasn't going to share and she couldn't divine.

She smacked his hand away and rolled over.

16

NATASHA THOMAS-ENGEL

I'm honestly not sure what my parents think I do most of the time. When Elijah went away to boarding school, we agreed — or they agreed and presented it to me as if it were a "family agreement" — that we'd eat at least two meals a week together, Tuesday and Thursday dinners, and one meal on the weekend that could be either brunch or dinner. But that was almost four years ago and now one of them usually has some other scheduling conflict, so it's usually just one meal a week, and half the time one of them has to step away from that one meal to take a call.

Most mornings I'll run into Mom in the kitchen making her matcha, and there will be some inane comment about whether I have the right item of clothing for whatever the weather is, but Dad is already long gone, like before I even wake up. The truth is, I interact more with Malaya and Aurora than with my parents on an average day because they're already there in the mornings when I leave and they're still there when I get back. Plus they seem more interested, which I guess makes sense. Because if I were cleaning, shopping and prepping meals for a family like ours, I'd at least want to have some insights into what they do with their days, and what they like and dislike. Right? I mean just so you feel invested. Otherwise, it would really just feel arbitrary and probably just stoke some sense of resentment that you're doing all this work, year after year, for this family you don't even know, and what's the point other than the paycheck. Not that a paycheck isn't enough, it's just that it'd be more meaningful if you feel a connection, which is what I get from Malaya and Aurora.

For example, sometimes Malaya will leave a prepared snack

or meal in the fridge for me with a note saying something like "hope the test was good today xoxo" if I'd told her earlier that I had a chem exam that was stressing me out. It's the type of gesture Mom might have done a few years ago.

I guess the point is there are big chunks of time when I'm finished with school and my two extracurriculars, lit club and fencing, when my parents have literally no idea what I'm doing, and apparently don't really care. I mean they'll ask how school was or what I'm up to, but it's nothing like my friend Brook's mom who pretty much sits her down and interrogates her every night, and tracks her phone constantly, and loses her shit if Brook forgets to text when she's leaving school and then again when she arrives back at their apartment. But Brook's an only child and her parents recently divorced and her mom is definitely a bit extra. Like Brook is always telling her she needs new meds, or at least a higher dose, and then the other day she told me that if her mother doesn't emotionally recalibrate soon she's going to crush up these hard candy edibles she has and put them in her mom's cereal or coffee "to mellow her the fuck out."

My parents are probably more hands-off because they already went through it with Elijah and he basically turned out okay, at least on paper. I guess they assume I'm just this introverted kid who reads when I'm not at school or lit club or fencing. Fine.

But thinking about all this the other day got me wondering about their days, or really anyone's days. Like all the little moments and interactions and habits and secret routines that fill our waking hours that we don't share and that nobody really witnesses, or nobody could witness unless they were following you. Like, for example, it was only this February or March that I started stopping at the bakery on 74th and Amsterdam and buying a pain au chocolat most afternoons after school. The employees there know it's become a sort of ritual for me, but they're the only ones, because by the time I get home, I've already finished it and dropped the wax paper bag in the trash can on the corner of CPW and 75th. So that's a sort of innocent but private routine I have. Which begs the question: what are the routines and rituals and habits Mom and Dad have that they don't share and that I've never witnessed?

The more you think about it, the more it's like what a book can do. As a reader, especially as we're entering into the world of a book, like in the earlier chapters, we're traveling alongside our protagonist for all these quieter, more private moments. Or sometimes we're even in their heads as they deliberate about something, and it's these moments and thoughts and small choices that reveal the true essence of a character that we might end up loving or hating or thinking about for years to come. And it's really an accumulation of the smaller moments that helps us understand why a character might make the bigger choices they do, like falling in love with someone who appears to be their polar opposite, or sabotaging a rival out of jealousy, or even killing their nemesis. As a reader, if we can relate to and believe the little moments and choices, then we'll believe in and have empathy for the bigger, more dramatic choices our characters make. At least that's what I think a good writer does. Like they lay all the smaller bricks so that when you pull back and see the entire wall or the full building, it makes sense and is beautiful or revelatory or confusing, but in a satisfying way.

Maybe I'm getting lost in the metaphors. The point is, with my parents, I realize that I don't know these more granular moments and character details, and so really you could argue that I don't really know them. Which I think is actually pretty much true. Take my dad. Most days he leaves the apartment by 6 a.m., which is something he must take pride in, because he talks about it all the time, or used to when Elijah was younger and preparing to head off to school.

"Always make it a point to be the first one in, last one out," he'd say.

Apparently this was something his father and maybe his grandfather said and did too. A tradition, like a badge of honor. Whatever. Seems childish, honestly, or cliché that this is what you choose to take pride in. Especially since "The Family Office" is our family, and he's the one in charge of the office. I mean he could just as easily declare to the world that he's organized his life around having leisurely breakfasts with his wife of 23 years, and how they go to pilates three times a week together because they value and prioritize their relationship and their health and, in his vast experience, health is true wealth and they plan to live to 125. It all just seems kinda random. Also, the reality is that he could probably never ever show up at The Family Office and the machinery he's got in place would keep doing whatever it's doing, all the "due diligence" and "asset allocation" and "tax-advantaged giving" or whatever. Basically, the thing would stay on auto-pilot and the net worth would keep going up, which I guess is the main point. "The beauty of compound interest" and all that. I don't really know what I'm talking about with the lingo but that's the general idea. "Capital begets capital," like my classmate Rohan Zindler kept talking about last semester in our History of the Industrial Revolution class, I guess quoting Karl Marx. His father is a professor at CUNY and Rohan likes to tell anyone who will listen that he's been a neo-Marxist since the 6th grade, which is ironic because he's been attending a private day school that costs 65k a year since pre-k. He also likes to talk about disavowing the trust he's set to inherit when he turns 18 but, again, because he talks about it so much, I'm not really sure what's true and what's just a desperate cry for attention. Mainly I think he's just really horny. Like in math class if I ever glance over he's usually all agitated and it's clear he's attempting to hide a boner under his baggy vintage corduroys, which don't seem to be the right choice, because they form a very visible teepee that's just pretty disgusting. There's a lot about Rohan I don't understand, like psychologically.

But back to my father. There are definitely some aspects of his character that are revealed by him always wanting to be the first to arrive at his office, but the reality for me is that once he closes the door behind him at 6am and before he returns home, usually after 8pm, I really couldn't say with any certainty what he actually does. My mom too. Like what do adults do with all their time, all day, for years and decades and full lifetimes?

With my mom, at least I can pull up a mental visualization of her during the day, at different times. I know she goes to her showroom and office, and talks with her designers and the people that manufacture the furniture, and she also goes to pilates and meets her therapist a few times a week, and goes to the gym. I know recently she's also been on the phone with relatives and doctors down south a ton. And that she goes to charity functions maybe once a week, all the causes she donates money to, because sometimes I'll go with her to those.

———

So anyhow, the other day I decided to get up before anyone else and leave the apartment before anyone else and stand on the other side of the street so that when my dad exited our apartment building, I could watch him enter into his day, beyond where I've seen his day begin before. Turns out it was a stupid idea because he basically exited the building, smiled and said something to our doorman, Eddie Velazquez, and then climbed into the waiting car. Which of course if I'd thought about it for like half a second I'd have known would be the case, but in my imagination I'd seen myself following him down the block, like fifty paces behind, and that I'd learn a bunch of new details, like maybe he stopped in for a croissant too or maybe he'd come up behind the skinny old woman walking the two Irish Wolfhounds and he'd pause to pet them, or even pull a treat for each of them from his blazer pocket.

Point is I thought I'd learn more. Instead he stepped down off the curb, climbed into the car, Eddie closed the door behind him, and I couldn't even see his expression because of the tinted windows as his driver took off. So it was something, a few more brush strokes on the canvas of my father's day, but not much. I did like how he smiled and said something funny to Eddie. Like maybe he prepares a new joke to tell him each day? Or maybe he asked Eddie about his family? Or maybe he said how Eddie looked sharp with his new haircut? Something. He was engaging with the world and I liked to see that, how confident and at ease he looked in his own skin. So I decided to continue with my sleuthing and took a car downtown to his office building later that week, again up and out before anyone else, and I watched him exit his car there and enter the building. Again, I noticed how he seemed to be liked by those with whom he interacted. His driver, and Eddie, and the doorman at his office building, they were always smiling or laughing together. But then I thought maybe this is the dynamic only because he pays them, and whoever controls the purse strings is always the funny one, if that's how they are presenting themselves and want to be perceived.

Which reminded me of a short story I read about how some rich boss of some garment factory thought he was just hilarious because all his employees always laughed at his jokes. They'd laughed until tears flowed. They'd slapped their knees with their palms. They'd hold each other up so they wouldn't collapse to the floor in heaps of laughter. But then something happened, and the boss lost everything, was bankrupt from one day to the next, and had to lay everyone off and even sell his country estate. The only thing he knew he still possessed was his undeniably good sense of humor. So he got dressed in his one remaining suit and walked out into the streets and started sharing all the jokes he'd collected over the years, the ones that had been so successful in his earlier life. But no one laughed. No one even smiled. His wife got so sick of him trying the jokes on her, over and over, that she left him too. I think the story was written by an Eastern European, maybe Czech or Polish. It was super depressing but also really stuck in my mind because it reveals something true about human nature. Maybe my father thought he was funny because he was rich and had the power to fire basically anyone he interacted with, in effect anyone who didn't laugh at his jokes. Anyhow, seeing him interacting with even just Eddie and his driver made me more interested in understanding what was going on. So over the next few weeks I started following my mom and my dad. I followed them around without them knowing, sometimes in the morning before school, more often in the afternoons and evenings.

17

NEIL ENGEL

There were probably 50 qualified candidates among the almost 500 applications received by my HR team, but only one really stood out after the initial round of interviews. And once we met in person, there was no doubt in my mind. If we were going to survive and thrive during and after the shock, this guy needed to be in the mix. It wasn't just the training he received as a member of the 75th Ranger Regiment, or his ten subsequent years in special ops with Delta Force. There were other candidates with credentials along those lines, including two prior members of Seal Team 6. Turns out there are plenty of adept killers out there, most with extensive combat experience followed by lucrative stints doing the dirty work for dictators, drug cartels, and billionaire paranoiacs.

What struck me about Gavin wasn't only that he was a badass in terms of protecting assets, neutralizing threats, and planning and executing complex missions. It was also that he grew up on a family farm in Nebraska. The Haines family had deep roots in Platte County, he told me, going back to the early 1800s. He knew about crop rotation, seasonal variance, what to plant when and where during prolonged droughts. I hadn't thought it possible, but we were getting the mercenary muscle as well as the agronomist, all in one package. So I offered him the job at $350,000 a year, for a two-year contract. Walk away with $700,000 net, all other expenses covered. Once he'd agreed in principle, and my team had run background checks and scheduled physical and psych evaluations, of course he wanted to know more specifics himself. So I had him come into the office at 6am, two hours before any other staff members would show up.

"Okay, so am I understanding right that we'll be living above ground until you decide even that's too risky?" he said.

We were sitting in my office, with views out over Battery Park to the Statue of Liberty, Ellis Island and New Jersey beyond. It was a beautiful morning. Clear skies. Traffic still light on the streets below. I'd been describing the overall scenario, and my expectations of him, and he'd begun to pepper me with questions in return.

"Well, it's not really me deciding, but yeah. The algorithm calculates threat levels and then recommends an action plan tailored to our specific circumstance. Basically, it ranks options for us. If there's nuclear fallout or some pandemic spreading via unknown means, then it'll recommend we go below ground, with estimates on how long we'll need to hunker down. We're stocked with five years of supplies, for up to eight adults."

He nodded, eyes on me, assessing.

I gave it a beat. Stared straight back. Didn't want it to seem that I was selling this too hard. Also, I wanted him to recognize that I wasn't your typical prepper, just parroting language that had been circulating on the web for decades. There was an extremely sophisticated model involved.

"Of course before that, chances are good we'll already have relocated. Maybe due to social unrest resulting from markets collapsing or some shock to global trade and commerce. Or even the implosion of regional or national governments. Point is, phase one is relocation, and living above ground on a 250-acre compound with water, farmland, livestock, game we can hunt, fully fenced, fully self-sufficient. Also totally isolated. You've got thick forest as a buffer for thousands of acres in all directions, and accessed only by air at this point."

Again, he just sat there, focus unwavering, confident in his skin, no doubt tabulating and re-tabulating pros and cons. And also trying to get a read on my character, his potential boss for a job that couldn't fully be envisioned for either of us.

"I'll definitely want a site visit before signing on, but yeah, I'm interested," he said.

"Glad to hear it."

"Also, it'd be good to get a list of the other families or individuals who have signed up. Owners of the other units. We'll want to do some due diligence there."

I grabbed a folder on my desk and handed it to him.

"On it already, but will definitely want to hear your thoughts."

He opened the folder, began leafing through the documents.

I watched him. He really was a fine specimen, an archetype, really, in the same way Flor was. He was well-proportioned, handsome, self-confident but not in an arrogant way. His questions were targeted and pragmatic, nothing extraneous. And, just as important, he didn't seem to lapse into unremitting asskissing like so many of my other employees. Although clearly he valued the proposition I'd set before him, he wasn't going to blow smoke up my ass to get hired. He knew his worth. I knew his worth. This was someone who would share his assessments, opinions and recommendations whether I asked for them or not. And that's what I needed for this mission.

But watching him peruse the contents of the folder, I also couldn't help but speculate out farther, beyond this first in-person interaction. This was an actual person in front of me, endowed with his own unique set of prerogatives, desires and impulses. It was this person, Gavin Haines, who was about to embody the hypothetical placeholder I'd been imagining for so many months.

Various scenarios began to unspool in my mind. If we, as a family unit of four, together with Flor and Gavin and some additional staff, are in fact forced to relocate, and then possibly live below ground in a bunker for years at a time, what sort of dynamic might evolve? And it's not only below ground, during years that would clearly tax each of us psychically and psychologically. What about after, assuming the world becomes habitable again? We might emerge as one of only a handful of human survivors. Would Gavin feel indebted to me at that point? Would he feel indebted to my family? Or would he kill me off, the old alpha for the new, and begin siring children with Flor and possibly Natasha. Would he let Zora live on, the old matriarch still valuable to the clan for child-rearing and household chores? Would he kill Elijah, viewing him as competition, or would he enlist him and train him as a fellow warrior, though forever of lower rank?

Gavin Haines. This handsome, unassuming man sitting across from me in jeans, boots, a casual shirt. He's unquestionably a leader. He's demonstrated that in the military and I have full confidence he'll demonstrate that in the years ahead. He's the right choice. The right choice in terms of our surviving the trials ahead, and yet, counter-intuitively, hiring him may also result in my demise. In five, ten, or twenty years he might decide, based on his calculus — a new calculus that we can only begin to imagine — he might decide that I'm redundant. One morning he might wake up and decide I'm deadweight, a drain on clan resources, that I add nothing in this new context other than competition. I can see it. With our two-year contract long up, and the realization that $700,000 is meaningless in this new reality, he'll make the determination that slitting my throat while I sleep is the best move in terms of securing his primacy and ensuring his biological imperative is realized. My forethought, my algorithm, and my high net worth will have enabled our small clan to summit the treacherous mountain. We will have survived against all odds. And yet this man before me may well decide that I shouldn't be allowed to enjoy the land of milk and honey below.

He looks up from the folder. "I'll do some additional research."

He stands and extends his hand. Smiles.

"And let me know when it works to do a site visit."

18

ELIJAH THOMAS-ENGEL

It could be any of them, really. Choate. Deerfield. Hotchkiss. Andover or Exeter. St. Paul's. All basically the same. So I guess just assume it's one of them. A feeder school. Endowments so bloated it's become like an arms race in terms of how extreme it can get with the aquatic and equestrian centers, the pimped out dining halls, the Gehry-designed science labs, the faculty-student ratios, the percentage of one-percenters and, more recently, the fight over who can recruit the largest crop of "underserved" POC geniuses with refugee parents who didn't attend college and who can demonstrate they have a combined adjusted gross income of under 50k. Okay, rambling here, but the point is my suspicion was correct. When I got back from visiting Grandpa down South, with just the kernel of an idea beginning to form, I decided to check out my school's Makers Lab, and it didn't disappoint.

The place is huge, almost always empty and, when I asked for a tour from the Bangladeshi work-study tutor on duty — who apparently posted a perfect SAT score at age 12 — I wasn't at all surprised that there were six different 3D printers just sitting there. Available to me at all hours. Because that's what you get from an endowment of $631 million and a tuition of 76k. Anything remotely "educational" better be at your fingertips at a whim's notice. And if it's not, some dean will be soliciting someone to write a fat check by day's end and said educational item will be delivered and installed in a nice new building with a nice new Mr. and Mrs. So-and-So donor plaque before whatever bright young mind smokes another bowl of chronic and spaces on what his/her/their whim might have been.

My whim's a little different, although there's been plenty of press about it, and also attempts to get the relevant info removed from the web. I'd read that some Swiss researchers printed and assembled a model called the Liberator with a plastic called acrylonitrile butadiene styrene. Again, not hard to order. Or, in my case, available in the Makers Lab. So that was it. I downloaded the plans, inserted the styrene and fired up the printer when the lab was empty. I figured it was best to print one piece per visit because, individually and unassembled, you'd have no idea what I was going for. Which is also my plan for transport when and if the time comes: unassembled and therefore no red flags raised.

The Swiss researchers clocked the speed of bullets exiting the Liberator's chamber at between 138 and 172 meters per second, which I guess is about half as fast as a normal bullet from a normal pistol, but still plenty fast. Particularly at close range. On another site, I'd read that the styrene can easily be dissolved in a solvent like acetone. Just pop it in the fluid, leave overnight, and it's gone, like a tooth in Coke. Which I guess is why law enforcement types are shitting their pants. I had 13 of the 31 pieces printed by Spring Break.

————

I'd told my folks I was going to St. Louis with Liza again. In reality, I'd booked a ticket to Montgomery, since my mom didn't seem interested or able to go, and since I'd proposed a paper about it for Peace & Justice, my final humanities class of high school. Liza agreed to go with me. Not sure what she told her parents, but probably something about visiting my family in Alabama. Something that would appeal to their ideological outlook. Nice little story about their socially-conscious, socially-engaged daughter traveling to the reddest of Red States with her "mixed" boyfriend to visit his impoverished Black ancestors. So brave. So committed. So awake to

The Moment. I imagine that kind of anecdote would have mad cachet in her parents' world of enlightened liberal scholars, artists and philanthropists. A little nugget they could toss out at their next dinner party as their peers jousted over which of their offspring was whateverthefuck champion or whose kid was recently accepted early action at whogivesafuck.

Harrowing. A word I'm sure is often used. Gut-wrenching. Heinous. Evil incarnate. I'll probably use all of them and more in my essay for Dr. Nasser. But despite the take-away the museum wants you to have — which I guess involves an acknowledgement of the brutality and general fucked-up-edness of the myth of racial difference, and the centuries of slavery and incarceration that resulted, and how through an acknowledgement and maybe some token reparations our country must continue to limp toward a "more perfect union" — the truth is there are really all kinds of possible take-aways from a visit to the National Memorial for Peace and Justice and The Legacy Museum. For example, just read the MLK quote they've got displayed front-and-center on one wall:

True peace is not merely the absence of tension; it is the presence of justice.

Okay, yeah, except who's defining justice here? We talking Old Testament or New? We eye-for-eyeing it or turning the other cheek? And when Martin phrases it like that, seems there's never been true peace anywhere on earth for any population ever. Because there's never been justice. And the "presence of justice" is gonna be different for anyone who has suffered an insult or injury. If I'm a devout Muslim in the mountains of Afghanistan whose child bride runs away, then justice might look like a public flogging or beheading. And obviously the child bride has some other sense of justice if she's willing to make a run for it, imperiling her life and shaming her entire family.

And then they got this on another wall, staring you right in the face as you come through the main entrance:

For the hanged and beaten.
For the shot, drowned, and buried.
For the tortured, tormented, and terrorized.
For those abandoned by the rule of law.
We will remember.
With hope because hopelessness is the enemy of justice.
With courage because peace requires bravery.
With persistence because justice is a constant struggle.
With faith because we shall overcome.

Come on, though, is that really enough? To remember with hope and courage? To persistently remember? And I'm not even sure what to remember "with faith" would look like. Seems way too fucking passive to me. What about to build a case — which the museum does an excellent job of — and then use it to prosecute these motherfuckers who continue to benefit? No justice, no peace.

But you do gotta give it to 'em. The curators, and whoever put up the cash for this place. Because all the artifacts and stats and videos paint an irrefutable picture about the past, but also the present and probable future. They got a whole wing on mass incarceration. And obviously we're talking about Black and Brown men here. Stats saying that one out of three Black boys born today — "at the dawn of the 21st century" — will end up in prison at some point in their lifetime. They don't break it down, but it would be interesting to see how colorism and family net worth impacts that prediction. I'm sure my pops could get some assistant to dig that shit up.

Because they're Black, the staff at the front desk and the

docents in the exhibit halls can tell I'm part of the story. The diaspora. The middle passage. The legacy. Yeah, one part of my story is definitely represented here. Not that they or Liza know the specifics. But they can tell I'm not just another white Northerner trying to wrap my head around the history that sits at the crumbling foundation of my privilege. They can tell because of my hair and maybe my nose. They know I'm part of the "one drop" story, and they nod in acknowledgement. Which, not gonna lie, feels good. To be here in a place that puts it all out there on display. An institution that, unlike my family, acknowledges the fact that my mom's cousin, my namesake, was lynched. Strung up in a camphor tree. That a noose with 11 loops was cinched so tight around his neck that the police had to use a razor knife to cut it off.

Liza and I stood under one of the 805 steel rectangles that hang down over museum visitors, each one representing a US county where a lynching took place. That's 805 counties out of 3006 in the country. 4407 documented lynchings of African American men and women since 1877. Each rectangle is the size of a coffin. I stood under the Mobile County block and I read his name, inscribed there on the bottom. I read his name and several other names out loud. Liza didn't know why and didn't ask why, but she must have recognized that we share a first name. After that, she just sort of trailed me, silent almost the whole time, maybe thinking that because this is my history she didn't have the right to say anything or interrupt my thoughts. Or maybe she could sense that the reason I came here was greater than just to do research for a school paper.

Later, at the hotel, we just lay there, her head resting on my chest, listening to my heart. The fingers of her right hand were intertwined with mine and she held on tight. I'd thought we'd order room service and fuck until my dick got sore again, but that didn't happen. Neither of us were in the mood. She fell asleep and I just kept thinking about my namesake, and the fact that his name was engraved on the bottom of a massive steel rectangle hanging in a legacy museum, 300,000 visitors per year walking under that remembrance. And even though that's cool, to know his name is forcing all these people to reckon with our ugly history, it still feels like he didn't get justice. Even though each of his three murderers died in jail over the past ten years, Namesake Elijah didn't get peace. He didn't and we definitely didn't. Not my mom. Or Auntie Mita. Or Shawna. Or me. Or LaVonn, who probably got the worst of it, and who I'd never even met on account of him being locked up. As I lay there, that seemed like the natural next place to go in order to understand the real legacy that's not depicted in the museum.

———

Woke up with my dick in Liza's mouth. She was smiling up at me, a twinkle in her brown eyes. She held my gaze, unblinking, as she worked my knob with skill and enthusiasm, exhibiting that same self-confidence that always rattled me. Where did it come from, her ability to be so self-assured in all her choices? She's like the polar opposite of the neurotic Jew stereotype. Hands-down the least anxious teenager I knew. She's confident in class. Confident on the sports field. Confident in social settings even when surrounded by conventionally hotter WASP girls with their long field hockey legs and humble brags about weekend trips to St. Barts. She was confident that I'd be happy waking up with my cock in her mouth. Which of course I was.

It was actually my first time waking up this way. Highly recommend it. Especially pleasant for me after our visit to the museum the day before and the fitful night I'd had, where I kept thinking about, or maybe dreaming about, my mom as a girl. And the story she'd told me about going fishing with LaVonn. How he'd been a quiet, sweet kid, a few years younger than her. And that it was hard to imagine anyone with the deck stacked more against them. She'd listed it all out for me, maybe when I was 13 or 14 and had been acting like an entitled little prick. She'd told me how he was the victim of a system that didn't recognize his learning differences, didn't recognize his need for therapy following his father's murder, didn't in any way steer him away from the default path of crime and incarceration. Just like the museum documented. He was one of the "every three." Like a poster child for that particular stat.

All this mental chatter was momentarily pushed aside as I exploded into Liza's warm mouth. She smiled up at me and swallowed, and it made me wonder how much of a factor something like this plays into the equation of saying and meaning the words: "I love you." Really. I'm not fucking joking right now. Her eyes watered as she swallowed a second time, getting it all down. I mean what she did, and how she did it, speaks to me about who she is and why I feel the way I do about her. Her swallowing my cum, smiling, swallowing a second time, then opening her mouth and sticking out her tongue to show me she'd swallowed it all... it almost brought me to tears. That she can do that and it's not even remotely demeaning. That it actually seems to give her pleasure while also giving me so much pleasure. The sincerity of it all. She means it. I mean it. And it's not some bs porn role-playing situation.

I smile down at her, shaking my head in awe and gratitude, as she climbs up onto my naked belly and rests her warm, naked chest on mine.

"Thank you."

"You're welcome."

"I think I love you."

"No. No fucking way! Sorry," she says. "Not allowed to say that after just blowing a massive load in my mouth."

"Thought maybe you'd say that."

"Thought right, then." She kisses me and smirks.

"Remember Wilkes' class? How the male brain doesn't fully mature until at least twenty-five."

"Yeah. What's that got to do with anything?"

"Pretty much means you don't know what the hell you're doing or saying, especially when your dick's involved."

"Okay, maybe. What'd he say about the female brain again?"

"Thought you got an A."

"I did."

She smiled again. Kissed me again.

"We're like three years ahead of you, developmentally. Also, later, we don't get dementia as frequently. And we live longer. So, yeah..."

Smart as fuck and sexy. But I still mean what I said, despite my stunted male brain. It's gotta be love, this feeling.

"So there's something else I wanna do while we're down here," I say. "Another place I'd like to visit, if that's cool."

"Of course, yeah, but first I gotta eat something. Need to try that Shrimp and Grits Breakfast special."

She rolls over and grabs the phone. Presses "O".

"Want one?"

I nod. Definitely.

———

A prison guard got stabbed here last year. And two inmates were killed in the last six months, the murders still unsolved and most likely gonna stay that way. Apparently, no one gives enough of a shit to really investigate. And that's how the place looks when you roll up. Like the walls and fences topped with big loops of barbed wire get their strength and menace from decades of beatings, rapes, and shivs to the jugular. Also all the lonely deaths, clock just running out on so many forgotten lives. It's an 8,200 acre facility that opened in 1928 with a working farm and manufacturing plant. I'd filled out the paperwork a week before coming down, in case I decided I wanted to do this. After the museum visit and the fucked-up dreams, and also the fact that it was only an hour south of Montgomery, I figured what the fuck. Plus Liza seemed cool with taking a drive and seeing more of the South. Not that either of us was prepared for this.

There's really no other way to express it other than LaVonn looked super fucked up. Like he's the embodiment of The Broken Black Man, with a front tooth missing and one of the lenses of his prison glasses cracked right down the middle. He looks like he weighs under 100 pounds, with sunken cheeks and deep eye sockets. And his hair is all lopsided like all he does is lie on his bed on one side, probably in the direction of a cinder block wall.

"You know who I am, right?"

He nodded at us through the plexiglass, his eyes unable to not wander to Liza.

"Zora's boy," he said. "I know who you is. Know you got the same name as my daddy."

I nodded. Liza glanced at me. I hadn't told her much. Really anything other than my mom's relative was in jail. She didn't know anything about the lynching.

"Heard your granddaddy ain't doing real good."

I nodded.

"This is Liza," I said. "A friend from school. We're both about to graduate."

"Girlfriend?"

I nodded. He looked from me, to her, and back. I found Liza's hand beneath the formica counter and squeezed.

"Other'n my grandmama, you the first person visited since they locked me up." He couldn't keep his eyes off Liza.

"Is it okay if I ask you about your father?" I said.

LaVonn shrugged.

"How old were you when it happened?"

"First or second grade."

"You remember him well?"

LaVonn shrugged again, shifted his weight in the chair, eyes blinking rapidly behind the cracked glasses.

"See... now why you even here asking me these kinda questions?" he said.

I wasn't really sure. Maybe because my mom never wants to acknowledge the 800-pound gorilla in the room. Or elephant in the room. Not sure which expression works best in this particular situation, but the point is she doesn't want to confront it, or can't confront it, whatever the fucking animal. She never wants to talk about it, and neither does Shawna.

"It's part of a project for school," I said.

"Kinda project?"

"History class called Peace and Justice."

"You in the class too?" He was addressing Liza now. She shook her head.

He stared back at me. His lips were chapped, his skin dry. We must have looked like aliens to him and everyone at Fountain Correctional. Other than the warden who'd signed us in, everyone we'd seen was either Black or Latino, inmates and guards. As soon as we stepped out of the rental, all eyes immediately went to Liza, then clocked me for a second, then back to her with a mix of confusion and then a hardening gaze of pent-up lust. Prisoners stood in the yard, barbed wire fencing separating us, as we walked toward the building to check in. It was like their eyes were disrobing her and assaulting her. Bending her over in the parking lot and fucking her from behind over a car, fistful of hair in hand, jamming her face into the hood. This was animal instinct, brutal and short-lived. They didn't want to see her face or expression. That's the violence I saw in their eyes and postures, but maybe she didn't experience it like that. Hope she didn't.

"I'm writing a paper about our family," I said. "About what happened to your father, Elijah."

"Who else you talkin' to?"

"No one, really. My mom won't talk about it and I figured I should probably talk to you before asking Auntie Mita. Don't want to upset her."

He nodded. I couldn't figure out what he was thinking. Or really what he knew himself, or experienced himself, other than the fall-out of his father's murder, the single event that propelled him to this hellhole.

"But I've done some reading," I said. "What was in the papers, about what happened and the two trials. I guess one of the questions I have is if you think justice was served."

19

LAVONN PATTERSON

LaVonn stared down at his hands. Cracked one thumb, then the other. What the fuck was this white boy with his white girl-friend really asking? It didn't make no sense, but something about them sitting there reminded him of dessert. The fancy kind of dessert you'd get at a fancy restaurant. They were like two pieces of cheesecake with some kinda of sweet syrup drizzled on top. Strawberry syrup. Over the top but also swirled on the plate. Pretty to look at but even better to taste. What did her nipples look like, he wondered. Pink? Light pink like the strawberry drizzle on the cheesecake? Like on that "Bake Off" show he sometimes watched in the cafeteria. She had real pretty brown eyes and a thin neck with a birthmark just above her left collar bone. Nipples just had to be that light pink color—

The boy was asking the question again, about a father he didn't know. About a hole in his life that kept getting bigger, swallowing more and more people. Sucking them in. Pulling them down and not letting them climb back out for air. The boy was asking about justice. Which means what? He'd definitely had a gun, an illegal gun he'd bought for $125, and he'd used it in a robbery that went in a direction none of them thought it would. No one was supposed to get hurt. That was the deal. They'd even talked about going in there with empty chambers. But the woman behind the counter, this woman they didn't know, she'd ended up dead. She'd reached for something under the counter and everyone got nervous and so they'd shot her. And even though he hadn't pulled the trigger, he ended up with a life sentence because of the priors. So was that justice? Did her family think that was justice? He wasn't sure what justice was supposed to mean or look like, for him or his father or the dead woman who had smiled at them when they came in and greeted them in some soft foreign accent.

His Grandma Mita had talked about it. About how his father's killers got the book thrown at 'em. As a teenager, when he was beginning to get into trouble, she'd pulled out and read the newspaper articles she kept in a drawer in the kitchen. She read about how all three of them went to jail for the rest of their lives, and that it was one of the first times when white men went to jail for killing a Black man in the South. They'd been Klan members, but times had changed. They all got thrown in jail, even though the jury was almost all white. She'd read him the articles and she'd read him plenty of passages about righteousness and giving himself over to the Lord. Every time, she told him that the only judge who really mattered was the Lord. Salvation, peace, justice, it all flowed from the Lord and the words written in the holy book. But scripture didn't speak to him like it spoke to her. She didn't seem to have the same questions rattling around her head at all times of day and night. Questions about each of the steps along the way that landed him in here, and if he was really the one responsible for his actions or if some of what he was and what he did was actually because of what happened to his daddy. And if any part of his actions, his crimes, was because of what happened to his daddy, how much would that be? And if he let himself believe that some part of it was because his father was murdered, then maybe it wasn't actually his entire self that entered that office supply store with a loaded gun and watched as the small woman behind the counter collapsed into a puddle of her own blood. He could take some responsibility for his actions, definitely could and did, but should he take it all? And did any of this really matter, questions of justice and responsibility, given that nothing was going to change for him anyhow?

He wondered whether the Mexican had these same type of thoughts when he got visitors and they asked questions about the past. He'd made it clear through his fists that he didn't want the Mexican to ever talk to him, but he was beginning to think talking to him might not be such a bad idea. Except he wasn't actually sure how good the Mexican's English was.

White Elijah just kept coming at him with the questions.

ELIJAH THOMAS-ENGEL

It wasn't clear to me if LaVonn heard my words. Or maybe it was an issue of whether he had the capacity to really understand the questions. And I mean, fuck, asking someone in jail whether justice was served for the murder of his father is a pretty loaded and heavy question. Especially because he didn't even know me. But even without a response, the answer was clear as fucking day. LaVonn is a billboard for collateral damage. For the fact that justice wasn't served and probably never can be served. He's not at peace. There's not even the absence of tension. He lives in tension. His body carries the scars of trauma. His mind is corroded by PTSD. He's the victim here, and there's no one stepping up to avenge him.

"Don't know much about justice," he finally says.

I nod, still holding Liza's hand beneath the counter. He looks at her, then back to me.

"But if you got it, wondering if maybe you could leave $50 with the warden at the front desk. When you headin' out. So maybe I can buy me a new pair of glasses."

NEIL ENGEL

Our first meeting was at the Plaza, which she said felt stuffy and overwrought with its clawfoot tub, chandeliers, gilt headboard. It was backward-looking, she said, needlessly trying to replicate the grandeur of Old Europe.

"And why? If you want that, go to Europe. For me, this country is about this time we are living now. And also the future times to come."

I realized she was a bit of an architecture buff, and so the next time I booked us at the Standard, which quickly became our standard. She likes it for the way the massive cement columns rise up above the High Line, above the old industrial landscape, together with the clean lines of the glass facade and the interior woods. She also likes the views across the Hudson, especially at sunset.

Today, like most days, we end up in this, her favorite room, and she stands naked at the floor-to-ceiling window and stares down at the teeming masses on the High Line 23 stories below. I ask if she thinks they can see her standing there. She shrugs.

"It'd be a gift," I say.

"What?"

"If anyone happens to glance up and see you there. More beautiful than Lady Liberty. Definitely more memorable."

"You do not need to give complements," she says. "Even if you did not pay for me, this is not necessary."

It's honestly too much, the whole package, for a man of my age who's forgotten this feeling. How perfect she is — her form, coupled with the thick, buttery accent. And the ferocity in her eyes when we're fucking. But also when we're not. The way she stares right back, unblinking, as if witnessing the full spectrum of my being, in a way no one ever has. It's as if she sees my strengths and successes, but also my blights and imperfections, my frailties. And they don't revolt her. Maybe this is the radical honesty people talk about. Because I do feel like I can share my full and true self with her in a way I never can with Zora. And I'm willing — eager, in fact — to witness her true self in all its multifaceted complexity.

Of course my friend Ben just says I'm pussy whipped. He says it was like this for him when he bailed on his first marriage and started dating his second wife, and then again when courting his new fiancée. And of course you do have to wonder if it's like this for all the men who pay Flor for her services.

"I need to ask you something," I say.

She continues to stare down at the cityscape below, with its ant-sized humanity hurrying here and crawling there.

"I've been working on a program for several years with my team. It categorizes and ranks all the various risk factors out there. All the things that threaten our survival as a species."

She turns toward me, her silhouette backlit by the setting sun. It's almost cliché how the golden orb behind her illuminates the tiny triangle between the top of her thighs and her shaved pussy. I'm sure there's a name for that, the space where the sun now peaks through. It's a vision like some 1980s Penthouse spread my tween friends and I might have salivated over. She waits for me to say more.

"Right now, the time we're living in, it's arguably the most precarious in all of human history. The most dangerous time."

She smiles.

"What?"

"I think it has probably always felt this way for many people at many different times," she says. "Since the beginning of time. For example, this is how Caracas was for me six years ago. For example, it could happen that I walk on the street and I am shot in the middle of the afternoon and no one would do anything to stop this. Or you don't know if there will be food to buy the next day or next week. Or if the money you have saved will be worth anything in one month's time. But now?"

She smiles and gestures at the tray on the fold-out table next to the bed, at the champagne on ice and her half-eaten burger and sweet potato fries. "Now there is room service."

I want her to come and lie on top of me. Just rest her warm, perfect form on top of mine. And I want that feeling to last. She turns back to the window.

"When I look, these people down there look happy. Yes. They are eating ice cream. They are kissing. They are pushing their kids and walking dogs. Maybe they have gone to the museum today. Or maybe to the Apple store for the new phone. Or they met with friends for coffee. I think they do not have whatever program you are talking about that you have developed for two years, this program that says life is so dangerous."

She's right, of course, about the people down below. And they will likely perish because they are oblivious. Or maybe she thinks their experience of life, all the singular moments that give them joy, in aggregate, make for a more fulfilling human experience even if it will be cut short. Even if it will end in brutality and privation like she experienced in Venezuela. Maybe she believes living in the happy present is enough, and is far better than fretting about and planning for the inevitable. I certainly can't enjoy the moments in the same way anymore, knowing what I know, and knowing that I am in the unique position to save myself and a few select others.

"I have a question for you," I say.

She turns and waits.

"Okay. So if I were to pay you $250,000 a year, for a minimum of two years, would you be willing to come live with me?"

She moves to the bed and, as if reading my earlier thoughts, climbs on top of me. She straddles my torso, looking down at me as I lie back.

"You have a family, yes?"

I nod.

"A wife?"

I nod.

"Okay, so you want to leave everything to live with me for only two years?"

I shake my head.

"Then explain me, please."

I love when she says this. "Explain me." I wish I could. I wish I knew her well enough to explain her to her, and to understand her myself. I wish I knew myself well enough to explain me.

"It's probably easier if I show you," I say. "Where we'd be living."

She stares down at me, intrigued.

"This is some special mystery you are talking about? Are you making a joke?"

"No, I promise."

"And one hundred percent you are saying you would pay me half a million dollars to live with you for two years?"

I nod.

She leans down and kisses me with her full lips. Her nipples touch my chest. Her eyes are open, as are mine. She smiles and drops her full weight onto me. I feel her warmth, top to bottom. She smirks and rests her head on my chest.

"You should know that it is possible that I would say yes for less money. But now I think this is maybe only your first offer, so we will have to see. You show me the place where we will live and then I can decide how much more you will need to pay for me."

Opportunistic. Powerful. Ruthless. And well-equipped for the life ahead. I feel myself getting hard again.

22

NATASHA THOMAS-ENGEL

If I didn't read like I do, my reaction to what I uncovered would be totally different. Like if I hadn't read so many books about people being stuck in relationships or marriages that don't bring them joy but instead drive them to seek happiness or love or purpose in other ways or with other people. Obviously, that's the theme at the center of AK. Lots of the Russian lit I love basically uses this as scaffolding for all the interesting characters. People are stuck in marriages that are slowly killing them. Or they're trapped by class or lack of money or societal expectation about what they are allowed to do and who they are allowed to love. Virginia Woolf is another, obviously, in terms of what she writes about in her books but also how she lived her life; marrying a man and then having many affairs with women, and being sort of unabashedly public about her decades-long love of Vita Sackville-West (which is a pretty badass name, btw, Vita Sackville). If you read more about the artists and writers who were part of the Bloomsbury Group, and I have, then you realize it was all about this. They chose to veer off from the cultural norms and create the art they wanted to, and support one another in being unconventional, and pretty much sleep with whomever they wanted to, man or woman, because ultimately I guess they thought life is too short to suffer jobs that crush your soul or partners who repulse you. This is what VW wrote:

> *We were full of experiments and reforms. We were going to paint; to write; to have coffee after dinner instead of tea at nine-o'clock. Everything was going to be new; everything was going to be different. Everything was on trial.*

I like that. *Everything on trial.* Like just don't sit there accepting whatever is expected of you because it's expected of you. Or suffer endlessly and needlessly because you're surrounded by people who are annoying or doltish. She talks about her brother Thoby bringing friends home from Cambridge and their regular Thursday night salons where they'd sit around, I guess drinking coffee instead of tea, and discussing subjects like beauty and goodness and reality and the nature of love. And what she really goes on about is the fact that these young Cambridge men didn't seem interested in marrying and also weren't attractive enough for her to want to sleep with them or marry them. So basically they were ugly but super smart. Edwardian nerds, and I'm guessing probably queer. In her words:

> *It was precisely this lack of physical splendour, this shabbiness! that*
> *was in my eyes a proof of their superiority. More than that, it was,*
> *in some obscure way, reassuring; for it meant that things could go*
> *on like this, in abstract argument, without dressing for dinner, and*
> *never revert to the ways, which I had come to think so distasteful.*

Of course they were all British aristocrats and Virginia and her siblings had inherited enough money to buy a house and live without having to work. That was a point we talked about at length in the class that included some Victorian and Modernist lit, and it was a valid critique according to our teacher, Miss Varda. She agreed that bucking convention is made possible, or at least made much easier, by financial independence. But she also impressed upon us that these individuals did suffer because of their radical ideas and life choices. I mean VW filled her jacket pockets with rocks and drowned herself in the River Ouse, after all, though some say that was because she was bipolar and didn't get any treatment. But my point, or one of them, anyway, is that it's pretty close to the class situation at my school and definitely at Elijah's boarding school. And even so, you have all these people today who are crippled by anxiety and in therapy or on meds or self medicating because of the weight of societal forces they perceive to be crushing them. I see that in my own family with Elijah and my dad, or at least I did. Elijah definitely feels pressure, which has made him lash out a few times, to the point where I thought maybe he was actually going to rebel and chart his own course, but ultimately he's basically following the exact path Dad hoped for, almost like it was pre-ordained for the firstborn boychild of the family.

But of course now, because of what I witnessed when I was following him, there's a whole new dimension to my father. And I'm trying not to immediately rush to judgement because, again, I've read these books that have forced me to consider all the ways we as humans can or should choose to live. I mean, okay, I'm not saying it wasn't shocking, or isn't still shocking, what I saw. My hands literally started shaking so much that I couldn't unscrew the top of my water bottle. That was my first physical reaction and my mental reaction was similar. Like totally scrambled. I saw what was undeniably happening right in front of me, but it still took a moment to assemble the puzzle pieces. I was sitting in the lobby of the Standard Hotel High Line. That was the setting. And I was in the disguise I'd used several times before when following my dad: sunglasses and my hair in braids, tucked under a baseball cap, wearing my mom's leggings and a T-shirt that made me look like I'd been jogging in Hudson River Park or at some stupid spin class. Basically an outfit I'd never wear and activities I'll never do. My father was across the lobby by the bank of elevators and, yes, OBVIOUSLY, the woman he was stepping onto the elevator with was his MISTRESS. Or an ESCORT, CALL GIRL, WHORE, PROSTITUTE, SEX WORKER. This was now obvious to me because it was the second time I'd witnessed them together. The first time was exactly one week prior, same place, same time. That time I thought maybe it was just a business meeting or an interview situation, and that they were heading up to the restaurant. This time the reality of the situation smacked me upside the head and smacked me hard. I'd be an idiot not to know what this is.

First of all, she's gorgeous and probably 22. So, honestly, what would anyone think, especially the way he stepped aside to let her on the elevator, and the way his open palm touched the small of her back to guide her in, just a little lower than would be right if this were a platonic situation. I mean it'd be far-fetched to think she's his daughter or a work colleague. Also, she's wearing jeans, boots, a puffer jacket, with her hair back in a ponytail, so not exactly business or business casual attire. I guess in some leap of fantasy he might be some media exec or agent and she's either an actress or influencer and they're meeting about some new project, but the reality is, even that would be bad optics at this point in time. Especially to be meeting at a hotel.

She looks maybe Puerto Rican or Dominican, complexion a little darker than mine, really pretty, definitely sexy. So the elevator doors close and I'm sort of left in a daze of not knowing how to react or what to do, and it isn't until maybe 30 minutes later when I'm outside walking on the High Line, still trying to wrap my head around what I saw and what it all means, and I look back up at the hotel and scan the windows, and I'm pretty sure I see her standing in the window on the third floor from the top and she's completely naked, looking out toward Jersey and the setting sun. Everyone on the High Line is doing that too, looking West, but I'm staring back at the hotel and her. And the questions had already been stampeding circles in my head, but seeing her there, what her nakedness represented and confirmed, it just ramped it all up even more, so now it was like millions of buffalo hurtling toward me across the plains, thundering hooves and snorting nostrils and big slobbery mouths as far as the eye can see. Like what does this person mean to my father? Other than she's obviously super attractive and he likes her naked in his hotel room on a random Tuesday evening? And what does this mean in terms of his relationship with Mom? Or is it possible that Mom knows? And if she does know, does she care? Or are my parents trying an open marriage situation? Like is Mom also having an affair or having her sexual needs or emotional needs met in some other way? And how common is this? And if I brought it up to him or to Mom, what would happen? And on some level I feel like I should be angry or emotional but instead I'm more thinking about it from Dad's perspective when I'm looking up at this woman. Like he's obviously not getting what he needs from his relationship with Mom, and went to the trouble to book this hotel and somehow meet this woman, and it's clear from the way he and Mom interact that she's not really into him anymore, so maybe this is somehow acceptable if you toss out the wedding vows and institution of marriage and heteronormative expectations and all that, which to me makes sense, honestly. At least in the abstract. Like if you have a Bloomsbury perspective on this, and we're sitting around drinking coffee instead of tea at 1 a.m. with a bunch of queer Cambridge nerds.

But then of course you also have to ask who this naked woman is and is this degrading or demeaning or exploitative for her? Like what are her feelings for my Dad? Does she laugh at his jokes for real or because he's paying her? Does she love him? It's hard to imagine she'd find him attractive, given what she looks like, and all the attention she must get, but maybe old bald white dudes are her thing. Daddy issues, like they say. And, really, is she a mistress or a sex worker and is there a difference anyhow? For example, maybe he pays her rent in return for their weekly meetings. Or maybe he pays her rent and has her on "retainer" as a "consultant" at The Family

Office, which would be sort of ironic. Wouldn't surprise me if he's figured out a way for this to be a tax write-off. And is she choosing to stand there in the window, like an exhibitionist, or did he tell her to do that because it's some weird fetish, some power play where he gets off on her following orders? What exactly is the power dynamic? And how did they meet, anyhow?

Just like when I was watching my dad interact with Eddie Valazquez, our doorman, now that I'm staring up at this woman, who's naked and so, so beautiful, this whole scenario shows me again how much we don't know and maybe can never know about other people, even if it's your own father. She's standing there and the warm evening light is hitting her but also reflecting back in the glass as she turns her back to the window. Maybe he said something to her. Maybe she's listening to the next command. Now it's just her back and her ass and her legs, which look really strong, and I pull out my phone and zoom in and snap a pic. And just then she steps into the shadows of the room and the sun sinks behind the buildings of Jersey City or Hoboken or whatever city that is across the Hudson. And I hear a kid losing his shit and look over to see a mom and dad and two kids, one in a stroller, coming toward me on the High Line, and the kids are eating bright red popsicles and juice is running down the younger one's chin and onto his shirt and it looks like blood. And he's just noticed and is screaming his head off, panicked, his feet thrashing and his arms flailing.

23

NEIL ENGEL

Zora and the kids flew down again yesterday afternoon because, apparently, it's real this time. He's in his final hours, and in some ways, you have to envy him. To be clocking out now, just as life as we know it is about to get a whole lot uglier. I mean this is a man who can still look back on his time in the Navy with a sense of pride, despite the racism and stunted opportunities he must have faced. He can reflect on advances in social justice, in living through the Civil Rights era, despite the recent spasms of BLM and its violent counter spasms. Born into a segregated South, he's now able to drink at any water fountain, dine at any restaurant, shop at any store without fear of arbitrary arrest or violence. He's seen the first black president get elected twice. He's watched the black CEO of American Express talk business on the nightly news, and Oprah, JZ and Michael Jordon ascend the Forbes billionaire list. He was a member of the first generation of black men to legally marry a white woman and not get murdered for doing so. Not that he received the respect and deference he deserved, but at least what he experienced and witnessed represents some form of progress over the course of a 76-year lifespan. History bending ever-so-slightly toward some approximation of justice. And better to be able to reflect on that arc of history than to die a year from now, amid a society ripped apart by civil strife, environmental collapse, and global chaos.

It takes thirty minutes from Gulfstream touchdown at MOB to the hotel. To enter our suite and find the kids asleep, it catapults me back to winter trips to Martinique and Kauai. Happy times when they'd be out in the sun all day, frolicking in the pools or ocean, hiking in the jungle, kayaking with whales, and then just collapse after dinner, completely spent, leaving me and Zora to be adults for a few precious hours. To share a cocktail. To sit on a balcony and watch the moonrise. To make love to the sound of waves breaking on the shoreline below.

Now they're giants, our kids. Creatures with massive limbs hanging off the beds, lost in complex, troubled dreams, and far from innocence. And even if Zora's father wasn't dying, our time wouldn't be as easy and loving as it once was, despite what I might want. Which isn't to say I see myself as innocent in what's happened.

Zora's in the master bedroom on the other side of the living room. She's in bed with her laptop open, hair in a towel, face free of make-up and illuminated by the screen. I sit down beside her and take her hand, kiss it. She glances over.

"Finally signed the do-not-resuscitate paperwork," she says.

I nod. Makes sense based on what she's told me about his condition.

"You know if Horowitz contacted his cardiologist?" I say.

She nods and pulls her hand from mine, returning it to the laptop. I'd had one of our NY doctors call to make sure all that could be done had been done. His heart is barely able to constrict anymore. Without 24-7 ICU care, he'll die. Even with it, he's going to die. They've already resuscitated twice, breaking a rib in the process, and it seems cruel to keep it up.

Her eyes are back on the laptop, fingers attacking the keys.

"What're you working on?"

"Announcement email," she says. "And the obit."

On task, even in the middle of what must be a storm of emotions. On task like when I first met her at Cipriani's twenty-four years ago. I was still working in the private wealth division at Brown Brothers and was representing the firm at a benefit gala. Her modeling career had recently ended and she'd pivoted to "giving back" by working at an NGO focused on women's health in the developing world. We'd emailed about what I was going to say on behalf of the firm and what size check I'd be bringing. From the emails, I didn't know how stunning she'd be, or that she was black, or biracial, which left me totally caught off guard when we met in person. But I wanted her, immediately. I remember sitting there and watching her move from table to table, greeting and smiling and thanking the many white benefactors, and just marveling at how evolutionary science was right about the benefits of genetic mixing and variation. Her beauty, her seemingly good health, her obvious intelligence, she just appeared to be a superior human specimen than everyone else in that room, synthesizing the best attributes of the genetic lineage she embodied.

I wanted to fuck her, definitely, but I also wanted more, and immediately began scheming on how best to sweep her off her feet. I'd dazzle her with my expansive mind, my sense of humor, with spontaneous weekend trips, expensive gifts, grand gestures. The latter, I recently read, is a telltale sign of a narcissistic personality. The study detailed how the "grand gesture" strategy in early courtship — usually undertaking by men, but not exclusively — is an attempt to quickly disrupt whatever social network the recipient of the grand gesture has, and to make the grand gesturer the very center of what the article called the "victim's universe". Sort of like a shock-and-awe Blitzkrieg that disorients the recipient. You come in big, blindside them, dominate the airwaves and communication channels, isolate them from their friends and family, and then sit back in the position of power for the duration of the relationship. The study claimed that once you establish this kind of relational imbalance, from a psychological perspective, it's virtually impossible to evolve toward parity.

Initially, reading the study pissed me off. But once I got over the narcissism critique, I couldn't deny the fact that it matched the pattern of our courtship. Not that it was totally asymmetrical. She had money from her modeling career, but nothing like the money I had. And it wasn't only material plenty that mattered here. I also went hard at her emotionally and culturally. I took her to plays and art exhibitions. I bought her a Basquiat print for our first Valentine's Day, starting a tradition of purchasing her art that continued through this year. I even went back and found some poetry I'd written in college and reworked it with her in mind. And it paid off. Within six months, she agreed to marry me. Soon after that she quit her non-profit job and turned her focus to remodeling our first country house in Sag Harbor. It was only once the kids came along that my centrality, or maybe even supremacy, began to slip. And, I'll be honest, it wasn't only the kids. It was also her desire for independence. I think she realized she'd been shock-and-awed, and that the resulting wasteland, with me standing at the center, wasn't going to be enough. It was also about that time that her father came back into the picture, and she began connecting with her family down here in Alabama.

She sets the laptop on the bed beside me and rotates the screen. I begin to read:

*It is with great sadness that I write to you about the passing of my father, Darnell Morris, Jr. As many of you know, he suffered from heart failure over the past few years, which left him with limited mobility and significant discomfort. He passed on **[date TBD]**, and is finally at peace.*

Darnell was born in Biloxi, Mississippi, the second child of Henrietta and Darnell Morris, Sr. The family moved to Mobile when he was a teenager, and he graduated from Mattie T. Blount High School, where he played on the varsity basketball and baseball teams. A star shortstop, he dreamed of playing professional ball, and for several years played for minor league teams including the Jackson Senators and Jacksonville Jumbo Shrimp. He claimed he was a better ball player than teammates such as Amos Otis, and didn't achieve their level of success only on account of a knee injury.

Later, Darnell joined the Navy, where he served for four years, traveling to ports in the Philippines, Japan, and Hawaii. As anyone who met him knows, he had many stories to tell about his travels, especially how different the foods were from what he grew up with down South. He met my mother, Elise, in San Francisco in 1972. The marriage lasted only two years before he returned to Mobile.

Other than baseball, his other great love was music, especially playing the bass guitar. In addition to working as a janitor, and for many years working as a short-order cook, Darnell played in many local bands, and across many genres, including R&B, funk, soul and for many years at his church, Stone Hill Baptist.

*Darnell was predeceased by his second wife, Colette, who passed just over three years ago, and their son, Coleman, who died as a teenager. Memorial services will be held on **[date TBD]** at Stone Hill Baptist Church.*

I set the laptop on the bed between us. "It's good. I think it says what you need to say."

"You don't think I need to mention what happened, right?"

"No. I mean anyone who really knows him, knows the history. And those who don't, not sure what it adds."

She picked up the laptop to reread the announcement.

"Why, do you think he'd want you to include something?" I say. She shrugs. "What were they, cousins?"

"First cousins."

It's the second time Zora's referenced the lynching in the past few weeks. She mentioned Elijah had asked about it, and had asked her about whether she'd ever been to the museum in Montgomery. It's still part of her, like a deep-tissue wound, but clearly not something she wants to talk about with me. From what I gathered, she didn't want to talk about it with our son either.

What lies 275 feet beneath a forest in upstate New York is what I want to talk about. Our place of safety away from this dark family history, and away from a set of contemporary concerns, regrets, even hopes that I believe we'll look back on with nostalgia for being petty and inconsequential. I want to tell her that the refuge deep beneath the forest is large enough that we won't be on top of one another, and that it's supplied with enough food and drink to withstand and outlast whatever scenario is thrown our way. That's the conversation we should be having.

After Darnell's death, once we're through with the funeral and grieving, I'll need to call a family meeting. I'll tell them about our bunker, my estimated timeframe for relocation, and the rationale. Then I'll share info on the other four who will joining us. I'll do that because — depending on how events unfold — those others might be the way in which our family line is perpetuated. Perhaps how humanity is perpetuated. We're privileged enough to have the opportunity to live through a cataclysmic event that may well kill off over 99.99% of humanity. Because of that, the onus is on us to have these tough and rather strange discussions.

I look up at Zora, so focused on what will happen in the next hours or days, and I want to tell her it's comparatively trivial. What I've been working on is a generational problem set. A world-historic problem set. And I've come up with a very good solution to a very dire and distressing reality. For the four of us. I've done this for us.

ELIJAH THOMAS-ENGEL

Amazing the insulated cocoon she lives in, my sister. You gotta assume that her internal world is rich with fantasies inspired by literature. That in the few waking minutes when she's not reading, her mind must take her to intricately plotted worlds with all kinds of colorful characters. Like when she's lying in bed at night drifting off, or showering, or in the minutes between finishing one book and starting the next. But during the course of a normal day, she misses so much of what's actually happening around her due to the simple fact that she just doesn't lift her eyes above the top of whatever tome has her in thrall. It must be like some sliver of a horizon line at the top of her visual frame with color and action and noise that, to her, just pales in comparison to what her brain can do with page after page of black print on white paper.

Which in this instance is fine. Way better, really. I prefer that she doesn't register where we're at or what I'm doing. Because an explanation as to why we're idling in our rented SUV on the corner of Lee and Hershel streets, in a working-class neighborhood fifteen minutes northwest of downtown, catty-corner to a cinderblock bungalow, while Mom and Dad are at the hospital with Grandpa, who's definitely dying this time, well... it isn't fully formed in my mind yet. Like how to articulate it. The motivation to find this address and then drive here is one of needing to see something concrete, to connect the historical dots, but whatever action or actions that may result, that hasn't come into focus just yet, though I'm almost certain it has to do with the 31 pieces I finished 3D printing last week and brought in my luggage, unassembled.

Shawna would have asked me what I'm doing by now. She'd

be calling me crazy for even being in this neighborhood. She'd be hunched low in the front seat, muttering and cursing. But Natasha couldn't give a shit. Her book is her world.

Maybe it's not even working class, this neighborhood. Or maybe working class doesn't even exist anymore, at least the way it used to be represented, with tidy streets of modest homes where parents have jobs in manufacturing and kids go to decent public schools. Where the promise of upward mobility is evidenced by industrious young Johnny down the street who got a full ride to college because he worked hard and his teachers and parents loved and supported him.

Whatever that ideal is, this definitely isn't it. This neighborhood is poor and white, with houses needing paint jobs and rusting vehicles slowly becoming entombed in tall grass and kudzu vines. If not all white, it's gotta be close to ninety percent. Because as we drove out here we started seeing more and more Confederate bumper stickers and MAGA flags, and fewer and fewer Black folks. Honestly, the set-up would seem too cliché if I were writing about it for some school essay, but here it is. No denying the facts right in front of us. There are the pick-ups with gun racks, the bumper stickers and flags and, again being honest but also sounding cliché and probably discriminatory, almost everyone you see is fifty pounds overweight. Or more.

We read in health class that "morbidly obese" is anything over thirty pounds overweight, which is definitely what the woman struggling to get out of the shitty old Buick is. Not sure what sixty pounds overweight is, but that's probably closer to her reality. Morbidly obese XXXL? She beeps the horn twice and hoists herself from the front seat, eyes on the door of the bungalow. And when the door opens, it all just clicks. He's probably my age, maybe a year older. And, just like his mom, or maybe it's his grandma, he's carrying the extra pounds. But in this case, it probably helped him letter as a varsity lineman. Maybe even a college prospect. That's what he looks like. Just over six feet but must weigh in at close to two eighty, neck like a tree trunk. And as he pushes through the door and down the steps, it's like he's some kind of walking Red State poster child, with the jeans, the tank-top, the Auburn baseball cap on backwards. I've done some due diligence and it's definitely him. Troy Shelton, grandson of one of the three men who strung up my mom's first cousin, once removed, in a camphor tree. 11 loops around the neck.

Grandma pops the trunk and says something to rosy-cheeked Troy. He nods and grabs four plastic grocery bags and heads into the house. Such a good boy. Such a good ol' boy.

25

ZORA THOMAS

The first time I did a silent retreat I thought I'd lost my mind by Day 3. Hours and days, days and nights, minutes and hours and days, they melded into one extended moment of staring at the ceiling, staring at a flower in my private garden, staring at the pulsating geometric pattern my mind created when my eyes were closed. The only thing that tethered me to the rhythm and reality of the outside world were meal deliveries. Twice a day I'd hear a tray being set on the floor outside my door, accompanied by the delicate ring of a bell. This would pull me back into the here and now and quiet the voices in my mind competing for dominance. It would push back the visions that washed over me. Not that it mattered. The point was that I wasn't interacting with anyone else for twelve days. All I was expected to do, both by the center and myself, was sit in my spartan room and look within. To look within and see what was really there at my very core, once everything extraneous was peeled back. The husband. The kids. At the time, my fledgling home furnishing business. Also the fact that my father was ill and beginning to want more from me, emotionally, to make up for what he called "all that lost time".

By Day 5, a new clarity descended over me. A clarity about my shortcomings. For the first time since childhood, I began to recognize myself again, or what I began to think of as my essential self. I was a person holding conflicting narratives, embodying a set of stories about self and family that were passed down from my mother, and another set of stories about self and family that were assembled from fragments, patchworked together. More sensory experiences and memories than something told orally over many years. Memory bursts of short trips down South as a child. The feel of my grandmother's hand as I held it, calloused but warm. Her smile. Her dentures floating in a glass beside her bed in the morning. The feel of sitting in the front seat of my father's pick-up as he drove me to meet some relative on a sweltering afternoon. The stench of decaying fish my cousin and I had caught, now belly up in a cooler whose ice had melted days ago. And these dual narratives were informed by the language and messaging of pop culture as represented by magazines, billboards, TV shows. Narratives about what it meant to be a Black girl or Black woman. And yet here I was at the retreat, once again in a majority white space. A space decorated with all kinds of ethnic and cultural flourishes and appropriations, from Buddhas to Sanskrit signage no one could decipher, to Native American totems, all with the aim of inspiring inner peace within the hearts and minds of wealthy white women. White women who had the resources to set aside two weeks to look within. To seek the essential. To mine, extract and then have the courage to proudly showcase "our true and authentic selves" to the world.

By Day 8, I was enraged for even letting myself do this. Not only the retreat, but the life I was leading. I was responsible for this. I let myself be lured into modeling by promises of glamor and riches. I'd been plenty warned, mainly by my mother. She told me I'd end up anorexic or bulimic or coked out in some New York loft getting groped by some European photographer or creative director feigning sophistication but really just lusting for fresh meat. But I was 18 and she couldn't keep me from signing with Ford. I had agency, and now a top modeling agency, and I wanted to get the hell out of small-town New Mexico and all the self-righteous spiritual seekers in my mother's friend circle. They wanted to abandon material possessions for spiritual enlightenment and artistic freedom? Maybe. What they didn't see was they were only able to make those privileged choices because someone in their family had accumulated the resources that allowed them to drop out and be unconventional or countercultural in the first place. With my mother as Exhibit A. Numerous times during my upbringing, I'd heard her claim to be "a single mother living below the poverty line." What she conveniently forgot or ignored was that when she was in her mid-40s she inherited a paid-off house from her parents, which she sold, and which enabled her to quit her conventional job and dive deep into her world of spiritual seekers, massage therapists, crystal healers, and eco-feminists.

But, again, who the hell am I to judge? That's what was abundantly clear to me on Day 8 of that first retreat. Who am I to judge anyone given who I married, the business I've built, and the world I now inhabit.

And why is this coming up now, as I sit alone in the ICU with the man my mother hasn't seen in over forty years. Her dying ex-husband. My father. Who I finally don't resent for not being there when I was growing up. The nuance informs the bigger picture. The context and nuance you don't see or understand when you're eighteen, partly because you haven't heard the stories or shared the lived experience.

I hold his hand, this large black hand, and think of all the bass lines these fingers have played. All the hours this hand encircled a mop handle as a janitor or a spatula as a cook. And earlier, all the times this hand pulled a ball from a baseball mitt and threw it with precision to first base. This hand that at one time sought out the white hand of my mother, at a time when that was a risky move, a revolutionary move, a gesture which, depending upon location, could have had him strung up in a tree like his relative.

Did the risk add urgency and energy to that first interaction?

Certainly it did for my mother, who was already running from convention. Taking that hand, and leading that hand and that man back to her apartment was, for her, a repudiation of the small-minded and racist life her parents had given her.

The beeping starts again at 3:14am, building in urgency and volume. He's flatlining again. But this time I've signed all the do-not-resuscitate paperwork. His heart is worn out.

And so I sing to him, softly, as the nurse and doctor step through the door. I sing the Bill Withers song he once sang to me, or at least sang over and over during my first visit to Mobile, when I was six or maybe seven. Of course, now I realize he may have been singing it with someone else in mind.

Can we pretend
That from now on
There is no yesterday
Paint a portrait of tomorrow
With no colors from today...

26

NATASHA THOMAS-ENGEL

I noticed him at the funeral. Three rows behind us and across the center aisle, sitting between what I guessed was his younger sister and grandmother. I felt his eyes on me, but not like in a creepy way. Just that whenever I looked over in his direction he'd be looking back at me, and then quickly glance down at his hands, which rested in his lap. There was something sweet about his large brown eyes, his long eyelashes, the way his collared shirt and suit jacket were too big for his skinny neck, like his grandmother bought the outfit knowing he was going to fill out any day now.

Later, at the repast in the church cafeteria, he was standing in line at the food table when I went to make a plate. He smiled and gestured that I should cut in front of him and make my plate first. I smiled back, thanked him, and told him my name was Natasha, which he obviously already knew because we were the grandkids at our grandfather's funeral and it was all spelled out in the program, who's who and from where.

As I took a paper plate and plastic cutlery, he said: "Natasha means birthday of the Lord." Which is true. And, honestly, always kind of freaked me out, that my name had such strong religious connotations. Or more than connotations, really. The fact that it's like so central to the genesis of the whole thing, like the actual Lord's birthday. And, by the way, how's that even possible? Or what does that even mean, that a deity would even have a birthday? Because wouldn't that also mean that his/her time ruling over us mortals, and all creatures of this planet, and I guess the universe, is actually just temporary? And that he/she would also necessarily have a death day? Which I guess has maybe happened in that I keep reading about how more and more people identify as agnostic or even atheist, myself included. And, okay, since we're going down this divine rabbit hole: if the Lord was born, had an actual birthday, then what does that mean in terms of who his/her parents were? Who birthed the Lord? Is it Christ and Mary we're talking about here, or the overall concept of the Lord? Because I thought this was monotheism. Or are we saying the Almighty One was the product of non-deities. And, okay, like what even existed before the Lord or his/her parents existed? Maybe it really is only about Christ. I should probably do some more research. Like I said, sizable rabbit hole and one that makes me anxious just thinking about, given my atheism. Guess I actually prefer if people don't know the meaning of my name.

Except in this case. Because it was a solid icebreaker. Point is, in this instance, the fact that he knew the meaning of my name, and smiled with his perfect white teeth framed against his dark skin, which was also perfect, like no blemishes at all, somehow I found it all totally endearing. Southern boys are so polite, especially at church. He introduced himself as Milton Riggs, Jr. I have no idea what Milton means but it seems old-school Mobile to me. Or maybe my association was based on my thinking about old blind John Milton and *Paradise Lost*, and how that quote about "solitude being sometimes the best society" didn't, at this particular time and place, make sense to me, although I'd often thought it was written specifically for someone like me. So much so that I'd written the quote on the front of my last laptop with a Sharpie to inform the world, and remind myself, that I didn't need friends, per se.

Anyhow, Milton and I moved down the table of food together. Being a vegetarian limited my options substantially — to mac & cheese, fried green tomatoes, okra, and Caesar salad drowning in dressing. The collards looked good but had bacon. He smiled as I bypassed the ribs, shrimp and grits, fried chicken, fried catfish. He told me he knew my grandfather from church. Said Pops was always talking about his grandchildren up North. Me and Elijah. How proud he was about who we were, and what we were doing. Milton said he'd missed seeing my grandfather at church over the past six months, and how sorry he was when he heard he'd passed on. Then he smiled again with those 1,000-watt teeth.

My mom was off talking to relatives I didn't know, and I couldn't find my dad or brother in the crowd, so I decided to sit with Milton at a table in the far corner of the cafeteria. He unfolded and laid a napkin on his lap, tucked another below his chin, closed his eyes in prayer for a moment, and then began to eat with a shocking degree of focus and enthusiasm. That's when I decided I wanted to kiss him. When I saw how his entire being was like completely engrossed by the food, body bending around the plate, hands cradling a rib, napkin dabbing BBQ sauce from one side of his perfect mouth. It was like he was a conductor, or a whole orchestra and conductor playing some impossibly beautiful symphony. I was transfixed and he was clueless that I was transfixed. I really needed to kiss him. And maybe more.

So after we'd eaten I told him I wanted to show him something and headed out into the church entrance hall. I'd noticed steps leading down to a basement. Down I went, pretending I knew where I was going and what I was doing. He followed, looking a little nervous, checking over his shoulder to see if his grandmother or sister were watching.

At the bottom of the stairs was a long hallway with three doorways to one side. I tried the first door, but it was locked. Tried the second and it opened into what appeared to be a preschool room. Or maybe Bible study for youngsters. Sunday school? There were small chairs around tables and bookcases along the far wall. A circular carpet in the middle of the room. What did I know about what might happen in a space like this? My parents never took me to church unless we were down here, and for that we were always the special guests, not part of the fabric of everyday activity.

As I stepped into the room I reached behind me, found his slender fingers, encircled them with mine, and pulled. The room was dark, lit only by the faint green of an emergency exit sign. I closed the door behind us. We were surrounded by silence. I moved closer, feeling the warmth of his body. I stared into his large unblinking eyes. We were the same height, which put me at ease, because normally I tower over everyone, and I know it makes people uncomfortable, especially insecure boys and short men.

Then I kissed him. Gently. And he kissed me back. Warm, generous lips, flavored with a hint of BBQ sauce. This was the first boy I'd kissed since Timothy Whitehead kissed me on our 5th Grade trip to Mystic Seaport, and that had come as a surprise on the bus ride home. This time I was the instigator. I was in control. It was thrilling.

I reached for his waist and pulled his body closer. His hands were still at his side, as if paralyzed. I eased even closer and my breasts touched his chest, sending shockwaves coursing up and through my body. One of his hands found the small of my back. And then the other. Our mouths were open now, and our tongues entangled.

27

WILLAMITA PATTERSON & ELIJAH

If interrogated, she'd have to admit that Stone Hill Baptist was a respectable church by almost any measure. It was older than hers, grander, with a bigger congregation and a history dating back to the early 1800s. Famous civil rights leaders had spoken here. Any politician worth their salt made sure to include a meet-and-greet and photo op on the front steps at the very top of their campaign schedule. And it was clear to everyone why. The pastors, the deacons, the parishioners were "of consequence". They were middle class or higher, employed, younger than they were at her church, most with college degrees, and they certainly voted. And probably brought a friend or relative along to vote with them too. Willamita also viewed them as two-faced.

You could sense it the moment you walked into the place, even without the benefit of vision. It was in the way they spoke, how they greeted one another, how they moved about in the space, always seeking out the most advantageous pew to sit in, the most high-powered cluster of folks to sidle up to in the cafeteria. They attended services not to be closer to the Heavenly Father, but to rub shoulders with others who also had decidedly earthly aspirations. Ascending the social ladder, or maintaining one's already elevated position, was apparently more important than humbling oneself before the Almighty. And there seemed to be no shame! That's what irked her more than anything. These people were interested first and foremost in what the "Stone Hill family" could do for their careers, their financial well-being, in how a short conversation in the parking lot might ensure placement of their child in the right school, with the right teacher.

The fact that the place irked her wasn't out of some sense of jealousy. Willamita could have been one of them. She'd been invited to join the church on several occasions. In fact, they'd lobbied hard after Elijah's murder, telling her they — out of the hundreds of churches in Mobile — were best able to advocate on her behalf for justice and financial restitution. And yet she felt the offer wasn't strictly out of Christian compassion. She could feel it, the way they wanted to use her as a means to bring attention to their church, their mission, their congregation, their collective status. The pastor and his assistant sat there in her living room, a huge basket of food before them — "just a small token of our congregation's love and concern" — and told her they were ready to hold a press conference as soon as the very next morning. They'd already taken the liberty to reach out to Reverend Jesse Jackson. He was willing to join them, they said. He was willing to speak on her behalf and stand at her side in solidarity.

All she could think of at that moment was the maxim about all press being good press, and the sense deep down within her soul of how that wouldn't be the case for her. Even if the murderers were convicted, which eventually they were, it wasn't going to be good. And even if the civil penalties went on to cripple the regional KKK, which they did, it wasn't going to be good. All press was not good press for her and her family. All the knocks at her door, the TV crews camped across the street, the many times her car was followed by those trying to do her harm, trying to scare her. No, she and her family suffered plenty and still suffer, and all that press was not good. She felt fine, looking back, that she didn't accept the offer from the Stone Hill pastor and his eager assistant. Reverend Jackson had spoken on her behalf anyhow. Not at her side, but on national television. Reverend Al Sharpton had visited and met with her too. Her son's murder was shocking enough, gruesome enough, that she didn't need Stone Hill to be stepping into the spotlight with their grandstanding.

———

Willamita had yet another observation about Stone Hill, and this was based on today. It had to do with the funeral service itself. In her opinion, the music minister was wielding far too much power, which was a failing in almost every church she stepped into these days. Because if it's the music and song getting folks to attend, well, you've already lost the battle. Anyone can feel the Holy Spirit through song and instrument. Can stand from the pew to stomp and clap. Can throw their head back and bring down the rafters by belting out a praise song. That's the easy part. She knew folks thought she was old fashioned on this point, especially the younger generations, but she was too old to care. In her opinion, if you're not reaching people through the gospel itself, through verse and scripture and the spoken word, then souls simply aren't gonna be saved. They might be touched in the moment, but that's just scratching an itch. No, she knew that a gut-punch is needed if you really want someone to find and walk the righteous path, and that comes only through listening to the spoken word and daily study of the written word. She'd told this to ministers and parishioners for decades now, had fought the idea that a music minister should be paid the same or more than a pastor, but she knew she was losing the battle, in her church and every church in the country. The battle had certainly been lost a long time ago at Stone Hill.

Point is, she'd known many of the parishioners and ministers at Stone Hill over the years, including her first cousin Darnell, who was now dead and laid to rest. God bless him. He wasn't always good, Darnell. Wasn't always kind. Certainly didn't always act in a godly manner, particularly when he was younger and carrying on with multiple women at the same time. But in the end, judging a life simply wasn't up to her. She knew that and accepted that. It was between Darnell and his Maker, and she felt sure he'd found the righteous path later in life, through Bible study, through building a relationship with his daughter and grandchildren, and through a firm belief in the promise of salvation.

———

Elijah opened the front door and, cradling her elbow, helped his great aunt Willamita up into the SUV. His mother had asked him to drive her home after the funeral.

"You a good boy, Elijah," Willamita said as he took her cane and placed it on the seat behind her. "Gonna make your family proud. Make a name for yourself. I can see that clear as day, even though I lost my vision a long time ago."

She felt him sit into the driver's seat beside her, heard the muted thud of the door closing. Everything about the vehicle spelled luxury to her, even though she had no idea of the make or model. The engine purred to life.

"Shawna said you'll be attending the same college as your daddy."

"That's right, yeah, starting in September."

"Yale University," she said.

"Yes."

"I heard about that college. Everybody has. On the news, in the paper. President Bush went there. Clintons too. Plenty famous people."

"Yes."

"It gonna be mostly white kids then?" she said.

"No, it's changed a lot since my dad attended. They said over forty percent of the incoming class are students of color."

"And what's that supposed to mean, exactly? How many Black kids they got?"

"Maybe like ten percent? They don't say it outright, but I'm pretty sure the philosophy at a lot of these schools is basically to try and have each class reflect whatever the country's overall demographic is. Ethnic and geographic diversity."

"Sounds real good to me, sure does. Get people talking to each other, make 'em see we more the same than different, no matter the shade of skin. No matter where we grew up—"

Willamita heard a chuckle from the back seat. She knew immediately who it was, and wasn't happy he'd decided to join them. Although, being honest with herself, she'd expected he'd have shown himself earlier. During the service she kept thinking she'd see him sitting in the pews, nodding along with the music, that look of mischief on his face. Or maybe waiting in line to view Darnell in his casket. Or standing in line to get a plate of food. She fought the urge to shush the chuckle.

"See, now, why don't you go on'n ask him where he's actually drivin' to?" said her dead son, the apparition in the back seat. He was happy, relishing this moment.

Willamita shook her head. Clenched the bible in her lap.

"Everything okay, Auntie M?" asked Elijah.

Willamita nodded.

"Ain't that cute, way he say that! 'Auntie M'. Like he grew up talkin' like that—"

"Shush, be gone now!" she snapped.

Elijah looked over at his great aunt, could tell she was distressed about something.

"You need something, Auntie? You want me to pull over?"

At that, Elijah the apparition cracked up in the back seat, smacked the leather beside him with an open palm. He leaned forward, close to his mother's ear, and whispered:

"Go on, Auntie M, why don't you ask him what all he's been

doing while he's been down here? Where he's been driving off to, what all he's plannin' and plottin'."

Willamita shook her head. In her mind, she turned around, stared him dead in the eyes and said:

"Told you once, told you a thousand times to leave him alone! Ain't nobody interested in your opinions. Don't nobody want you stirring up trouble!"

He just smiled back at her, one leg crossed over the other, dressed like everyone else in his best suit for the funeral. Except she'd actually never seen him in this combination of suit, shirt, tie, these dress shoes. Which made her wonder, for the thousandth time, how this actually worked. Did he possess a wardrobe he could just access anytime he felt like he wanted to torment her in some new and particular way? No, this was all just a figment of her imagination! This was a suit and wardrobe that sprang from her head, her brain! Whenever he appeared, it was she who had dressed him with her imagination, just like she used to dress him as a child with her actual hands. This was a sickness within her own mind! Her flesh-and-blood son was long dead! But even though she knew this to be true, and told herself so, she couldn't rid herself of the vision of him, the namesake of the sweet boy now driving her home.

"You need anything from the store, Auntie? Before I drop you home?"

This was a real voice, coming from a real human who was sitting beside her in a real vehicle.

"Bless you, but I got everything I need. Always plenty of food in the pantry and freezer."

The vehicle turned in a direction that didn't match where she imagined them to be. As she tried to visualize their location, the voice from the back seat chimed in again, evermore gleeful.

"Just don't say I didn't warn you now! Because I did. Told you how he has his own plans. Oh yes! Because out of all of 'em, he the only one that learned what really happened. Only one that decided he wanted to do something about it too—"

"Said shush!" she blurted out.

Elijah braked this time.

"Sorry... Everything alright?"

Willamita smoothed her skirt with one hand, clenched her bible with the other.

"Yes it is. Everythin' just fine," she said. "Didn't mean to scare you. Jus' trying to quiet a voice in my... well, in my mind, Elijah. You know how sometimes you end up conversatin' with yourself? Or conversatin' with people that used to be in your life but ain't no longer?

"Yes."

"Well that's all that is. Sometimes, and it probably comes from living alone too long, but sometimes you ain't sure whether the words are on the inside of your head or the outside. It ain't that I'm crazy."

"Yeah, can imagine how that would happen," he said. "I mean sometimes it happens to me if I've been studying or reading for too long. I just start saying stuff, or sort of talking to the characters in the books, but in my mind. Or maybe some-times out loud too."

"Then you know exactly what all I'm talking about! Despite what they gon' tell you, it ain't that my mind is slippin'. It's just that the inside and outside voices sometimes seem the same to me."

Stopped at a light, Elijah glanced over at the old woman. She was losing it, no doubt, like he'd heard his mother and relatives talking about for several years now. She was repeating herself and she looked rattled, her wig askew, with a streak of what might be BBQ sauce on her cheek. Her lips were parted as if she wanted to say something more. Or was listening to some-one, waiting to respond.

"Go on, why don't you ask him where he's driving to!" said the apparition from behind. He was leaning close to Willamita's ear again. "Go on, mama. Ask if he lost his way or if he knows exactly where he's at, and just what he's fixin' to do."

28

ELIJAH THOMAS-ENGEL

My calculations on how long the service, burial and repast would take were pretty much right. Because it's dusk. I was also right about how mom would respond to my offer to drive Auntie Mita home. Driving your blind great-aunt home seems like the perfect alibi, not that I'll need one.

I pull to a stop in front of the vacant lot across the street from the house. The neighborhood's quiet, just like when I drove here with Natasha. No kids on bikes. No fathers working in the yard or barbecuing. I tell Auntie I'll be right back and step out of the car. Close the door and stand still for a beat.

Yeah, no one's outside because it's still too fucking hot. Better to stay indoors with the AC cranking, TV blaring, pounding Dr. Pepper and shoveling fried food into your pie hole.

Go ahead, tell me I'm an elitist asshole. Tell me I'm stereo-typing. But then shut up and break out the statistics on obesity in this state. Or diabetes. Or coronary artery disease and life expectancy. And once you've got all the metrics in front of you, go ahead and shut the fuck up again. Thank you. Because I'm not ascribing blame or even being judgy. I'm just relaying personal observation, which also happens to be substantiated by easy-to-find stats from the Centers for Disease Control and Prevention. Which I used for one of my writing assignments. Alabama's got the third highest obesity rate in the nation at 39.9% of the adult population. And FYI, they define obesity as someone with a Body Mass Index (BMI) of 30 or over, and give as a hypothetical an adult male who's 5'9". Call him Mr. Average Joe. To be "healthy", he'd have to weigh between 125-168 lbs. Obese, with a BMI of 30, would make Average Joe 203 lbs. So he's carrying at least 35 lbs more than he should, and that's on a pretty short frame.

In terms of life expectancy, Bama is third to last out of all the states, one decimal better than Louisiana. 73.2 years. Right across the border, just one County over in Mississippi, life expectancy is 71.1. On the other end of the spectrum, you've got Hawaii at 80.1. California at 79. New York at 77.7. Basically you're gonna live like 10% longer if you're not born here. Turns out it's pretty much a red state-blue state situation if you look at it from that macro perspective.

———

Auntie Mita appears to be a statue when I glance back through the tinted window. She stares straight ahead, hands cradling her bible. Except her lips are moving just a little. Almost like a tremor. Probably praying or talking to the voices again.

Okay then.

No one's around.

The living-room light is on in the bungalow across the street, but the sedan isn't there.

Just the old pick-up.

Grandma's not home.

So I guess we're good to go.

Being from up North, and mostly from the City, I don't have much experience with weapons. Dad never took me hunting or to a firing range. No one ever opened up the gun locker to show me their collection. The thing about a ghost gun is that it doesn't weigh much, or weigh as much as I imagine a normal handgun would. I can hardly feel it in my right jacket pocket as I begin across the street. I reach in to double-check, to make sure it's there. It is. With all its deadly promise, and also its capacity to disappear forever, untraceable, once its acrylonitrile butadiene styrene body is placed in acetone.

I reach into my other pocket and pull out gloves and the stocking I stole from my mother's closet back in the City, and already cut and tied off. I pull it over my head and face as I step up and over the curb, beginning across the patchy front lawn.

These people are poor, maybe even poorer than my Black relatives. They can't afford to water their lawn. Can't afford to paint their house or resurface the driveway or redo the roof. And it feels right, these facts. They've already been diminished. They've been taken down several societal pegs by court battles, lawsuits, incarceration of their patriarch, the blinding scrutiny of the press. It feels right that they're teetering on the precipice of family ruin, bankruptcy, one medical emergency away from losing this house too, maybe even the shitty pick-up. They're just one final kick to the balls away from the shame and trauma that will mark them for generations to come. Let's make this shit epigenetic.

It's Old Testament justice, what I see here, but it's also narratively cohesive and satisfying. Our family suffered hundreds of years of humiliation, torture, and subjugation, but to them, to this exact family, apparently that wasn't enough. They couldn't just let that history be. No, their patriarch felt compelled to assert his hatred and aggression one final time by murdering my namesake. Okay, maybe it was rooted in some feelings of inadequacy. Or because he felt the sand shifting beneath his feet and needed, one last time, to demonstrate that he was still the protagonist in his own life, still belonged to the dominant race, still operated above the law as a white man in Dixie. Who fucking knows? He didn't take the stand in court and he never gave an interview to the press. Point is, he miscalculated and personally paid the price. His family did too, to a degree.

But not to an equal degree, and that's the point. Despite the fact that they can't pay for better sod or can't pay the bill to water this lawn, it's still not analogous, their generational pain.

Until today. Until right now. See there's a logical arc to this story that, up until now, no one in our family saw as necessary or possible. But the world has changed, the calculations have changed, and my action will bring some equivalence. There's a narrative elegance to this, a beauty even.

So here I stand on the front steps. Concrete beneath my dress shoes. Gloves on. Stocking over my head, distorting my facial features beyond recognition. The gun rests in my right palm, loaded and cocked. One final glance up and down the street and I ring the doorbell, step to the right side of the door, as planned, so he won't see me if he looks through the peephole. I wait.

Footsteps inside and then the front door opens. The screen door next. It's slow motion. He takes a step out onto the concrete landing, a confused expression on his face and, before he can turn to look at me, I depress the trigger and the gun aimed at his left temple fires its single bullet at what the specs promised would be 564 feet per second. It's louder than I thought it would be, maybe because of the overhang above the front door. The gun kicks back so hard I almost drop it, my hand vibrating, but these are minor details. It's the results that matter in situations like this. The planning and envisioning that yield the desired end. And the results are irrefutable. I stare at them.

Blood and bone shards and clots of brain splattered all over the open screen door.

Troy's massive frame crumpled on the cement below.

It's one more data point that will lower life expectancy in the state. One more body who died with a BMI over 30.

I notice that he wears a Roll Tide tank top and black athletic shorts, Nike slip-ons, white socks pulled to his thick calves. His left eye, wide open, stares out toward the street. Still confused. The other eye is a mess. Not really an eye anymore.

I hurry back across the street and open the trunk, open the

64 oz. bucket of acetone, drop the gun in, close the container, climb in beside Auntie Mita and pull off down the street. As we turn from the side street onto Springhill Rd., I pull the stocking from my head and the gloves from my hands.

"Almost home now, Auntie."

29

ZORA THOMAS

I received the call sometime during the whirlwind of planning for the funeral, but didn't listen to the voicemail until we'd returned to New York. Elijah was back at boarding school for his final month before graduation and Natasha was at some Fieldston event. Neil was having dinner with his insufferable Yale friend. The apartment was quiet. I stood staring out the living room window, across the treetops of Central Park, and played the message on speaker.

Hey there Zora! Hope you're doing great! Patti Laybourne here. We met at the expo in Atlanta a few months back. You gave me your card. Anyhow, just wanted to say we took a closer look at your company and, my gosh, the team and I just really really love what y'all have built. The website and social media presence is so strong. Just a beautiful, consistent aesthetic through-and-through-and-through. Anyhow, I don't want to fill your mailbox with too much of me just gabbing on. Point of the call is to say we think there might be some really amazing synergies here. As mentioned, we're in the middle of acquiring several outfits similar to yours, and think Palmetto might be a perfect addition to our overall brand strategy. So, there ya have it. If you're even remotely interested, I'd just love to set up a time to hop on a call and discuss. Or, even better, hop on a flight and come meet you in New York. Always good to have an excuse to visit the Big Apple! Okay? Well, bye for now! Really hope to hear from you!

There ya have it. A bulldozer of a woman with a small mountain of platinum hair, fair skin, flushed cheeks and an unabashedly strong southern accent, wants to buy my home furnishings company. Patti Laybourne from Fort Worth, if I'm remembering right. Talks as if we're sorority sisters from back in the day. Talks of amazing synergies.

In Atlanta, she'd shown up at our booth at the end of the final day and plopped down on one of our loveseats. She sat there for a few minutes, taking in our demo living room, fingering every texture within reach of her meaty hands. Then she started gushing about how she just loved the area rug and artwork. The coffee table too. And how the grain of the coffee table complemented the wood accents of the loveseat and couch so perfectly. Which it did, obviously. Which was intentional, obviously.

"I mean, and I'm being honest with y'all right now, but if I were actually someone else, like someone not as tacky and loud in my interior design predilections, I mean I could really imagine myself living in a house like this. I really could!" She reclined back into the loveseat, snapped a few photos.

"Seriously, y'all! I mean in a living room just... like... this! That is if I didn't have three teenage boys who run around demolishing anything pretty and valuable and getting their grimy feet and Cheeto-y fingers all over everything! I mean that'd be the key, obviously, if you're gonna be living in a place like this. You're gonna have to be single, or maybe a real sweet gay couple with one of them well-mannered pugs!"

She laughed, like a cascading waterfall laugh, and slapped her knee with delight. At least that's how it plays in my memory.

My assistant Selena was standing off to one side rolling her eyes. Her tolerance for loud white women was even lower than mine. I was tired and just wanted the day to be over, the expo to be over, but by now I'd learned that you never know who's going to end up ordering product at these shows. Could be the most unassuming or the loudest and tackiest; the one decked out in big bling or sporting last year's Marshall's pantsuit. And sometimes big deals happened in the last hour, on the final day, as the other venders were already heading for the exits.

So I sat down next to Patti with our catalogue and told her about the operation, how we'd started with one storefront, expanded to six, but soon realized that online was our sweet spot. I explained how we'd built out our manufacturing operations in Alabama and North Carolina, how our prices were higher than most competitors but our quality was better, and how we paid our employees a living wage and weren't afraid to market as such. She asked probing follow-up questions and I realized even then she knew her shit and might have an agenda beyond only ordering a few couches and coffee tables.

Of course she ended with the inevitable: "My gosh, you're just so pretty! I mean like model pretty! What's your background, anyhow?"

And so, yet again, I had to explain my heritage. Which made her nod and smile and offer up that tired old "truism" about how mixed babies are simply "more beautiful" babies.

"It's just a fact!" she said, nodding vigorously at me and Selena, wanting us to concur.

Selena gritted her teeth and smiled back, another beautiful mixed baby. I had to fight the urge to ask whether her great granddaddy had raped one of his slaves and sired some beautiful babies himself, and whether she had heard from any of them now that Ancestry.com was setting off a global genetic reckoning. Maybe she had hundreds of second or third or fourth cousins who embodied the truism. Maybe she should sell one of the fat diamonds on her fat fingers and launch a #FamilyReparations viral movement...

It was late and I was tired. I had to check myself. Had to step back and remember: who the hell am I to march off down this self-righteous path, making judgements without knowing any real facts?

But then again, at this point in our nation's history, even if you're cocooned in the world of Fort Worth white privilege, I'm pretty sure someone like Patti already knew the answer to her "background" question before she asked it. And maybe it'd just be better for all of us at this point to just let that question lie. Just hold back and let's refrain from wading into the complexity and quagmire...

Or maybe that's impossible. At least it seems that way to me. Not to get sucked in or wade in. I mean even without her asking that question. Because, to be honest, I can't meet one of these southern belle types without later googling their family name and seeing if their in-your-face privilege can't be traced back to some sprawling family plantation and, if the linkage is there, going deeper to find out how many slaves they owned and for how many generations. Also what levers of political or economic power they controlled then, and therefore still control.

It's not healthy, I realize that. And I've spoken with my therapist about it and she's given me empathy exercises. She reminds me that the sins and transgressions of our ancestors are not the sole determiners of who we are now, of who a woman like Patti is today. For all I know, she might be like Sandra Bullock's character in *The Blind Side*. Not that that whole white savior premise wasn't problematic and blew up in everyone's face once the true story surfaced. Also, turns out that when I reversed it and asked my therapist whether she could relate, she admitted to having done the exact same thing when she was invited to a seminar at Vanderbilt. Googled the shit out of her fellow panelists. Dug up all sorts of dirt which then informed how she went into those interactions. So I guess that's just where we're at. Google is our Pandora's box.

I'm sure if I tell Neil about Patti's message he'll be able to tell me what my company is worth based on our sales and growth trajectory. Instantaneously spit back a number. He'd love nothing more than to lift the hood and dig around, see what I've been doing. Share his wisdom. I'm sure there's some online tool to generate the number too. But in listening and re-listening to her message, I realize it's gonna be more complicated. It isn't only about the money. Can't be. I can't help but see this in the context of just another Black-owned business selling to some bigger white-owned conglomerate. Should that be the first lens I look at this through? Don't know. I wish it weren't, but there it is. Of course if I'm being really honest with myself, there's probably a big enough number that makes that lens or context or calculation go away. Because if that number is big enough, I can step away from everything, including my husband.

30

NEIL ENGEL

Since its founding 228 years ago, this place has graduated one president, three vice presidents, four Supreme Court Justices, two Nobel Laureates, eleven billionaires, and now my son. My beautiful boy.

He sits up there in cap and gown and stares back at us. At a sea of parents and grandparents in rows of white folding chairs, some bursting with pride, like us; some no doubt questioning the value proposition, as not even this school's pedigree ensures everyone an Ivy acceptance. Those days are long gone. Elijah told us 32 students applied to Brown and only five were accepted. He's one of only two who will be attending Yale.

What does he see, our son, when he looks out and sees me sitting here? Sees us? What does he feel?

The Pulitzer-winning commencement speaker, an alumna herself, reminds the graduates of what they've been given by attending this remarkable institution:

...Because opportunity of this kind, what this school gave and will continue to give each of you during your lifetime, also necessitates that you act in a way that transcends the individual, the self. You're now bigger than merely the biological, hereditary, cultural, ethnic, linguistic, and educational sum of your identity. As you step into this next chapter, your intelligence, your connections, your wealth — whether literal or in terms of potential — now requires a daily, personal reflection on what can be done to improve the world for others. Why? Well, for one, each of you won the Mega Millions lottery ticket in this particular lifetime. Seriously, you did. Look around you, at one another, and recognize the time and place and circumstance in which you find yourself. For whatever reason, it's

you that's here today and not one of the other eight billion inhabitants of our planet. And because of that, the onus is on you. On us. Because of our remarkable good fortune, because of the whimsy of the fates, we each have the capacity to identify, expose, and strive to eradicate the rampant injustice we see in this nation and world. You possess the ideas, the energy and resources, and the leadership capacities to right the ship in terms of the climate crisis, in terms of...

On and on and on she goes with the hyperbole, exhorting the youth to shoot for the moon. But my question is what lives in the heart and mind of my son? What future does he see? Because he seems distant and moody since we returned from his grandfather's funeral in

Alabama six weeks ago.

The English department chair stands and approaches the podium. He begins to talk about a student who I realize is our Elijah, and his work. He tells us about an exceptional piece of writing that reflects the themes of the commencement address. He says the work is personal and raw, about the nuance, complexity and contradictions found within each modern American family. He describes how the essay harkens back to the injustice at the heart of this great nation, the original sin of slavery, but also strikes an "enviable balance" with moments of self-effacing humor and poignant confessional. At its core, he says, the prize-winning essay addresses questions of personal responsibility when faced with injustice. What to do with rage and guilt and jealousy. How to recognize and harness such impulses for the good. He says it's one of the best student essays he's read during his 30-year tenure at the school and wants to share the final page. He clears his throat, pulls on his readers, stares out at us for a moment, letting us recognize the gravity of what we're about to experience next. "Here goes," he says, and begins reading:

Despite advanced glaucoma, my great aunt Willamita is anything but blind to the facts. Behind the milky pupils is a steel trap of a memory; a repository of the granular, the minutiae. She can rattle off birth names and married names, when and where folks were born and died, where each of us sits on the family tree. She also retains the regional and national history, in her mind and her body, from which Category Five hurricane ravaged the Gulf Coast in 1969, to the rape, church fire-bombings and lynchings perpetrated against her African-American community for decade upon decade, century upon century. These are the history lessons recently banned at the state house in Montgomery. History lessons no longer taught to the Black and Brown children at the school on the corner of Monroe and Stocking; the neighborhood children still suffering the legacy of that history. Auntie Willamita is also aware that, unlike her, I find no solace in scripture, no balm within the dog-eared King James Bible that's always in her hands or resting on her lap.

Newton's Third Law states that for every action there is an equal and opposite reaction. This makes sense to me. Unlike my great aunt, who believes the 'reaction' to all the injustice she and her loved ones have experienced in this life can only portend eternal peace in the heavenly hereafter, I cannot sit idly by with the awareness of what's been perpetrated against her and the members of one side of my family simply because of their Blackness. A Blackness more visible, more profound than mine. My cousin's prospects in life are irrevocably stunted because of this history. My mother's cousin, almost 150 years after the end of slavery, is broken because of this history. Broken and in jail for life, a preordained fate based on where he was born, to whom he was born, and because his father was brutally murdered.

Except when I take a beat, when I look around and reflect, I'm not even sure what an appropriate 'equal and opposite reaction' might look like? Are we talking reparations? Stronger and more targeted affirmative action policies? An actual 40 acres and an actual mule? Because that seems fanciful and far-fetched in our current political and cultural climate.

But I'm here in Mobile today — a light-skinned alien dropped in from my Northeastern privilege — to attend the funeral of my maternal grandfather. This is a man who, if he'd been white, would have had a life expectancy of six to eight years longer than what he actually lived. A man that if he'd been from a higher tax bracket might have lived an additional six to eight years beyond that. We're talking potentially twelve to sixteen more years of playing the music he loved to play, driving the pick-up he loved to drive, continuing to rebuild the relationship with his once estranged daughter, and sharing his love and experiences with us, his grandchildren.

I'm here in Mobile and I know that doing nothing when faced with this awareness, these statistical truisms, this panorama of a life curtailed, defies one of the most profound laws of physics. So I open the door and step out into the sweltering day. Action necessitates an equal and opposite reaction. And that reaction will necessitate another action. The cycle will continue, but without me as yet another victim of color. I act and react for my grandfather, for my cousin, and especially for my namesake, Elijah, my mother's cousin, who historians believe was the last lynching victim in America. I act and react because they didn't and they couldn't. I step out into this day empowered to act."

Our son's teacher looks up and finds us, my wife and I, our daughter, and nods. There's a pregnant pause before everyone around us erupts in claps, cheers, whistles. Our son stands to accept the award. He shakes his teacher's hand, raises a hand to the crowd, smiles at Zora and returns to his seat. Class salutatorian. Winner of departmental awards for writing and mastery of history. Captain of the tennis and fencing teams. A young man clearly loved by classmates and teachers alike. I look up at my son and I love him so much my heart aches. I want him to experience this adulation, these accolades, and this love forever.

But of course that's not in the cards. I know that. I know that because of what life will become in the months ahead. As of last week, the bunker is in the name of our family trust. Next week, we will tour the complex as a family and go over the various contingencies that would lead to each of us being picked up by a member of my team and transported to our future, and hopefully temporary home.

31

NATASHA THOMAS-ENGEL

He's always been The Golden Child in the eyes of Dad and Mom, but now that we're here and he's sitting up there on stage in cap and gown, I can see the bigger perspective too. They all love him, his teachers and classmates, and now I see that it really goes back to the beginning. Like it's all been some self-fulfilling prophecy that was set in motion on the day of his birth which, when you think about it, isn't really that different or unique than how it's been for thousands of years, at least in the West and in terms of Anglo cultures. Or really most cultures. All hail the Firstborn Boy Child! Primogeniture is the rightful way, as God on high hath ordained. Hold him high above your head and let the gathered masses witness his beauty and inevitable might. Love him now, fear him later.

I'm guessing that if Elijah were to ever reflect on all this he'd probably have to admit this is basically the way it's been. He'd have to acknowledge that from Day One he was the center of our family's love, hope, expectation and promise. I mean pretty much from birth he must have begun to internalize the fact that he was somehow special, like the focal point of a vast reservoir of emotional and material resources, the pinch-point of a dam, with all this force just propelling him toward inevitable success and glory. Because it never seems like he struggled or struggles. He was the planet around which Mom and Dad and then our nanny Esme orbited for those formative years and, because of that, when he was deposited on the steps of NY's premier pre-K, he already possessed this very healthy confidence and sense of entitlement. And then that institution, which has been educating future leaders for almost two hundred years, sees this beautiful boy who's already so gifted academically and socially and decides there's something about him that's special and so they provide him with extra attention and love and care. Because out of all the future leaders in their classrooms — and we're talking classrooms full of the offspring of the City's most powerful and wealthy — he's the one with the best shot of bringing their institution even greater fame and fortune in twenty or thirty years. Not exactly sure what their calculations are, but it's clear they're anticipating extensive Wikipedia entries about Elijah and his accomplishments, with "early life" links to their "notable alumni" section, and articles about his vast fortune and largesse.

So he's held aloft like Simba and all the other animals see him as the Chosen One and this pattern basically just repeats and gets reinforced over and over until we're here and he's getting the love, support and validation of the premier boarding school in the nation. Plus he has the prettiest girlfriend. Plus he's off to Yale to study what dad wants him to study so that in maybe five or ten years he can take over the Family Office and I guess make sure that his offspring will step into the world with this same sense of belonging and manifest destiny.

And I guess when you look at it this way, it kinda does resemble the royal families of other countries and the question, at least if you're me, is where I fit into this picture and this lineage? Not that we're like the main royal family in this American context, because at different times we've both been in school with Rockefellers and Vanderbilts and Rothschilds and DuPonts, and they're definitely at a different level where they see themselves in some grander sweep of historical significance, and seem to walk around more comfortable in their skins, as if this is in fact their rightful place in the world. Probably there's also that thought in their minds that if I'm born into this lineage then maybe there is some bigger preordained master plan and God maybe has given me this position for some good reason. And if that's the case, then they're probably thinking that it's okay to act and be the way they are, as if they're a distinct and very rare human breed with a completely different set of rules of conduct that others will never understand, and it's also okay, and actually makes sense, that others treat them this way because the others know their family name and, deep down, they must also see that God or whoever is in charge must have a plan for them *not* being born into one of these royal American families. Anyhow, our family isn't at the Mellon or Guggenheim level but, if I think about it, we're definitely distant cousins to these rulers, the modern day kings and queens. And, from my perspective, it's like my brother must have been born on some auspicious day, with the gods in a great mood, or maybe drunk and focused on something else, because he seems to be ascendant in this whole royal tableau, whereas I'm clearly a secondary character in the story. Maybe even in his story, which is how I've felt my entire life.

It's a reality I first recognized when I became aware that Esme treated us differently. My memories are of her first, by the way. Her taking the two of us in a red and brown double stroller to places like the Natural History Museum and the Central Park Zoo to see the sea lions. I remember the outings and I remember how she always listened to Elijah's requests or heeded his tantrums first. One time in particular — and this might even be my very first memory — was when I needed to pee but Elijah was losing his shit because he'd dropped some toy in the dinosaur exhibit and, instead of taking me to the toilet first, Esme hurried us back to find the toy. And I couldn't hold it and I pissed through my brown tights. I remember the yellow puddle growing in size on the white marble floor and Esme being super mad.

And then pretty soon I became aware of the same dynamic with Mom and Dad. And honestly I'm fine with it, especially now. Of course, I can see how someone might say I'm fine with it because that's all I've ever known, and this is some kind of conditioning where I've just grown to accept and be happy for whatever scraps fall off the edge of my brother's bigger and more bountiful table. But now that I'm looking at him up there on that stage, and literally feeling the pride and hope and expectation that's emanating off the bodies of my parents who sit next to me, I realize that it's way better to be a lesser figure with fewer eyes on you and fewer expectations. Because I really don't want the weight of that wish-transference or whatever it's called on my shoulders; shoulders which everyone is always saying are already stooped because I hunch over when I'm reading.

Also, by the way, as I sit here, I realize that no one ever asked me if I wanted to come to this boarding school. And that's fine too. No one until this year asked me where I was thinking of applying to college, even though I remember my father talking to Elijah about Yale, and taking him to visit the campus, when he was in like seventh grade. Maybe they thought I couldn't handle it here, or maybe mom couldn't take having an empty nest so soon, but it just seemed logical to them that I stay at Fieldston all the way through. And obviously it's not like it's any worse than this school and for me it's probably better not to have to follow in Elijah's gilded footsteps. Always in his shadow. But looking at him up there it's not like he seems that happy to be graduating or that happy with what his teachers are saying about him, about his bright future and boundless potential. He doesn't tell me anything but I know on some level he resents how Dad has such specific expectations of him. But so far it seems like he's basically just going along with the path laid out before him. I mean, why study economics at Yale where dad studied economics if you're not really into it? It's not like every time I look over, he's reading some econ textbook or watching videos about entrepreneurship. And, really, like how much money do we actually need? Does anyone actually think about any of this? Seriously! I mean I don't know the details but any moron can see we have plenty, probably too much, and so why should the main focus of the Golden Child's life be to double or triple or ten-X our family net worth? Especially if ultimately it doesn't make him or anyone else in the family happier, which is what I gather from what I read, that at a certain point money just doesn't make you happier. Like I read somewhere the cut off is something like eight million. Up until that amount you might get happier but once you hit that it plateaus, because that's the point at which you don't ever have to do the menial tasks like cooking and cleaning and doing laundry unless you choose to. Definitely true for us, like it becomes a choice, some special occasion when Mom wants to cook the one recipe that some old friend taught her when she was living in Paris, or Dad wants to barbecue fish or steak when we're in Amagansett and some guests are coming over. He likes to wear his bespoke leather apron and be The Grill Master, but only once or twice a summer.

So I guess when I look at it this way, like in terms of class and everything, there's really nothing new going on here that Tolstoy or Dostoyevsky or I guess even Shakespeare didn't already write about. Like it's emotions such as love or jealousy or resentment from some real or perceived slight that animates what everyone's doing. If anything, I guess Elijah might resent Dad, and that might be what drives him to do something different at some point, but so far, he hasn't acted that out in any way that I can see. I see anger in there, but maybe that's just me. Maybe I'm angry that he doesn't make different choices because, from the outside, it's like if this person on this stage doesn't have the ability to do what he wants in life, to act on what he desires, to create what he dreams of, to live the way he wants, to love who he wants, then we're really doomed as a species.

What would Milton Riggs Jr. think of all this if he were

sitting here? He's a firstborn too, but living under the watchful eye of his grandmother without much money, who clearly has a plan laid out for him. And so far he seems to be abiding her wishes by doing well in school, being respectful and courteous, talking about attending college and maybe studying pharmacology, which strikes me as an odd choice for a 15-year-old to set his hopes on, except I guess he's heard from his grandmother or teachers that it's a well-paid and respectable occupation. My point is that others seem to be operating with a scaffolding of expectations and if I think about it, I've honestly never thought my parents have any particular hopes or desires for me in terms of what I do, where I do it, with whom I do it, etc. Which is both freeing and also a little depressing, depending on how you look at it. I mean would I want to be sitting up on that stage in my brother's seat? Definitely not. But, being honest with myself, I have to admit that at times I do wish Mom or Dad would ask what I'm interested in doing so that maybe I'd be forced to think about it and make some first steps in that direction, and maybe they could tell me how to get from point a to b. Like everyone in my life has known since first grade that books are where I find my joy and comfort and solace and excitement and sexual turn-on and revulsion and rage and hope and fear. But Milton Riggs Jr.'s lips on my lips in that dark Sunday school room in the basement, and the way his fingers started to explore my body, made me want to live more outside of books than inside of them. I'm sure it sounds naive or cliched or adolescent, and in a few years I'll probably want to puke thinking this is what I would say, but to put it in words, I want to eat life and get punched in the face by life and punch back even harder and fuck and get fucked and love and get loved and break relationships and heal relationships and understand relationships and see what's behind my mother's sunglasses, what's going on in her complicated mind and damaged heart, and learn more about why my father is so obsessive about his spreadsheets and our family legacy or whatever, and why he's meeting that woman at the Standard, and whether Mom knows, and whether she cares, and really I'd like to be transported back to the basement of that church on the afternoon of my grandfather's funeral and relive the exact moment when I leaned in and kissed Milton Riggs Jr. on his soft, sweet lips.

32

ELIJAH THOMAS-ENGEL

My new roommate — Kai Nakashima from Kane'ohe, Hawaii — was already off at the Marx Science Library studying organic chem. This was the second day after move-in, and three days before classes officially started. We were still in the middle of new-student orientation which, honestly, wasn't that different from the orientation I'd suffered through at boarding school four years ago. Plenty of cringy bonding exercises, forced sharing of personal anecdotes, rousing speeches about boundless possibility, topped off with an info-geyser about the mental health, academic and career supports available to us 24-7. "Because without you being your best and authentic selves, we can't be our best institutional self!"

I needed a break and bailed on the afternoon hike to West Rock overlook. Kai feigned jet lag, grabbed his laptop and scurried off. Even though he presents as if he's all chill with the Locals flip-flops and "always aloha" baseball cap, roomie is clearly out to prove he's deserving. I guess of being admitted. Maybe it's a first-gen issue. Or that he's on financial aid. Or maybe he's just intimidated by the global assortment of brainiacs, royals, Olympians and moneyed legacies that comprise our class, "the most competitive and accomplished in university history", according to the bs press release my dad forwarded but that I'd already seen.

Anyhow, I was lying on my bed and glanced over at what was supposed to be Kai's empty bed. Except it wasn't empty. At first it was just the eyes, which I recognized immediately. But then, as my own eyes adjusted, or maybe as my imagination kicked in to overdrive and fleshed out the full vision, it was the body lying there too. A body twice the size of Kai's. He was lying on his back, arms behind his head, wearing the same outfit as the last time I'd seen him — red and black Roll Tide tank top, Nike shorts, athletic socks pulled up high on his thick calves. He smiled across at me.

"Kinda ironic, right?"

It was the first time I'd heard him speak. He had a strong southern accent, as expected, but the pitch of his voice was higher than I'd have guessed given his massive body.

"What is?"

"Where we're at right now," he said. "I mean, given the fact of who you and your roommate are an' everything."

"Not following you, bro," I said.

"You even know what the college you're a member of is called?"

I nodded.

"Ain't talkin' about Yale. But that's kinda ironic too. I'm talkin' about..." and he air-quoted here... "Grace Hopper College."

"What's your point?"

He rolled his body toward me, on his side now, one hand supporting his head, and smiled.

"Seriously, what do you want?" I said. "And why the fuck are you smiling like that?"

"Well, guess I got some time on my hands on account of you. So, yeah, been doing some thinking. Also some reading, which normally ain't my thing."

He nodded and smiled again. Lay back on the bed again, hands behind his head. He crossed his legs, slow and deliberate, a show of making himself at home. I looked away, trying to break out of this little fantasy. Shit was all in my head, after all. I'd conjured him into being on account of allowing myself this downtime. Probably should have gone to West Rock after all. Or, like Kai, maybe should get a jump on my reading. I knew we'd be discussing the Nash equilibrium in our first week of

Game Theory, one of the econ classes I'd signed up for, which my dad seemed pleased about. Which kinda pissed me off, honestly, even though the class seemed pretty cool. Course description read: "Ideas such as dominance, backward induction, evolutionary stability, commitment, credibility, asymmetric information, adverse selection, and signaling are discussed and applied to games played in class and to examples drawn from economics, politics, the movies, and elsewhere."

Or maybe I should call Liza. She'd started at Pomona last week. We'd promised to talk every day but had already lapsed, which bothered me. I missed her. Not sure exactly why, but ever since what happened in Mobile, I'd been unable to appreciate her in the same way. Her humor. How frank and honest she is. Her optimism. The way she doesn't give a fuck who's in earshot, on the other side of whatever wall, and just screams her head off when I pleasure her with my tongue or she's riding cowgirl. But for the last few weeks of school it was like I was watching from the outside, almost floating above and observing what was happening, feeling maybe 50% of the experience. Felt like I was half-anesthetized for graduation, saying goodbye to classmates and teachers, moving out of the dorms. Same over the summer.

Troy was still there on Kai's bed. And he was smirking.

"Guess what I'm saying is that I found it pretty interesting when I read that your college wasn't named after that scientist lady until 2017," he said. "Especially because of how old it looks, like it's Hogwarts or something."

I knew this. I'd read the history. Plus my father had been an undergrad at this same college. I chose not to respond, thinking that if I didn't engage maybe my mind would pivot back to the real here and now; the reality that I was here about to begin college, lying on my new dorm bed, with my mom and sister back in the City and my dad, I don't know where, maybe still prepping for end times. In which case what was the point. Like why did he seem so invested in me being here, studying econ, continuing the legacy, if bunker life or a violent death was imminent for all of us. Shit made no sense.

"Thing is, they called it Calhoun College for over a hundred years," he said. "Yeah, named after what everyone thought was an 'eminent' alumni until, well, I guess from one day to the next the higher-ups decided he wasn't. John Caldwell Calhoun. Still plenty about him in the library. He ended up being a Congressman, Vice President, Secretary of War, even one of the college 'Worthies', and you got only eight of them. They still got a big ol' statue of him over on Harkness Tower—"

"Already know all this, okay? Definitely don't need to hear it from you!"

"Gotcha. And it's not like I'm tryin' to provide some history lesson, 'cause I think we both know you're the educated one between us. One who's gonna just add more knowledge on top of all the knowledge you already got. Plus all the important people you already know. Connections and network an' everything. Which is the part of it that maybe I didn't realize until visiting you up here. I mean, seems like that's basically what it's really all about, right? Just sorting people into the right categories. Like who's gonna run this, who's gonna own that. Who's gonna be a Congressman or President. Who's gonna marry into that fortune right over there so combined you get some even bigger fortune. At least that's the idea I came to when I was readin' the alumni magazine. Pretty interesting, what all y'all end up doing. That Bulldog pride they talk about seems real strong."

I stared up at the ceiling, willed him to be gone. But chatterbox kept fucking going.

"Like I was saying, though, I do just find it a lil' ironic that you're a member of a college that used to be named after a real famous slaver from South Carolina. And that you're going to a college still named after Elihu Yale, who most people say was basically cool with slavery. Most historians, anyhow. That he didn't mind getting served by slaves at all the fancy functions, and didn't mind that his own family members owned 'em—"

"Okay, what's your fucking point already?!"

He smiled. Nodded. Took a moment. This whole situation reminded me of when Auntie Mita was talking about that membrane between the voices inside her head and the ones outside her head, and how sometimes it was hard to distinguish the difference. Which at the time had made me think of schizophrenia, and now had me remembering that I'd read somewhere that schizophrenia usually manifests in early adulthood. Starts with people hearing voices, then the voices start telling them certain things that they need to do, which become compulsive. Fuck me!

Troy was sitting up now, legs dangling over the side of the bed, hands clasped in his lap. Kai's bed sagged in the middle under his weight.

"Alright, I hear ya. I do. So I guess if there is an actual point, if you're not cool with us just, you know, shootin' the breeze and getting to know each other better, I guess my main point would have to be that you're a hypocrite like everyone else is a hypocrite. Yeah, maybe that's it. Like maybe you're as bad as any other person that ever lived. As bad and also probably as good. But definitely no better. Because I'm imagining you think you knew me. Knew enough about me and my family that you could come to some conclusion about who I am, or was, and what all I represented. And whatever that thought process that got you to that conclusion was — conclusion that I needed to be exterminated — that was somehow justified in your mind. I deserved it, in your thinking. You were righting some kinda wrong. Like my life was of no more value than some cockroach or vermin because of what I represented, and what lived in me because of my family and what all they did in the past. And because you thought you understood that, understood us, that you had some special way of knowing what lived in my heart and mind, you thought I wasn't worthy of living out a natural human lifespan."

He looked over at me and waited. Again, it didn't seem like it was worth responding here. He wasn't going to understand what I understood, all the historical recapitulations and reverberations, the family nuances, the reactive and active forces at play. It was an equation beyond his capacity to comprehend. An equation that was always shifting and morphing, even in my own head.

"Probably think I wouldn't understand, that you're too smart for me," he said. "And maybe that's right. But let me ask you this, then. Might be comin' out of left field, but lemme ask you this. Because you probably wouldn't never have guessed that I asked a Black girl to prom. Am I right?"

I didn't know this and didn't really care. And didn't give him anything as far as a reaction either. He smiled, satisfied, and glanced off through the window toward the green of the quad below.

"Keesha Williams was her name. Shoot, still is her name. Her brother was on the football team with me, real nice fellow. Brandon. A year ahead of us. Was on the team the year we went to States and now plays for North Carolina Central. Which is the best HBCU football team in the nation, in case you didn't know, which I'm guessing you didn't. He'll probably end up gettin' drafted."

I grabbed P.K. Dutta's book "Strategies and Games: Theory and Practice" from my bedside table. Opened it to Chapter 1.

"Which I guess is another question I got, actually. Yeah, like how come you never even considered an HBCU?"

Fuck this guy. Or fuck this voice in my head.

"No, I'm serious though! I mean I'm not pretending to know anything about this, but is it maybe that you're not Black enough? Like you think maybe you wouldn't be accepted by other students at a historically Black school on account of how light complected you are? Brown paper bag and all that—?"

"Hey, I'm fucking reading!" I said. And I realized I said it out loud. Loud enough that someone walking by in the hallway might hear. This whole interaction or mental tangent, whatever it was, was spiraling.

"I hear ya, okay? Relax, 'cause I'm planning on wrapping this up real soon anyhow," he continued. "Lemme just get to the end of my thought, or I guess question. Or actually it's more like an observation. Which is, maybe you wanted the advantages of identifying as black when you applied to a place like this, but didn't want to actually go deep on the lifestyle, the history, the culture like you probably would've been forced to if you went to some place like North Carolina Central or Morehouse or Howard."

"You don't know what the fuck you're talking about, okay?!" My voice bounced around in the room, again out loud.

"No, you're right. You're probably right. I guess my only point is you sometimes don't know either. Because I went to prom with Keesha even though it made my Nanna real uncomfortable. See, she thought it would be some story that the press would pick up on. That there'd be all sorts of unwanted attention. Headlines like 'Grandson of Klansman Jailed for Racial Murder Goes to Prom with Black Classmate', or maybe 'Reconciliation Possible in New South'. Or maybe somethin' about mercy or redemption."

He stood from the bed and walked to the window. Stared out.

"Point I'm making is that I had a big ol' crush on Keesha. I mean I was real nervous, and you're the only other living soul I've ever told this to, but I was so nervous that when we got back to the motel we'd rented, like to have sex for that first time, I couldn't even make it work. Couldn't get it up, which had never been an issue before with my first girlfriend, Holly.

Not once, I promise. And it wasn't like I was drunk or nothin'. And the real messed up part was she thought maybe it was a race thing, that I wasn't attracted to her when I saw her in the flesh like that, and she got real angry at first. Which didn't help, obviously, because it made me even more nervous. Had to work real hard to convince her that I actually found her more attractive and beautiful than any other girl I'd ever been with, or even seen. Like I had real feelings and everything, and not just only sexual. Eventually we figured it out, on like the third try, like the next week or whatever. And I mean I'm always gonna remember that, remember her. Real beautiful girl, inside and out. Keesha."

This was so fucked up. He looked like he was about to cry. How did I turn this off or shut this down?

"Sorry, got a little distracted. Maybe seeing all them young people out there on the lawn." He gestured out the window. "Like how they're looking all happy, talking to each other, probably crushing on each other an' everything."

He turned to face me. Looked down at me on my bed.

"Main point with the Keesha story is that you didn't know me. At all, really. Thought you did but you don't. But I guess we're gonna get to know one another real good now."

He smiled and nodded, rueful almost. Like he wished this wasn't the case. Almost like he pitied me.

"If you thought this is some story that just ends with you blowing my brains out, don't think that's really how it works. I mean definitely my family's ruined, if that was your intention. Nanna's not gonna live much longer. I mean a person can only suffer so much heartache, even if those you're grieving for are viewed by the rest of society as evil or whatever. 'Cause no matter what you say, or what all my grandfather did to your mom's cousin before we were even born, the truth is my Nanna loved him. She loved my grandfather. And she loved my momma even more, my momma who got destroyed by this train wreck too. I mean she couldn't live with what her father had done, with the trial and all the press, all the whispering she'd hear at the grocery store, the pointing, the cursing and spitting. I guess drugs were the only way to numb herself, that's what I gleaned, and that ended up killing her. So that's already a dagger to my Nanna's heart. Death of a daughter. Lifetime in jail for her husband. And probably she loved me more than all of 'em combined, my Nanna. So yeah, she got nothin' worth living for now and I'm guessing ain't long for this world. For your world, the alive world."

He wiped a tear with the back of his giant hand. Reached back and wiped the hand on Kai's bedspread. Shrugged.

"But I mean you got me now as a result of what all's happened. I'm right here. I guess living right here, alongside of you."

He pointed at my head.

"Or living right inside there. Until, yeah, I guess something else comes along that pulls me toward something else. Honesty don't really understand how this all works. Who's in charge of what. Like is it me or you controlling what's happening right now between us?"

He smiled and shrugged. I felt pinned to my bed, unable to move or say anything.

"Right, well, guess we'll see. Anyways, back to that point I was trying to make in the beginning. Like if it's about all these connections you like to think about, big picture an' all, how about that you're a member of a college that was once named after and probably paid for by a man who owned one of the largest slave plantations in the South. Who had a Black wet nurse and claimed slavery was an actual benefit to what he believed to be the inferior race. What about him? What about what he's thinking right now? Like if Calhoun just opened the door and stepped into this room right now to find you and this part Japanese, part Hawaiian kid living here?"

He was back to fucking with me. I could tell by the glint in his eyes. He reached into his pocket, pulled out a folded piece of paper, and began to unfold it.

"Pretty interesting to think about, right?"

I shook my head, closed my eyes. But his voice was still there, inhabiting the space.

"Wrote some of his words down, passages I found in the library. Yeah, like this right here. Listen to what he said: 'I hold that in the present state of civilization, where two races of different origin, and distinguished by color, and other physical differences, as well as intellectual, are brought together, the relation now existing in the slaveholding States between the two, is, instead of an evil, a good — a positive good. I feel myself called upon to speak freely upon the subject where the honor and interests of those I represent are involved. I hold then, that there never has yet existed a wealthy and civilized society in which one portion of the community did not, in point of fact, live on the labor of the other.'"

I cracked open an eye. Sure enough, he was looking over the top of the paper at me, waiting for a response.

"I mean you're the one who's probably studied the history an' all. What do you think? Even if you put aside the race stuff, what about the wealthy part of society living off the labor of the other part?"

I closed my eyes again.

"Or, okay, did you check out what's on Elihu Yale's gravestone. Pretty interesting what that says too." He started reading again:

Born in America, in Europe bred,
In Africa travell'd and in Asia wed,
Where long he liv'd and thriv'd; In London dead
Much good, some ill, he did; so hope all's even
And that his soul thro' mercy's gone to Heaven

You that survive and read this tale, take care
For this most certain exit to prepare
Where blest in peace, the actions of the just
Smell sweet and blossom in the silent dust.

I heard heavy footsteps and opened my eyes. Troy had moved to the door. He reached for the handle, held it in his left hand, glanced back at me.

"I get it. You're losing interest. And it's not like we can't talk about all this later. But that quote or inscription, whatever you call it that's on his grave, that was real interesting to me too. I'll admit, I'm still trying to wrap my head around the exact meaning. That part about the actions of the just smelling sweet when right up above that it's talking about the ill he did. I guess maybe it's about redemption? Like how you weigh the good and the bad but can still come out in the positive column? I mean maybe you got some smarter way to think about it. Like maybe you can help me understand, sometime when you feel more like talkin'."

He shrugged, opened the door, looked both ways, then stepped out into the hallway.

33

LAVONN & WILLAMITA PATTERSON

LaVonn stared through the scratched plexi and knew this was the last time. Something was different. Something had changed. She sat there with her bible in her hands, straight-backed, eyes clouded and clearly not registering his face or any other detail of her surroundings. This was normal. What was different was she hadn't greeted him yet. Hadn't said anything at all. The ritual established the very first time she visited, so many years ago that he'd lost track, was that he was led to his seat and she was already sitting there waiting. The guard on her side of the glass would announce his arrival and she'd greet him by name and then immediately share a scriptural passage she'd chosen in advance. Then she'd ask how he was being treated and whether he was eating enough. At first, he'd hated how the visits followed the same script every time, and that it was only ever her that visited. Eventually, however, as the months and years wore on, he resigned himself to the reality that nothing was going to change unless he chose to disrupt the flow of their ritual. He'd have to actually share something beyond a yes or no answer. Even though he realized this, it took him several more years until he managed to come prepared with at least one item of information to share or one question to ask about life beyond the barbed wire of the peni-tentiary.

Today she just sat there, wig more off-center than normal, her lips — which were usually bright red — brown and wrin-kled. He didn't know what to do or say. He'd come prepared to tell her that the warden had finally agreed to schedule an appointment with the eye doctor.

"Shawna drive you?" he said.

No response. Not even a physical acknowledgement that she could hear him.

"You hearin' me, Gramma?"

He called for the guard to check the intercom, who assured him all was working as it should. The guard on the other side of the glass, standing against the back wall, gave him a thumbs-up too. He let the silence hang between them. Then leaned forward toward the glass.

"Don't know if he said so, but Elijah paid me a visit a few months back. Been thinking about that, wanted to tell you last time you was here. Other'n you, he the only other kin that's made the trip since I been locked up."

His grandmother just sat there, catatonic.

"Zora's boy, Elijah, from up North. Brought his white girl-friend too. Real pretty. She was quiet, just watching, but he had a whole mess of questions that didn't make no sense. Said he was writing some school paper or somethin'. About the family."

Maybe he shouldn't even bother talking, he thought. Maybe what she needed was to just feel she was in his presence one last time. Because the more she just sat there unresponsive, the more convinced he was that she'd come today to say her final goodbye — maybe by choice, or maybe because the way she was acting meant that the rest of the family was finally about to step in and lock her up in some old person's home for good.

He leaned closer to the window, adjusted his glasses to get a better look at her. Yes, this was the woman who'd raised him. Or at least tried. She'd always been there for him, before his father was murdered and after. This was the woman who drove him to school. Picked him up and fed him a snack before he realized he was even hungry. Taught him to read and write. It was this woman who prepared and set a meal before him every morning, noon and night. This woman who made sure he left the house in clean clothes. Who demanded he be polite to his elders and, when needed, used a belt to enforce her rules.

But it hadn't been enough. Her love — whether in the form of a tender hand wiping away tears or a firm smack to remind him of his manners — it couldn't inoculate him from what was destined to happen, or repair him once it did. Looking back, LaVonn thought that maybe it was during her darkest months of grieving when he slipped from her radar. She'd fallen into a bottomless vortex of what-ifs and why-us and didn't have the capacity to do more than make sure he was fed, clothed and housed. It was understandable. Thing is, by the time she'd clawed her way back out of the dark place, and had seen some semblance of justice realized — in the form of life sentences for the perpetrators and a civil settlement that gave her some financial means to support herself and him — LaVonn was already running with the wrong crew. She had the funds to enroll him at St. Ignatius, where the teachers were far better, but it was too late. Most knew his backstory and tried real hard to give him extra attention. But no matter their skills as teachers, mentors, counselors, they just couldn't compete with the adrenaline rush he'd already experienced when outrunning the police or a rival gang. The clarity of focus he felt when robbing a convenience store. The sense of belonging that enveloped him when smoking blunts with his boys after a successful carjacking. It was those sweet, fleeting moments that numbed the despair that sat at the core of his very being.

She'd tried. They'd tried. But there was no carrot or stick big enough to keep a boy whose father's lynching occupied the national spotlight for month upon month from seeking the most powerful escapism available: the camaraderie and glamour of crime, the solace of drugs, the bounty of girls ready to uncork another Dom in the VIP lounge at the club and fuck 'til dawn. He was 19 when he got sentenced to life without parole and broke his grandmother's fractured heart one more time.

She continued to sit there and he continued to observe her.

He'd had plenty of time to process it all now that his frontal cortex had fully matured. He'd read about that and, years ago now, spoken to a prison therapist who unfortunately got transferred. He understood that the woman in front of him had done her best given the shitty cards she'd been dealt. He was long past blaming her for anything she did or didn't do.

"Listen, Gramma, I need to thank you. For everything you done for me. All what I know you done, probably plenty I don't."

He thought he noticed a change in her expression. Maybe an eye twitch.

"You hearin' me? I need to thank you for all the years you shown me love. Before I got locked up and after. Also need to say I'm real sorry for what all I put you through. Didn't deserve that on top of everything else."

He hoped she registered his words because, before today, he'd never been able to say any of it. Not thank you. Not sorry. Not I love you. He realized it was the silence that let him share all this. The fact that for the first time in his life she was sitting there and not quoting scripture. Or lecturing him about the righteous path. Or begging him to accept the Lord and secure his everlasting salvation before it was too late. He stood up.

"I hope you heard me and I hope you know I appreciate you, Gramma. That I appreciate you and love you."

———

Later that afternoon Willamita lay in her bed, wig on its stand, dentures submerged in a glass on her bedside table. She was in her nightgown and had pulled on her hair net too, although now that she was lying there, under the covers, she wasn't sure any of this was necessary. She knew it was still light outside and that didn't matter either. No one was coming to check on her today, no one was fixing to call, and after more than three months of peace, she wasn't expecting the apparition of her son Elijah to visit either. The house was quiet.

She thought of her grandson LaVonn and the words he'd spoken earlier. She knew he looked older, probably didn't look good after all the years of being locked up, but since losing her sight she'd always imagined him as the young man who entered jail so many years ago. He was handsome like his father, which had been part of his downfall. Everyone always said so, and the girls thought so too. His teeth were straight and porcelain white and when he smiled at her it had always melted away all her anxieties, frustrations, her doubts. Disarming is what it was. Looking back, she was sure that smile distracted her from the discipline he needed at certain critical moments in his upbringing.

He'd been a happy child and she hoped he was able to remember that. There were many happy days before there weren't. She could still access those visual bursts of his smiling face, before the murder, when she felt promise for her son, for herself, and especially for this sweet gregarious boy. Yes, in one alternate scenario she could conjure up, her son Elijah had finished night school unscathed and found steady work with an appliance repair company, quickly moving up into a management position. He'd married a good Christian woman he'd met at church and they'd created a loving home for themselves and their two young children, a girl and a boy. They'd of course taken LaVonn with them too, the doting older brother who showed his younger siblings the righteous path. In her mind's eye, it was a middle-class life like you see in commercials, with the happy Black family pulling into their driveway in a new minivan, spilling out onto a perfectly green lawn, neighbors waving at them from across the street. White neighbors. Asian neighbors. Black neighbors. And LaVonn's smile was at the center of that tableau. A smile and sweet temperament that was met by teachers and coaches who recognized his goodness and potential and propelled him up and through high school, even to a degree from a four-year college.

Willamita lay there and imagined this alternate reality, how only a few adjustments to a life could have rendered something so different. But then she felt the weight of the book that rested next to her on the bed. The Book that reminded her that, despite her formidable imagination, she was simply not the one in charge of her own life or that of her kin. The Book reminded her that allowing herself to be led down this alternate path of what-ifs was in fact the Devil at play, as had been the case when she allowed her son's apparition to take up residence in her mind, and stay for so many years. Her actual life, the one guided by God's will and governed by His mercy, was the one that led her to this very moment, where she lay in this bed, on this exact afternoon, in this house on Savannah Street in Mobile. And as she lay there, she reminded herself that her only role in this lifetime was to recognize that a divine power far beyond her comprehension was in charge, and that only by giving herself over to His power would she attain the everlasting peace she so desperately sought. She closed her eyes. She rested her hands on her chest. Felt the rising and the falling. She was ready to let go, she thought. She was ready to be cradled in the warm embrace of an army of cherubim and carried heavenward. She imagined the sound their wings might make but just then the AC kicked on and overpowered them.

She waited and waited but her mind wouldn't quiet. What she still couldn't reconcile was the way in which Elijah her son, the apparition in her mind, and Elijah her grandnephew were somehow connected. She knew the apparition had hinted that he was making visitations to others, possibly even to his namesake. But was that her imagination at work or was there reality to this? Beyond her, was there any reality to the words he whispered in her ears?

For at least the hundredth time she replayed how Elijah her

grandnephew had driven her home after the funeral service. She recalled the sense she had that he'd traveled an unfamiliar route home from the church, and had made a stop. He'd exited the vehicle for a minute or longer. She'd heard a pop sound and then he'd returned and opened the trunk, closed the trunk, then climbed in beside her and driven her home. What had happened wasn't clear. He didn't say anything and she didn't ask. He'd acted as courteous as ever when he dropped her off, taking her elbow and escorting her up the ramp and into the house, making sure she was settled in her chair in the den.

What she did know with certainty was that from that day onward her son Elijah hadn't visited again. He had been sitting behind her in the car after the funeral and up until Elijah exited the car. He'd been tormenting her with cryptic words, asking if she knew where they were going, almost giddy about what was happening. But then he was gone. He hadn't joined her in watching the evening news, hadn't shown up smiling beside her in bed, hadn't snuck up on her in the kitchen and whispered nonsense in her ear. No, he'd just vanished, and she wasn't sure if it was her mind that finally turned him off or whether something her grandnephew Elijah had done had finally set him free from his limbo.

She felt lighter, thinking of this. The idea that perhaps her son was finally free. And that he was no longer tormenting others — herself included — on account of him having been so tormented himself.

But where was he now, she wondered. She realized her vision of the afterlife was more feeling-based than specific to a location or setting. She imagined the afterlife as a feeling of comfort and safety. A feeling of belonging, unburdened by fear and anxiety or bodily pain. But if Elijah was free of the purgatory of being tethered to the earthly realm, what was it that he might see if he opened his heavenly eyes. Were there even such things as eyes where he was now, and where she hoped to be going soon?

Returning to the here and now, to the earthly realm, she wondered what his moving on meant. How many living people still thought of him? On a daily basis, she was sure it was only her. Maybe LaVonn thought of his dead father a few times a week. She knew students and researchers at colleges might stumble across accounts of his brutal murder in old papers or on the internet. Police photographs too, which she hated would be how he'd be remembered by history, his body slung up in the camphor tree, feet only inches from the road below, neck at that angle that made her sick to her stomach. But actual personal memories, held by those who actually knew him and loved him, each day they were becoming fewer. And once she was gone, taking all her memories with her, he would be diminished to the point of caricature. She remembered what LaVonn had said about namesake Elijah asking questions and writing some paper for school, and that maybe he was the one who would think of his dead relative the most, and that was only on account of him being burdened with the same name.

She felt her hands rise and fall on her chest. Rise and fall. Her hands felt lighter. Maybe she, together with her Creator, could decide in unison when to inhale and exhale for the last time. Maybe it was a dialogue they could share, that maybe they were already sharing. She could let Him know she was ready to be unburdened by this life and he would finally believe her and accept her this time. By thinking of this, she felt she was letting Him know. And she felt, for the first time, that He heard her and understood her.

34

NEIL ENGEL

Pointed questions and irrational blowback was to be expected. It was a monumental reveal, both of my thinking on the future and the lengths to which I'd already gone to ensure our survival. The most efficient way seemed to be a site visit, as a family, so they could see this wasn't merely hyperbole. Rip the band-aid off in one go. No one was keen to clear schedules for a full day, especially without more details, but this time it wasn't optional. I said it involved estate planning — the subtext being inheritance — and they all shut up and arrived at Pier 6 early on Saturday morning, Elijah down from New Haven.

45 minutes later we sat cocooned in the back of the helicopter, a vast blanket of green treetops below. Each time I've made the journey, these final minutes of flight, with no man-made structures visible, only undulating hills of forest, higher peaks in the distance, reminds me that if we don't make it as a species, life on the planet will continue on just fine. A nuclear blast might flatten these trees or block the sun's rays with lethal particulate matter for months or years, but somewhere down there in the ancient biome one or more lifeforms will survive. They'll survive, exploit new opportunities, heed the biological imperative, and evolve. Whether or not that's the event that takes out humanity as we know it, at least for the four of us, the sheer size and density of this forest will most likely be a defining factor in our preservation. It will be one of numerous motes.

The helicopter banks. In the distance, a fenced square of gravel and cement blocks is visible. It's incongruous, an affront to the uniformity of green. The helicopter levels off and sinks to the landing pad.

Zora watches through her shades, unflappable. Natasha continues to read. Elijah leans toward the window, eyes on the razor wire loops that have been added to the perimeter fences since I was last here.

"What the fuck?" he says. "This some kind of prison?"

———

The facial recognition entry key works as promised and the doors to our dedicated elevator open. We could take the stairs, as I did last time, but 11 stories down isn't going to help my cause. We step in, the thick steel doors close, and we drop. Now that her face isn't buried in her book, Natasha looks confused. She stares at me.

"Okay, did I miss something?" she says. "What exactly are we doing, Dad? What is this?"

"For now, I just want you to notice the attention to detail, and the various security measures. It's all state-of-the-art."

Natasha stares at Zora. "Mom, what are we doing?"

"No, just hold on," I say. "I'm going to tell you a whole lot more in a moment."

Zora shrugs. She's checked out. Maybe on account of losing her father, and more recently, her Aunt Mita. Or maybe she's just fatigued by me. Everything about me. That's how it feels, lately. On a good day, I'm a hindrance deserving of derision. On a bad day, she doesn't even recognize my existence. The fact that she doesn't respond now with anything more than a shrug is the confirmation I need to lock down Flor. She will be a key variable in our survival equation. Populating the bunker with three or four others, in addition to us, will make life down here more tolerable and, just as important, might be essential in terms of continuing our family bloodline and maintaining sufficient genetic diversity for humanity's survival. Unfortunately, that's how you need to view this.

The elevator doors open and I lead the way into the foyer. The kitchen is to our right, bedroom suites off corridors on either side. Straight ahead, with vaulted ceilings of aspen above, the living room's digital windows feature a stunning tropical beach at sunset. Seabirds fly up and out of view in one direction, a distant yacht with full sails makes good time on the horizon. All the furniture has been delivered and is in place. Artwork on the walls. The apartment rivals any we've ever lived in, and this one is built to withstand the apocalypse. I turn back to judge their reactions.

They just stand there.

"Okay, look, I mean do any of us want to live in a doomsday bunker? Obviously not. But if it comes to it, we could do a whole lot worse than this apartment. Seriously, walk around," I say. "Our bedroom suites are that way. Staff quarters are down that hall, past the kitchen."

Zora still hasn't taken off her sunglasses. She stares straight ahead at the tropical seascape on the digital windows.

Elijah's eyes blink rapidly. He's on-edge, and I recall that when he was eight or nine he went through a spell of being gripped by panic attacks anytime we were about to step onto an airplane or even a subway car. It was hit or miss. Sometimes he was fine, other times he'd hyperventilate and lash out, physically forcing his way outside, screaming if he had to. It was something about doors closing behind him and not having access to a window that he could manually open, or some form of easy egress to the outdoors. We found a claustrophobia specialist who used a flight simulator and guided meditation that seemed to disrupt whatever behavioral pattern was forming in our son, but it took months. I'd forgotten that expression on his face, of impending panic, of the irrational grabbing the reins from the rational, and now I see it again for the first time in years.

Natasha stares off down the hallway toward the staff quarters.

"You said staff," she says. "Who are you hiring to live down here with you?"

"Well, first off, it would be with us, not just me," I say. "If the situation is dire enough, we'll all be living here."

"Okay, whatever, but have you already hired people or will we have a say?"

"It's in-process, yes. But I'm happy to share—"

Elijah starts pressing the elevator button frantically.

"I gotta get outta here!" he says. "Now!"

"Okay, like I was saying, the elevator requires the facial recognition—"

He spots the emergency stairwell and slams the bar with both hands, pushing through the door, desperate to get out. I see him taking two stairs at a time before the door slams closed again. He's gone.

Natasha steps forward and holds her phone up to my face.

"Did you hire her already?"

It's a pixelated image of a naked body standing in a floor-to-ceiling window.

"What?!" I say.

Zora pushes through the emergency exit door and begins up the stairs after Elijah.

Natasha pushes the camera closer.

"Her. Did you interview her for the job?"

I recognize the body. It's Flor. Standing naked in the window of what must be the Standard, maybe taken from the High Line. And, yes, I have interviewed her. And hired her.

35

NATASHA THOMAS-ENGEL

Okay, so if ur doorbell rings one afternoon and
it's me standing there, what do u do?

That was my DM to Milton Riggs, Jr. I hit send and waited.

It's a text I've been wanting to send for like three months now. Ever since we kissed in the basement at my grandfather's funeral. I'm honestly not sure why it's taken this long. I mean there are plenty of excuses I could make, like the school year ending and Elijah's graduation and my attempts at getting a summer job and my father showing us the bunker he thinks we'll all need to live in sometime soon if we're going to "survive and thrive", and how he looked like he shit his pants when I showed him the pic of his mistress or prostitute or whatever she is. But, in reality, it's really just fear. The kind of fear I came to know in middle school, which is the fear of being rejected or ignored or even politely dismissed because whatever you say or do or long for is somehow not in sync with whatever everyone else is saying or doing or longing for.

Milton was probably working at Books-A-Million, which is this huge bookstore out on Airport Blvd with a café. We've ended up there at least once during each visit to Mobile. Stopping in is always a good way to kill time between seeing one set of family members and another, or waiting for it to be visiting hours at whatever hospital or nursing home a sick relative is in. Mom knows I'll always go for a bookstore over going bowling or the water park or mini golf or the mall. The place has an impressive manga and graphic novel collection, which Milton told me at our one and only meal together that he's responsible for during his shifts.

If he isn't at Books-a-Million, I imagine Milton at band practice, playing his tenor sax and strutting up and down a football field in the hot sun. Maybe he's wearing the blue hat and uniform I'd seen on his feed. I want to see that in person, him in that uniform playing in that marching band, because the songs and routines they do down south always seem way more interesting than the sport itself. Like how they can play their instruments and at the same time do this crazy complicated choreo.

> guess i'd invite u in for some sweet tea since it's real hot

That was his response. And reading it made my heart kick into high gear and my palms got all clammy, which I really hate, because I definitely don't want to be known by everyone as that person with sweaty hands, like our ceramics teacher in 8th grade, Ms. Lazara. That's all anyone ever says about her if her name comes up now, even though she was a pretty good teacher and everyone had really nice holiday gifts that year to bring home. I wrote back:

> ☺ … and then what?

And he wrote:

> depends

And I wrote:

> on?

And he wrote:

> on how u respond to the invitation. like if ur
> actually thirsty and want some sweet tea or if
> ur standing there for some other reason that
> you haven't said yet

And I wrote:

> like what other kind of reason?

My thumbs were shaking as I texted and my mind was leapfrogging all over the place. Whereas he seemed real smooth and confident, like how quickly he wrote back. We continued:

> well that right there is something u gotta tell
> me, not the other way round 😊

> so it has to be one or the other? can't be that
> i'm thirsty and maybe also have something
> else in mind?

> hmmm...

> my ? to u: is ur grandmother or sister home?

Pathetic how I have to wipe my right palm on my jeans every ten seconds. Really, like I'm turning into Ms. Lazara before my own eyes, and it's going to end up being one of my defining features. People already comment on my bad posture and now they'll add sweaty palms to the list, and warn each other that shaking my hand is a bad idea unless they have paper towels or a handkerchief handy. It's a disaster. And, like, how is it even possible that you can sweat through your palms when no other part of your body is even sweating? Like I'm not actually hot at all! We continued:

> u mean home right now, or when u show up
> and ring the bell in your lil fantasy?

in the fantasy

> then it's up to u. u want em here, they here.
> you don't, they aint

listen, not like i have anything against them,
but i'm totally ok if they're not there when i
show up

> they're gone then. all day. late into the evening

nice

> yeah

so now what?

Again, my thumbs were practically sliding off the screen, trembling and sweating.

> so yeah, then i invite u in and i let u take my
> hand and i also let u lead me wherever it is u
> wanna go. u thirsty, ima pour you some sweet
> tea with just the right amount of ice. u have
> something else in mind, definitely cool w
> that 2...

I'd never done this before. Was it sexting if it was just words or did sexting need to include pics? Which, being honest, I would do if he asked me. I stood up and made sure my door was closed and locked, not that anyone was home. Then I lay back down on my bed.

i don't know ur house. where's the best place
to go?

He took a moment. Then wrote:

go for what?

I unfastened my jeans. Held the phone in my left hand and slipped my right into my panties. I wasn't good at one-handed texting, so started using dictation, which changed the way my texts appeared, with appropriate caps and correct grammar. I hoped he wouldn't notice.

Well, guess I'd like you to give me a tour then. Please.

it's not some big ol' fancy house, like probably what u used to. so the tour ain't gonna take real long

Doesn't have to.

yeah, okay, so we're walking down the hallway and u got my grandma's room on the left side right here. that door's closed. always closed. we got some family pictures on the wall on the left. pictures of when we were young and also of my great grandparents. a pic of my mom graduating high school. and then you got my sister's room. her door's open and her room is always real neat. bed made nice and she's got her favorite stuffed animal on it. a giraffe she won at the county fair. and then you pass the bathroom and then the next room is my room…

Is that where you are now? Like in real life?

yes

I'm in mine too. Lying on my bed.

I was. And my sweaty palm was wet for other reasons now, my forefinger and index finger. I kinda wanted to FaceTime him and see him in real life. See his face, his smile and those white white teeth. He wrote:

> i was reading but now u got me real distracted

I dictated back:

> No, that's what you did to me! So distracting!

> uh-uh, no! sorry. we all know u the one started
> this. all I was gonna do was offer u some
> imaginary sweet tea

> Okay, so if I was actually there in your room
> with you right now, what would you do?

> what u want me 2 do?

> I never told you this in person, but I really like
> your lips…

I said this slow and sort of haltingly, but the words formed on the screen and didn't show any of my trepidation. I was coming across as more confident than I felt.

> ok?

> Yeah. They're soft and full and I'd ask you to
> use them

> ok. so close ur eyes then

I did. But then realized I couldn't see what he was writing to me. I opened them again.

> close ur eyes and imagine that I'm kissing you
> real soft on the lips

I imagined that. And waited for more.

> and then ima kiss you on your neck. like just
> under your left ear. imagine I'm doing
> that now…

I did.

> and from there ima keep kissing u as i move down to ur collar bones, still kissing real gentle, right down to where they come together in the middle. which I noticed was real beautiful, right where they meet, your collar bones, and there's that little sort of hollow right there. like an indentation. it's just perfect right there and if i'm remembering right, u got a birthmark just off to the side...

I was in the room with him and his lips were on my neck, gentle and skilled. And my body was starting to shudder and tremble as my fingers worked below.

> i'm kissing that real pretty birthmark right now, like it's candy just sitting there waiting to be eaten. and then, if ur cool with it, i'm gonna pull your shirt off and take mine off and i'm gonna keep kissing u. wherever u want me to keep kissing u i'm gonna kiss u. and for however long u want me to keep kissing u, i'm gonna keep kissing u...

36

ELIJAH THOMAS-ENGEL

Dr. Salzman might have some ideas. Liza's father. Like some commonsense ways to process this. Because it's getting fucking weird. I mean it's not like I'm expecting him to absolve me or somehow make everything right when clearly it'll probably never be right again. But it does seem like he's thought about issues like this before, ethical and moral dilemmas for an individual, but an individual caught up in the context of bigger societal evils.

I'm fully aware of what I've done. And I can still totally relate to the rationale for doing it. The variables and logic, all the factors at play, it's still coherent to me, at least most of the time. It's just now my mind is always projecting the kid. Troy. It's like he's superimposed into my new reality and it's becoming an impediment. Like in my everyday life. Like in terms of meeting new people or even talking to a professor after class if I have a question.

At first, I could take his perspective at will, like some immersive thought experiment or something. I'd imagine what it must have been like to step out through the front door and, in a split second, recognize life was about to change forever. That it was about to be over. I'm sure time slowed down for him, that his brain was probably processing every minute detail, from the gun entering his peripheral vision, to the way the evening light hit the overgrown grass in the front yard, to the black SUV with tinted windows parked across the street. And then, from one nanosecond to the next, all these details must have evaporated into a swirl of color and light as the bullet exploded through his brain, left temple to right.

He wouldn't have experienced pain. That's what I've read,

that the adrenaline kicks in instantaneously. If anything, confusion was probably his last primary emotion or mental state. What was left of his brain must have struggled to assemble an explanation for why this was happening, or whether this was really the end. That's what I saw in his eyes, anyhow. Bewilderment. I saw that he didn't recognize me, and that my logic for what I'd just done wasn't something he would ever comprehend, a fact that would have been true even if 80% of his brain weren't splattered on the screen door behind him.

But it's not that anymore. It's not me sitting there imagining the moment I shot him, or even what his life was like prior to me ringing the doorbell. Now I'm unable to control the entry point and it's more like he's in control, like he can set up residence in my mind whenever he pleases.

Sometimes he'll just be sitting there when I enter a dining hall or classroom. Or he won't be there, but I'll scan the room anyhow, expecting him to be lurking in some far corner. If he is there, sometimes he'll just grin and wave as if it's the most natural thing, and then I'll get distracted and spin-out imagining what he's saying to the student next to him, or how he might respond to a question posed by one of my professors. And what's really fucking with my head is that he appears to be enjoying himself. Like college life suits him just fine. Suits him better than it does me. I can't tell if this is his normal personality, like he's just this big affable jock type, or whether there's an element of him taking pleasure in the fact that he's messing with me. Tormenting me, almost sadistic.

An example. The other day he starts a dialogue with Professor Halper, who's this young badass whose debut novel was shortlisted for a National Book Award a few years back. She's from St. Croix originally and teaches Caribbean lit. So Troy's sitting there when I enter, before class has even started, this oafish white kid from Alabama with a thick Southern accent, and he's yakking on and on about an Edwidge Dandicat story about a woman who throws herself into the sea. He's saying how he really liked the story, which I did too. And Professor Halper, she asks him what he liked about it. And Troy starts talking about the theme of despair in the story, and all the stories in the collection, and how he could really relate to the sense of self-doubt that the narrator in the book keeps circling back to, and the impediments that stand in the way of self-actualization for all of the characters. Some pretty heady shit, and Professor Halper seems genuinely impressed and moved that stories about these marginalized black women in Haiti seem to strike such a deep chord with Troy, who I'm guessing she assumed was some legacy student or football recruit. She nods and smiles at him like she's just real happy to have the opportunity to recalibrate her snap character judgement. Which Troy has pushed me to do several times also.

And so I guess my question is this: is this full-blown psychosis I'm experiencing? Like is it actually me having that discussion with Professor Halper, and my new reality is just informed by this imaginary character that's living in my head? This imaginary character based on a real character who I happened to murder a few months back? Or could more than one of these realities be true at the same time?

———

Again, really not sure how Dr. Salzman is going to help me untangle all this, but it's worth a try. Which is why I rented a car and am three hours into the Pennsylvania turnpike heading for St. Louis. I'm hoping the 32-hour round trip drive will be worth it because I remember the way he wrapped his arm around my shoulders when we were standing in the living room and looking at the photograph of his aunt or great aunt who was murdered in the Holocaust. I remember how clear and delib- erate everything he said was, and how sincere he seemed. I remember the kindness, and the depth of understanding, like he was able to recognize the horror and brutality inflicted every minute of every day, locally and globally, but also see it in the bigger sweep of history. If I remember correctly, he kind of indicated that all the good and all the evil from the dawn of time until this very second resides in each of us. Like almost on some genetic level. And because of that, each of us is capable of the very worst act and the very best act, depending on the circumstances we encounter.

But then he also mentioned there are these cycles, historical cycles, and if we don't believe that we as humanity can actually bend toward something better, like MLK said, toward some closer approximation of justice or equality, then we may as well throw in the towel. I don't remember all of it and maybe I've added layers to the memory that weren't actually there, corrupting it, but I do remember the feeling I had when we were standing there together. I felt calm and I felt like there was a mutual understanding, which also struck me as unique because of course I knew that he knew that I was fucking his daughter like three times a day at that point. In the back of his car. In his laundry room. In his basement every time Liza snuck down to join me on the fold-out couch.

He's also a tenured professor of psychology, so there's that.

The other thing I want to talk to him about is the text my father sent today, on the family text chain. It landed just as I was signing the rental car paperwork. I didn't respond yet, and may never, but it says:

This isn't going to come as welcome news, but
I'm confident in the predictive abilities of my
program. I shared details as to why when we
all met and toured the compound. The point of
this text: the current threat level is the highest
it's ever been. Because of this, I expect we'll
need to relocate within the next two weeks. Or
it could be within the next 24 hours. We just
don't know. You may have seen some of the
recent news that plays into this calculation.
Just know there are many other variables that
go unreported. It's a very precarious time.
Please keep your phones charged and on, and
your go-bags ready. As discussed, you'll be
picked up, driven to the nearest heliport, and
flown here. Mom and Natasha will fly together.
Elijah, you'll be coming solo from New Haven.
I love you, Dad / Neil

———

As I'm passing the exit for Bellefonte PA, he starts humming. Which is typical. Exactly what I've come to expect from Troy. Random shit at random times. And of course he's humming The Banana Boat Song. So I glance over and he nods and grins, adjusts his seatbelt and starts belting out "Day-o, day-a-a-o... Daylight come and we want to go home—"

"Stop!"

"Yeah, I hear ya. Probably too obvious a choice, right? Out of all of 'em?"

I'm not gonna engage. I focus on the road ahead. On the 18-wheelers blowing by in the left lane.

I did notice he's got his tank top on, and a baseball cap. Sometimes when he shows up he's got the big gaping hole on the right side of his head, and his right eye is almost falling out of its socket; other times he looks normal. Like tonight. As if I'm just driving down the highway with my massive friend, on our way to some kegger in rural Pennsylvania. Cow tipping.

I sense him turning his body toward me.

"Hey, listen, I know all you can probably imagine based on whatever you read in them papers or heard from your family is that we're all just real racist all the time. So I'm gonna tell you somethin' that maybe won't make no sense to you, but it's the truth. Was always just part of our family growing up. And this was before even my granddaddy got locked up."

I didn't respond or look over at him.

"You hearing me?"

I shrugged.

"That's right, I know you are. Point I'm trying to make is that my Nanna, my Momma too, they just loved to play that Harry Belafonte Christmas CD. Like over and over starting in early December and all the way through 'til New Years. I'm not even lying. That song 'Mary, Mary' would make Nanna tear up every time. I remember one time I walked into the kitchen to grab somethin' to drink and she's just sitting there at the table bawling her eyes out. Tears running down her cheeks, snot all over. And there's like this small mountain of wadded up Kleenex in front of her."

I'm not engaging.

"So that's just like another example of the power of music right there. Am I right? No matter the color of the artist, no matter who's listening. I mean you can have a grandfather with enough hatred in his heart to string someone up in a tree for no other reason than the color of their skin, and then right there at home he's got a wife so moved by the song of another black man that she can't even stand up from the kitchen table to even function!"

It was dark already, and starting to rain. I flipped on the wipers.

"Now of course I didn't understand what all was going on at

the time. I was only eight or maybe nine when I saw her cry like that. There's a chance she was crying for some other reason than the music, maybe 'cause she was reflecting on what all her husband had done. I'll never know. But it was still the power in the music, those words and that real buttery voice that triggered it for her. Because I mean he does, right? Belafonte? He's got that real smooth but also kinda melancholy voice. Or did. Did he already pass too?"

37

NEIL ENGEL

I await their responses to my text.

I struggled with how much to include because the threats are known and catastrophizing is a national pastime. Just look at news headlines or Hollywood plotlines going back to the industry's founding. And it's no secret why. Centering stories on the forces that threaten human survival is lucrative and timeless. And they're lucrative and timeless because they reflect something innate and primal. Namely that at the very deepest genetic level we operate with a biological imperative that says: 1) survive long enough to procreate; 2) procreate as much as possible to ensure the continuation of your bloodline; and 3) eradicate anything or anyone that may impede this imperative. That's hardwired in each of us. It's the animal instinct that trumps all else. Without it we'd be maladaptive. Without it we wouldn't be sitting here with the capacity to self-reflect on this truism in the first place.

It's the level of precarity that's unique. Individually and as a species. It's meaningful when the Science and Security Board of the Bulletin of Atomic Scientists moves the "Doomsday Clock" forward so that it now stands at 90 seconds before midnight — meaning we're the closest to a global calamity that ends human life as we've ever been. Closer than at any point during the Cold War, including the Cuban Missile Crisis. Their calculus factors in the ease by which a nuclear warhead or enriched nuclear material might fall into the hands of a terrorist actor, which they rate as higher than ever. It also computes how many dictators or despots have nukes at their fingertips and how probable it is that one or more might get pushed into a corner by sanctions levied by the international establishment and feel so humiliated they'll finally just say "fuck it" and hit the little red button. Plenty of candidates for that. They also consider aging nuclear arsenals, number of warheads, and the high probability of human error. During their annual press conference, they also like to remind us that it's been less than a hundred years since humanity invented the capacity for full global annihilation. We're still in diapers and it's inevitable that someone is going to shit themselves.

Of course the Doomsday Clock is only one variable to consider. The others often cited include: climate change; pandemics, both naturally occurring and released as weapons; AI run amok; and resource depletion resulting in famine, war, and/or disease. It's complicated to parse it, and to determine how best to weigh any of these main instability drivers, as each is almost incalculably complex unto itself.

Take climate change, which I view primarily as a crisis multiplier. In this case, I like to remember the civil war in Syria, which has dropped from the news cycle of late but represents an event with a long and enduring tail. It was often billed as a fratricidal battle between the al-Assad regime and various domestic and foreign actors. In reality, the war was rooted in the fact that the region began to suffer the most severe drought on record about twenty years ago, which displaced millions of farmers and their families, who migrated to the cities, where they couldn't find adequate housing or employment, which created societal stresses, which resulted in civil unrest, which metastasized into a brutal crackdown and civil war, which resulted in one of the largest refugee crises in the post-War era, with the unlikely result of permanently changing the demographics of Europe, in particular Germany, resulting in significant racist and right wing backlash, which in turn was matched by a hardening of Muslim identity within the refugee communities, particularly among young and unemployed men, which has many predicting, myself included, that we should expect one or more terrorist attacks in Europe in the next decade or two. So, if a dirty bomb or suitcase nuke is detonated in Munich or Berlin's city center in the next twenty years, what should we attribute that to? Is that a result of climate change? Arguably, yes.

This is where supercomputing comes in. And it's why three years ago I hired an unassuming but brilliant Ph.D. grad from MIT to design and run my simulations, in theory as a way for the Family Office to identify market risks but also opportunities. The program has evolved to the point where I believe it is far more accurate and comprehensive than the Doomsday Clock or similar programs developed by the Department of War.

Now of course there are those who claim it's always felt this way, that life — individually and collectively — has always been one random bullet or one asteroid hit away from extinction. Fine. I'm fine with those such as my friend Ben who want to maximize experiences in the moment instead of living with the ever-present, low-grade anxiety I've grown to live with and even appreciate. It's been an evolution for me, and certainly in my 20s and 30s I had a different set of interests and priorities. Having children changed me. The death of my father altered my thinking too. These mile-markers shifted my thinking about the historical through-line of a family, and for our species at large. Holding a newborn that first time, or sitting bedside as a parent takes their last breath, it's impossible not to begin thinking with a generational perspective. I began to see value in considering the meaning of legacy, and what concrete steps I could take to ensure ours might continue when most, if not all, might not.

The vast majority of preppers are ignorant. It's unfortunate. They operate out of a rightful sense of anxiety about the future, but get conned by quack experts out to make a quick buck. InfoWars became a billion-dollar enterprise by stoking fear and outrage and then, during commercial breaks, hawking all-in-one survival kits. For $399 you'd get all you needed to withstand the coming pandemics, marauding hordes of black and brown urbanites, g-men coming to take your firearms... whatever the threat of the week was. Sadly, the stats indicate that those duped by the ads are more likely going to die at the hands of their gun-toting and paranoid neighbors, or to shoot themselves in a moment of despair, than survive long enough to experience the coming global catastrophe. Their demo: white, rural, underemployed men in their late 60s. Who, ironically, died at a disproportionate rate during Covid.

On the other end of the spectrum, you have the Thiels, Gateses, Musks and Zuckerbergs buying up vast swaths of land in New Zealand or Montana or Hawaii and building fortressed Shangri-Las to ride out the coming tempest. One flight from Silicon Valley or Seattle and all is well. Coupled with their elaborate cryogenic and longevity plans, I'd wager at least a few of them will be around in fifty to seventy-five years, maybe more. Assuming they time it right. Which is where I believe my advantage lies. It's all about the timing. Pulling the ripcord in time. Hunkering down in time. And then possessing the resources to ride it out.

Key variables include location, self-sustainability, security measures, structural integrity, system redundancy, means of communication, storage and supplies, and ways to support and maintain physical and psychological well-being. Based on my research, ResoluteX checks the boxes best. In more of a slow-emergency situation, where societal chaos may be raging, where national governments may have imploded or been overrun but there hasn't been a release of nuclear or viral contaminants, we'll have the ability to live above ground, grow and hunt our own food, even interact with the residents of the other seven units on the premises, all of whom I've vetted. It's who you might imagine in terms of who's already bought units:

several hedge fund founders, a medical device engineer and patent holder, an ex-professional athlete and his new wife, and an eccentric old-money bachelor who looks like he might not survive long enough to actually relocate. One of the selling points for the complex is that interaction with other residents is voluntary. Each unit is fully self-sufficient, with redundancy in energy supply, air filtration, water supply. If we elect to communicate and share resources, we're able to. If we want to be hermits, that's fine too. Ultimately, should we all emerge from some catastrophic scenario, of course how society and governance and breeding is reimagined and reconstituted is TBD. Hence Flor, Gavin and several others being part of our immediate family unit. Their two-year contracts will be a pittance when you consider some of the various outcomes.

I'd be lying if I haven't played out a scenario in which I sire children with Flor, or Elijah does, and Gavin ends up fathering children with Natasha. I realize it's borderline demented to be going so far down these various hypotheticals, but the more comprehensive the envisioning, and the more detailed the planning, the more likely we'll survive, lineally. Just because it's unpleasant and uncomfortable to play out these thought experiments, doesn't mean it's not of value. If we survive, then the imperative will have been heeded. We will have listened to the one true and constant voice that lives within our genetic code.

38

ZORA THOMAS

Possible responses to Neil's text:

- Sorry, won't be able to make it. Hope it goes well.
- Sorry, won't be joining you in the doomsday bunker. I wish you well.
- Sorry, won't be joining you in the doomsday bunker. Neither will the kids. We love you and hope you find peace.
- Really sorry, but we can't make it. Wish I'd been able to love you in the ways you needed, so somehow this wasn't your response to the state of the world. As expressed, I think you need professional help. xox, Z
- Sorry, won't be joining you in the doomsday bunker, because your entire plan and all the money you've already spent, without ever consulting me, is a clear sign that you're out of your fucking mind. Maybe this is a midlife crisis on steroids or a psychotic episode or a desperate cry for help. I don't know. What I do know is we've grown distant over the past few years, I guess in part because of my father's illness and the fact that my company has demanded more of me. I can accept that I haven't been as attentive to what's going on with you as I used to be, before babies, and before you encouraged me to start my business. I'm sorry about that. But when I look around, this seems to be the norm with our peers who have managed to stay together as long as we have. Life gets full. It takes more work to feel connected, something that when you're in your 20s,

and newly in love and without children, you can't
imagine or really plan for. I definitely haven't put in
the effort recently. I think you have to admit you
haven't either, other than telling me you still find me
attractive as we're undressing for bed, or passive-
aggressively hinting that you want and need sex at
the most inopportune times. Sorry, it takes more
than that. At our age it takes more, which we've been
told hundreds of times in therapy and still neither of
us has prioritized. Anyway, whatever got us here,
we're here, and when I got your text, it was crystal
clear to me that there's no way in hell I'll ever join
you in your high-tech bunker. More than that,
before you fly off, I really encourage you to see a
professional who might provide another
perspective. Because, for one thing, if you know me
at all, you'd know that in a million years I'd never
have agreed to any of this if you'd shared the plan
earlier. And I'll never let our children join you
either. I'd rather die in the streets still hopeful that
humanity might pull itself out of its nosedive than
live in some luxury bunker for how many years?
Seriously! How many years are you imagining you'll
live this madness?! How long have you spun this
warped little fantasy out? What does your model
predict is the logical outcome of living underground,
slowly losing your mind, staring at the same tropical
sunset or mountain vista on your video wall? Are
you prepared to watch your children slip into
crippling depression? Or blow their brains out? And
if you survive the apocalypse, then what? You'll
emerge into some contaminated new world as the
self-declared ruler, issuing orders and decrees to
whom, exactly? The 50 other people in the

compound? I mean what about the other hedge fund geniuses who also bought bunkers and are also stepping into the light with their offspring and mini tribes, no doubt with equally inflated savior complexes? Will you join forces or murder them as threats? And what about our children, assuming they didn't blow their brains out after three years of underground misery? Are you going to demand Elijah begin the repopulation of the planet by knocking up the young, fertile staff members you brought along? Or will you be impregnating them in order to retain your alpha position? You see how fucking sick this gets, right? Right?! And what about Natasha? You'll have your bodyguard impregnate her for the sake of humanity's survival? Seriously, is that the future you imagine, because I know you've explored all these hypotheticals, you and your "proprietary" AI. It's a sickness, Neil, to let yourself do this. And now that it's come to this, I can look back and see it's the logical outcome of your lifelong fixation on building wealth for wealth's sake and not building wealth to realize something of value in the world. Like a company with employees you know and care about. Or a fund that supports entrepreneurs in emerging markets. Or even a philanthropic division that uses what you've amassed for causes you believe will leave the world a better place than we found it. Where is that? Why isn't that equally deserving of your attention, skills and intelligence? Because you possess these amazing talents and it's sad. Partly it's sad because I let myself be party to it. I didn't ask the questions I should have. I didn't push to know what you were doing and why. And I clearly benefited materially from what you've done and what your father and grandfather built. I'm complicit, no doubt about it. But I won't be with this. No, fuck you for doing all this behind my back and then revealing it to our children without giving me some warning or ability to rein you in before it corrupts their minds and hearts... Fuck you for assuming that they should hitch their wagons to your warped reading of history and current events and not to some other vision that says, yes, the world is dangerous and troubled, but rather than cloister ourselves away we should roll up our sleeves and try and improve it, even if that means we'll all die at the hands of an angry mob or a dirty bomb or a super storm. Because whether it's a year from now or 50 years from now, on some lonely planet populated only by nutcase survivalists, it's going to happen. We're all going to die. You're going to die. And it seems clear that you and I won't be dying at one another's side. I'm angry, Neil. At you and at myself. So fuck you. But also, I hope you find peace somehow. Because clearly you're suffering, and I'm sorry I didn't do more. Love, Z

39

ELIJAH THOMAS-ENGEL

"Yeah, right here, look, you got like twenty of 'em within maybe five miles."

We were parked on Wyndown Blvd. and Troy's face was illuminated by the phone in his hands. He held up the screen so I could see. Google maps with dots. Each dot a gun shop.

"Guessin' we'll have to wait until morning though, unless they got like a 24-hour option. Lemme check on that."

His thumbs started dancing on the screen again.

It was raining and dark. Across the street, a light was on in the kitchen. I imagined Dr. Salzman making tea and then heading for his home office to review some academic paper, wearing fleece-lined slippers and a cardigan.

What the fuck was I doing?

I hadn't slept in over 24 hours and was hallucinating that Troy, the ghost of the kid I murdered, was sitting next to me, encouraging me to buy a gun and blow my own brains out instead of walking up the front steps of Liza's house and ringing the doorbell. Ever since I told him where we were heading, he'd been trying to convince me that Dr. Salzman could never understand my situation. According to Troy, it didn't matter that he was a world-renowned professor of psychology. He wouldn't be able to comprehend me and what I'd done because it made no sense. It made no logical sense and it made no sense in terms of a conventional psychological classification or diagnosis. No, a bullet through my temple, going in the same direction as the bullet I'd shot through his temple — in through the left, out through the right — made the most sense to Troy. And I had to agree it had symmetry to it, visually and also from a narrative perspective. If it was fiction, it would make for a solid short story. Like Norton Anthology or Paris Review caliber. If non-fiction, we're talking some long-form article for the New Yorker.

Somehow, I'd lost the thread on the 1136 mile drive from New Haven to St. Louis. What was I hoping Dr. Salzman would comprehend, exactly?

Why I did what I did?

Why I was now at the mercy of Troy, this figment of my imagination?

Why my father believes society and life as we know it is about to implode and that the only solution is to join him in his bunker?

"Nope, nothin', first one opens at nine a.m.," Troy said, looking up from the phone. "Must be state law that you can't purchase a firearm after dark."

I'd tried ignoring him but it didn't seem to make any difference. He kept showing up and he kept talking. He'd been sitting in the passenger seat beside me since the Wilkes-Barre exit on the Pennsylvania Turnpike. Kept telling me how much he loved road trips and wished he'd had the chance to go on more of them before his "untimely" death.

"So, what's your plan then?" he said.

"Same as before."

"Which is what, exactly?"

"Talk to Liza's dad."

"Okay, alright, but let's think about this then. So what you're tellin' me is you're gonna go inside that house and actually tell him what you did to me?"

Solid question. He was right. I hadn't really thought this through, whether I was going to talk to Dr. Salzman in some abstract way or tell him specifics.

"Because from what I can tell, at this point you're gettin' off Scott free. No weapon was found. No witnesses came forward. No motive. I mean the police asked around plenty, all over the neighborhood, all my friends, and no one's come forward to share any reason why somebody might have wanted to harm me." He grinned and chuckled. "Guess I was pretty popular after all, except with you."

The kitchen light switched off in the Salzman house, but it looked like there was still a light on beyond that, deeper inside.

"Tellin' you, shoulda seen the funeral. I'll be honest, kinda blew me away. All sorts of folks I never would've expected. Teachers and coaches from middle school and high school. Shoot, before that even! One of my pre-school teachers showed up. And definitely not what y'all would think. I mean you had plenty of white and black folks there. Almost half and half, 'cause of who all was on my football teams over the years."

I kept watching the house, imagining myself sitting across from Dr. Salzman in his study, me in the leather armchair, him behind his desk with his hands wrapped around his mug of tea, the Tiffany desk lamp creating a calming atmosphere. I liked that room. I'd stood in it late one night on my way back from the bathroom, books lining two walls, framed degrees and awards on another, my bare feet on the rug he'd said they brought back from a trip to Turkey. It was a welcoming space, a room that could accept secrets and confessions, and hold them tight.

"You even listenin' to what I'm sharing here?" Troy said.

I nodded, eyes still on the house. He jumped back in, adding complexity and nuance where I wanted simplicity.

"Now of course you got Keesha and her grandmother there, and I'ma tell ya, Keesha is a mess. Just hugging and holding on to anybody who'll let her. I mean just blubbering. To the point where I recognize, as I'm watching all this play out before me, I recognize that she actually loved me. It was way more than just a crush. And realizing that, that it was actually love, gotta be honest, it kinda broke my heart. Just gave me a real heavy and sad feeling. Also kinda made me angry. That we had that connection and whatever that was, that bond we had, well it ain't never gonna have the chance to become somethin' else, somethin' more."

It looked like Troy was about to start blubbering himself. He stared straight ahead into the dark, lost in memory, his lower lip quivering. Then he reached up and placed his hands on the dashboard, as if wanting to steady himself. He exhaled, his huge body sinking into the seat.

"Like... like you know how in movies, and I guess in real life too, sometimes high school sweethearts meet again after a bunch of years and realize they're actually meant for each other? Like they're soulmates, but were just too young and stupid at the time to realize that?"

What the fuck was this?! Troy was a projection of my mind and now it wasn't only him, but also his mental what-ifs and regrets and longings that were tugging at me, demanding my attention. He shifted his weight and looked directly at me, eyes brimming with tears.

"That's really what I think could've happened with Keesha, when I see it now, from this vantage. I mean she's off at Clark Atlanta, but maybe in like five years we coulda rekindled that flame we had, because that flame was real and was somethin' special. Like if she came home and saw that I'd made something of myself, had a good-paying job, that I'd fixed up my Nanna's house real nice. I mean I really think I could've loved her, or maybe do love her, especially now that I saw how tore up she was at my funeral."

He pointed past me at the house across the street. I turned and saw a figure walking down the front steps in a rain jacket and boots. It was Liza's mom, Nina, out walking Pavlov, their Labradoodle.

"So that right there, that's your girlfriend's house?" said Troy.

"She's in California. We basically broke up."

"She know what happened to you? What you did?"

I shook my head, eyes on Nina and Pavlov moving down the opposite sidewalk, away from us. It seemed like a good time to go ring the bell, with only Dr. Salzman in the house now.

"You open to hearing my take on this?" Troy said.

I shrugged. Knew I didn't have a choice, since his take was really my take, or one of my numerous possible takes.

"Well, if I'm you right now, I'm gonna at least wait 'til morning. Nine a.m. rolls 'round and I'm gonna go buy me a handgun. Then I'm gonna let myself sit right here in this car and hold that gun in my hands, just feelin' the weight, seein' how it feels. If it feels right. Because I mean only then are you gonna really know. Like to have a solution to this whole situation right there in your hands. Because maybe it doesn't even make sense to go talk to him, Dr. Whatever, if all that's gonna do is lead you down the path to a lifetime in jail or some maximum-security insane asylum. And when you look at it from that perspective, maybe just lifting that firearm nozzle to your left temple tomorrow morning, and releasing the safety, and pulling the trigger is gonna give you that relief you're seeking. The lasting relief. Or, being real honest here again, the relief that both of us are yearning for."

40

NEIL ENGEL

"I think maybe we should have talked about this before, papi, what you are thinking. You know, what happens for us."

Flor was standing in the doorway to the master bedroom in a tank top and jeans, barefoot, no make-up, stunning. She'd unpacked and settled into what I considered the best room in the guest wing, at the far end of the hallway, and separated from Gavin's room by a double room reserved for the two housekeepers I'd hired. She held a print-out of the contract I'd had her sign.

"Because you say your family is coming also, no? So, depending, it could get difficult if I don't know what you are thinking."

She held up the contract.

"And it says nothing about that right here."

She was right. For Gavin, the contract set out a series of expectations in terms of establishing and updating our safety protocols, keeping all weapons secure and in good working condition, how he would be in charge of all hunting and farm activities prior to our need to live exclusively below ground, should it come to that, and, once again, when it becomes safe to reemerge. I'd also shown him the location of the actual safe and explained the logic behind my allocations of precious metals and currencies. For Flor, the contract was much more general. She was under contract to live on-site for a minimum of two years and, as with all community members, "is expected to fulfill basic duties to keep the group happy and healthy."

"Come in," I said. "And go ahead and close the door."

She looked at me, raised an eyebrow, and smirked.

"Yeah. You can lock it, too."

I was sitting on the bed with my laptop, reviewing the threat level update that had just come in. She walked over and sat down beside me.

"I think maybe you have been lying to me," she said. "Maybe you don't have this wife and kids?"

I rotated my laptop so she could see the screensaver: a picture of the four of us at Elijah's graduation. She leaned close to get a better look.

"Oh, okay. Damn, she is so beautiful!" she said about Zora. "The kids too."

"Yeah, their mother made 'em pretty. Definitely not from my side."

Flor swatted my leg, playful.

"But I am serious! Why you even need me when you have this? Your wife looks like a model or something."

"She was, before I met her."

"Yeah, so like I say, why are you even bringing me here?"

"Where do you want me to start?" I said. "We've been together over twenty years."

"No, no, I get it. And, sorry, it is none of my business anyway. When you are married for this long, I cannot know this. Maybe you need different things. Or you grow apart, with the sex but also other things, the spiritual, whatever."

"Yeah, I'm sure you've heard it all before."

"Oh yes, stories and stories and more long stories."

She smiled at me. So beautiful, so matter-of-fact, so uncomplicated.

"But your family, they will actually come like you say?"

"I hope so. I told them yesterday that they should be ready to be picked up within the next 24-48 hours."

"And why do you say this? In exactly this many hours?"

Unlike Gavin, I hadn't provided Flor with the full picture. I hadn't shown her the program, shared the risk profiles, the threat levels, the thought process that led to me pulling the ripcord and arriving on site today. She placed her palm on my thigh, aware I was struggling to find the right words. I recalled the stories she'd told me of life in Caracas, and the way she told them, which had given me the idea that she possessed the strength and resourcefulness that would be needed to get through this, and therefore would make a good addition to our family.

"You remember that time you told me about what you experienced back home?"

"No, sorry, this is my home now, papi. I am a citizen of this country, just like you."

"Yeah, right, I know that. But remember when you told me about everything falling apart in Caracas? The smell of death in the streets, random violence, the fear in people's eyes—"

"Of course. My mother is there still—"

"Right. Well, that's going to happen on a much bigger scale, like any day. All over the world. Spreading quickly, that same desperation and violence. And the life we've become accustomed to here, in this country, is going to collapse."

She nodded, eyes finding the screen-saver image of my family again.

"And so you have told your family this idea?" she said.

"Yes."

"And what do they say back to you, when you tell them this?"

"Honestly, not much. It's possible they think I've lost my mind. What they don't realize yet is that I'm doing all this to protect them. Because this is what we need to do if we're going to survive what's coming. We need to be here. All of us. And that includes you."

She lay down on the bed beside me and stared up at the ceiling. I set the computer on the bedside table and lay down too.

"I have a dog, Alfonso. Alfi," she said. "I gave him to my

father and his girlfriend, and I tell them to take care until I come back for him in two years."

I took her hand and rolled toward her, watching her in profile.

"Maybe you will," I said. "I mean there's a chance I'm wrong. I think it's very small, that chance, but nothing is certain when there are this many variables at play."

"What does this mean? Variables?"

God I fucking love her accent. The Rs, especially. Just roll the Rs in my ear on my deathbed and all will be right. It sounds trite. I don't care.

"Variables are like factors," I said. "Different inputs. Like for a math equation?"

"No, you should know that I am not a lover of mathematics. One teacher, he always say that math is the language of the world. He say math is always right and true. That math can explain everything we see with our eyes, in front of us in this room, for example, and also everywhere in all the universe. He says that even the questions we do not know how to ask, math already has the way to explain. But then when I leave the class-room and look around, math does not explain to me the world that I know with my eyes and feel with my heart."

She rolled toward me and smiled.

"So you pay me two hundred fifty thousand each year for two years for what? To suck your dick and fuck whenever you say you need this? For me to stand naked in front of you, like I know you like for me to do? Of course I am okay to do this. I am happy for this. It is a good opportunity for me. But if your family is coming, I think it will be complicated for you, no?"

Hearing her talk about it made me want to see her naked right then, and I told her so. This power, the transactional power I possessed in our relationship, was always a turn on. Especially when it was her who acknowledged and brought it up. It was a turn on that she understood our compact so directly, and accepted it so fully and without resentment. We could go deep in our conversations, and I could fantasize about various outcomes for our bunker cohabitation and beyond, but there was never any pretense about the basis for our relationship. She was paid, and paid handsomely, to serve my sexual and emotional needs. And she felt like she was getting the better end of the bargain.

Of course she was also right. I didn't know exactly how this was going to play out with Zora and the kids. The maxim about leading a horse to water is true. You can flog them all you want, but if they're not thirsty, they're not drinking. When it comes to my family, it's a reality I don't really want to acknowledge, but ultimately the only power I possess is persuasion and threats. And apparently, I've yet to convince them, because none of them responded to my text saying they need to be ready to relocate at the drop of a hat. Unlike Flor, Gavin and the two Filipinas I hired to handle domestic chores and cooking, they're not going to relocate on account of a generous two-year contract. Of course once the shit hits the fan, I'm convinced they'll elect to come here of their own volition. And once they come, they'll be forced to acknowledge that I was the only one able to foresee the world-historic peril we faced, and that only I dedicated the time, effort and resources to organize safe passage to our collective future. And with that acknowledgement, I believe a new perspective will reveal itself within the group; a perspective that says that the rules that bind us together as this new clan will necessarily be different than the norms and rules of our prior existence. There will be different ways in which deference is shown, and a new set of expectations for what kind of life each of us can and should lead.

Flor stood beside the bed naked now, her clothes a small mound on the tile floor, her black panties a twisted knot at the summit. She smiled as my eyes took her in, feasting.

"Maybe they come or maybe no, your family," she said. "But I am here with you for two years, like I promise."

It was like she was programmed to say the precise words that would make a man in his autumnal years still feel relevant, needed, virile. My cock was getting hard but I wanted to slow the moment down.

"I have a question," I said. "If I'm wrong, and somehow the world is okay, what are you going to do in two years with the $500,000?"

She climbed up on the bed, placing a foot on either side of my torso, standing at her full height above me. She steadied herself by placing her fingertips on the ceiling. I was looking straight up at her shaved pussy and her perfect, dark nipples above. And, above that, her smiling face.

"Of course, before anything, I go to my father's house to pick up my perrito, Alfi."

"Of course. And then?"

"Then I use your money, and the money I have saved before, and I buy a house for myself. But not in the city. Maybe in New Jersey or even maybe I try California. And if I am lucky, I find a man that does not need me for my money, but loves me. He has his own business maybe, I don't know, and it is possible that I get married and have a baby when I am twenty-seven or twenty-eight. We see. I am not sure yet about this future."

She smiled down at me.

"And you? What will you do in two years, when you have spent all this money for nothing?"

No response warranted. I smiled and shook my head. Hers was a scenario that had less than .5% of coming true. And I didn't see the value in telling her that it was far more probable that I'd be the father of her children when we eventually reemerged into an unfamiliar world. I also didn't tell her that four months ago I'd reversed the vasectomy I'd had at age 42, a course-correction necessary once it became clear that firing blanks wasn't going to help humanity repopulate, and would in fact only serve to diminish my prospects of remaining the leader of our clan. If history tells us one thing, it's that bloodlines and lineage matter, especially if wrapped in a compelling mythology or religion. As the mastermind of our survival strategy, controlling the story of our survival will be key.

Flor continued to stand above me until I nodded. She understood and sank down, straddling me, and began to unbuckle my belt.

41

NATASHA THOMAS-ENGEL

Mom pulled me out of school and said we're heading to New Haven to get Elijah. She wants to talk to us about what's happening with her and dad which, depending upon the direction that goes, may force me to tell her what I found out about him and his mistress, or whoever she is, and then of course I'll also have to tell her the various reasons why I haven't told her this info before, which is complicated and includes me trying to understand the smaller moments and choices that, in aggregate, reveal the true nature of a person, and also my evolving ideas about love and happiness and finding meaning and my reflections on the heteronormative conditioning that basically creates so much inner turmoil and outward conflict. And in terms of the latter, if I'm being honest, I'm at a point now where I'm basically thinking about Milton Riggs Jr. all the time.

I wonder what his morning ritual is. Like what he eats for breakfast, if he even eats breakfast. And whether he takes the bus to school or rides his bike or maybe walks his sister hand-in-hand, sharing the few memories he has of their father and mother and reminding her of the reasons they're being raised by their stone-faced grandmother. I wonder what he looks like naked, stepping out of the shower after band practice. And I wonder if I really showed up at his door unannounced whether he'd freak and tell me to go away or play it cool and invite me in for the sweet tea he's promised.

Looking at my Milton Riggs Jr. preoccupation from the outside, being honest and objective, of course I realize this definitely all falls into the cliché of cisgender girl is infatuated with cisgender boy and creates this massive mental architecture about who she believes him to be, and what he could be if only he allows her into his heart and soul, like fully in, and of course what they could be together if the stars align and allow their love to blossom into its fullest and most resplendent potential. Like maybe this love is actually preordained. Like actually foretold in The Celestial Book of Eternal Love. And I get that my fixation may be problematic in a variety of ways, because when I think of Milton Riggs Jr., it's a combination of the physical and mental, the attraction I feel for him, and when I extrapolate out and look at it through the more patriarchal lens, which my classmate AJ used to always force everyone to do with everything, then I'm the one from the wealthy and entitled background who's totally sitting in the driver's seat on this one. I've got the agency and power that used to be monopolized by white males like my father.

I mean it's almost like I embody the patriarchy, and he's this sweet, innocent peasant boy or something, living with his grandmother and younger sister, and he just happened to be friendly, gallant even, while standing in line for food at my grandfather's repast. He let me cut the line and introduced himself like a gentleman, in the gracious way I've observed so many times in young people down South. And because he was polite and had that smile, and I was in whatever mood I was in, I basically lured him into the basement on a whim and got what I wanted, forcefully, and under my terms, which included my lips finding his lips and his hands eventually finding my breasts, but only with my encouragement, or more like mandatory direction, and in hindsight, I kinda wish I'd pushed it farther, like now I think about what could have happened if I'd unbuckled his belt. But he was so sweet and innocent, which I guess I am too, at least in terms of experience, and here I am now sending him provocative texts and considering whether I should follow through on the fantasies hinted at in those missives. I'm the aggressor or instigator, or might even represent the vestigial patriarchy, I guess, or at least some new form of female who will get what she wants and needs. Not that I don't want to hear and factor in Milton Riggs Jr.'s perspective on this, because I do and I actually plan to. It's just that I'm 100% positive my family and teachers and friends at school, if that's what they're even called, have no idea what resides in my mind and body, or what my real capacities are. To them, I'm bookish and hopelessly timid. I'm prey destined to be preyed upon, in a world of rapacious predators. But then again, they don't know about Milton Riggs Jr., where, if we have to look at everything from the perspective of who possesses power or who is the victim or who is historically subjugated, I'm definitely more of the apex predator with fangs and/or talons and he's the prey. And yet, ironically, he has the power to occupy my thoughts and emotions, even my physical sensations, and what results from that swirling mix of interior experience is probably going to dictate my outward course of action.

———

But back to my brother and New Haven, which is where we are and Elijah's not, and Mom is freaking out. His roommate, Kai, who seems really sweet but also super anxious about Elijah being gone and about Mom's intensity, told us that he hasn't seen or heard from him in two days, and that he seemed distracted and distant when he last saw him, and really since college began, which honestly is how I'd describe him almost every time I interacted with him over the summer, and really since his high school graduation.

Mom already yelled at the deans and campus safety officers plenty, demanding they review security footage and get the state police involved, but so far nothing. And Elijah's been avoiding our texts and calls and has the location app turned off. She's definitely not going to reach out to Dad and get him involved after the text he sent us about needing to be ready to relocate to the bunker.

So Mom checked us in at The Blake and I guess we're camped out until we learn more, with cable news as background noise, adding to the mental clutter and anxiety, the hourly cycling of reports on civil wars and drought and famine and firebombs engulfing entire towns and refugees and the financial markets teetering teetering teetering, about to collapse again, always again, and, honestly, I wasn't sure why I needed to be here at all until I was standing there at our hotel window and, in the distance, I saw a train making its way into the city.

It was like some beacon. Or a sign at the top of a trailhead with an arrow. Seeing it made me realize that other than the subway, I've literally never been on a train in this country. We took the TGV once in Europe, from France to Italy, because dad thought we'd enjoy going over the Alps, or through them, really, which we did. And also the bullet train in Japan when I was maybe seven. But never an Amtrak train in the US, which I know gets a bad rap, but still has some romantic, old-world attraction to me, because whenever I think of trains crisscrossing vast and unforgiving landscapes I'm reminded of Russian novels and all the scenes of reunions and goodbyes and rekindled love that play out on the platforms at stations in St. Petersburg or Moscow, or within train carriages as they traverse frozen countryside. Tears and kissing and billowing clouds of steam and porters carrying suitcases and elegant dresses and heavy overcoats and whistles and the rhythmic belching of engines beginning to pull away from the platform, building in speed and momentum and inevitability, and with protagonists whose hearts are also thumping and racing with excitement or despair or terror. Like when Anna Karenina senses someone is approaching on the platform and turns and sees it's Vronsky, and an "irrepressible joy and animation shone on her face." She asks why he's there, why he's boarding the exact same train she is on this dark and foreboding night, and he responds: "You know I am here in order to be where you are. I cannot do otherwise." And just then: "From ahead, a low train whistle howled mournfully and drearily. All the terror of the blizzard seemed still more beautiful to her now. He had said the very thing that her soul desired but that her reason feared. She made no reply, and he saw a struggle in her face."

It's scenes like this, pages I've probably read and reread at least ten times because each word rings so true and so right, where it's forbidden or dangerous but you know it's also preordained and the love just has to run its course, that has me thinking about Milton Riggs Jr.

Yes, okay, so I imagine him standing at a station waiting for my train to arrive with a bouquet of flowers in his hands, probably dahlias or peonies, the white of the flowers matching his perfect teeth, his warm eyes unblinking, and, this is maybe a little odd, but is it possible that he's at the station in his marching band uniform? I don't know. I mean since it's my fantasy, obviously it is possible, but it might be more old-timey and romantic if he's in some three-piece suit with a pocket watch and suspenders, polished shoes glistening, and as the train pulls in he lifts his top hat from his head and stands there beaming, peonies in one hand, hat in the other. Of course if we're going back in time like this, there are going to be all sorts of racial elements to factor in too, like there's probably a waiting area for "colored only", and of course segregated train cars, which means I'm either passing and in the first-class compartment or I'm not passing and I'm not, so how I wear my hair is key. And if I'm passing and a colored man with romantic eyes and intent is there to meet me, then clearly we're in trouble, as our love would be forbidden and could get him dragged to the nearest tree and lynched.

I'm getting lost in the weeds, maybe, because the main

point is that seeing the train in the distance with its interior lights glowing in the dusk, so warm and inviting, makes me want to be on a train and heading toward a very different reality than this one. One where Milton Riggs Jr. is there waiting for me, and smiling at me, and one where my mother isn't stressed and my father hasn't gone off the deep end with his visions of the perilous world depicted on our hotel TV engulfing us and our lives, and my brother isn't MIA.

Turns out, you used to be able to take a train from New Haven to Mobile, but the station was destroyed in Hurricane Katrina, which honestly sounds like a Russian name, Katrina, like Katerina, which seems like another positive omen. Although omen may not be the right word because I usually associate the word with the negative, so maybe what I mean is auspicious. An auspicious sign. Currently, you can take a train from New Haven to Atlanta, which takes 24 hours and ten minutes, and then hop on a connecting bus to Mobile via Montgomery, which also has its historical relevance given how important the bus riots were in the state of Alabama and all the Freedom Riders who traveled down South on buses to fight for justice in the 1960s.

So I guess what I'm considering is train to bus to Uber to Milton Riggs Jr.'s front stoop, and then my trembling finger pressing his grandmother's doorbell and hoping he'll be there and invite me in for sweet tea and more. And hopefully when he looks at my face and into my eyes, before he takes my hand and pulls me across the threshold, he'll see exactly the same truth that Old Man Leo wrote about in AK. He'll see the "irrepressible joy and animation shining" there, and hopefully I'll also see the same shine in his face and eyes and we'll both know, at the exact same moment, that this is all that matters in the entire universe, at least for right now.

42

ZORA THOMAS

Back on the Celexa. 40mg per day. Because my brain is serotonin deficient. And because I'm complicit.

Back on because my boy, my firstborn, the one who is closest to knowing who I really am, and knowing the full picture of who we are as a family, including our Southern legacy, our Black heritage, our mixed identity, has gone missing without warning and without leaving a trace. I am complicit in this fact. As his mother I should know more and intuit more.

On paper, or upon first impression, Elijah is exceptional by any measure. He's the model student and athlete, with the looks and social graces that will make him successful at whatever he chooses to do. The issue is I worry about what he may choose to do, or may already have done. There's a deep reservoir of turmoil beneath the surface. I see it in his eyes when he's unaware that I'm watching. I see it in his body, in his shoulders and neck, when his father enters the room. And I've done little to nothing in terms of tempering what's gaining force within his heart and mind, what's already taken root. I didn't stand up to his father, my husband, early enough or often enough. I didn't push back. I didn't insulate him from what I now see was a form of radiation that's been crippling and sickening him, and all of us, since the beginning.

The fact is, I let him guzzle the Kool-Aid in the form of Neil's endless anecdotes and stories of boarding school and Yale after that, the "unmatched calibre" of students and teachers he'd meet at these places, the way in which this singular trajectory, painted so clearly and often for him, would ensure a lifetime of opportunity, prestige and fulfillment. I now see that I allowed this, enabled this, because in comparison to my own story, these stories seemed so much more persuasive. Neil's campaign seemed persuasive; a campaign that was then bolstered over the years by teachers and coaches and guidance counselors and all the parents around us with identical aspirations for their own exceptional children. I now question everything about the path we set him down, both the means and the desired end.

But I'm a fool for interrogating the past when all that matters is WHERE HE IS RIGHT NOW! And yet no matter whether I yell or whisper-threaten or flirt or promise money, no one seems to know a fucking thing.

And so we circle back to the unending nightmare of what-ifs.

What if I'd only listened to my intuition and kept him home longer, closer to me, to his sister, to the richness and power of his Black heritage that I was still discovering for myself, and still am uncovering and discovering.

What if I'd left Neil when my babies were seven and three, that first time I saw clearly that beneath Neil's charm and wit and erudition lay a cancer that would slowly metastasize into and through each of us.

What if I'd managed to break free then and, despite the initial hardship, over time created a simpler, more intentional life centered around social justice and service as opposed to wealth accumulation and stifling exclusivity.

But all I see when I stare into the mirror is that I'm complicit. In all of it.

Neil poisoned Elijah's mind with a mix of expectations around money and status on the one hand and the impending apocalypse on the other, and I didn't see this clearly until now. I didn't protect him from the toxic floodwaters rushing toward him, swirling around him, pulling him under. I didn't see this because I was distracted by my father's illness, by my own blind spots, and because I'd let myself grow distant from my husband.

Or, no, that's laziness and deflection again. I didn't grow distant so much as push him away for many years, compartmentalizing. And by pushing him away, I didn't see the full impact and power he had over our baby.

Now Elijah is gone and I worry about his mental health. I worry the pressure imposed through word and example may have been too much. What were the triggers, environmental or genetic? What are the possible outcomes?

And then there's the fact that when I stepped out of the shower this evening, I found a note from Natasha on the hotel bed. It reads:

I'm on my way to Mobile to figure something out. Mom, you need to know that I'm totally fine. I have money and I'm way more capable than you and everyone else thinks. It's Elijah and Dad you need to worry about, not me.

xox, N

43

NEIL ENGEL

Three days in and we were growing more comfortable with the silences. Or I was. Gavin had always seemed comfortable and Flor seemed amused most of the time, happy to observe our preparations and, when asked, join me in the master suite.

We sat in the Adirondack chairs upwind of the fire-pit, looking out over the valley as the sun dropped toward the mountains, warm light reflecting off the spring-fed lake below. It's a vista few humans have savored over the millennia on account of its remoteness. According to the British colonist Thomas Pownall, the native hunters called this region "the Dismal Wilderness" or "the Habitation of Winter". There are no records of Mahican or Mohawk settlements before or after European arrival. The Adirondack name itself speaks to why we're here. Although they had no written language, the Mohawk name for the region means "eater of trees." In Iroquois, the name was a derogatory name for migratory groups of Algonquians who didn't practice agriculture and therefore sometimes had to eat tree bark to survive the harsh winters. Again, it's why we're here. No one wants to be here on account of how dense and formidable the surrounding forests are, and how harsh the winters can be. If anything or anyone manages to get close, we'll see them coming and have the means to neutralize.

I didn't feel the need to say anything. Gavin and I had spent hours going over logistics and supplies. We'd walked the perimeter fence, taken stock of the fruit trees and vegetable gardens, even met the owners of two of the other units, who had recently finalized contracts but seemingly had no intention of relocating anytime soon. I felt ready. Ready for the family to arrive and ready to persuade them of the merits of this new life.

Perlah and Isa emerged from the ground-level kitchen carrying trays of appetizers and drinks. Perlah handed me a Laphroaig on-the-rocks with a subtle bow, her eyes averted.

"You both should join us," I said. "Enjoy the sunset together."

They shot one another a glance and Isa, who was a year older and had worked for three years on a yacht in the Mediterranean, gave Perlah a subtle head shake.

"Thank you, sir. But we still have some preparations for supper," she said.

I nodded and sipped the Scotch, amazed to be sitting here with the world about to implode, enjoying a spirit aged for 25 years in barrels blackened by highland peat. I swallowed and felt the smoky warmth line my throat and chest. The era of trans-Atlantic trade, of globalism, of an interconnectedness the likes of which humanity has never seen and may never see again, is about to collapse. I'm guessing Gavin and Flor weren't thinking in such world-historic terms, but the drink in my hand, warming my chest, was a reminder that we stood atop a precipice; at the very end of an era that made the drink seem finite and precious in a new way. In the years ahead, I'd need to conserve the five bottles of Laphroaig we had for monumental occasions. A birth or death, perhaps. Or the day we decide it's safe to return to the world above ground. Or the day we set out from the compound to repopulate and rebuild a decimated world. I raised my glass to savor the view, savor the drink, savor the fact that we are prepared for the innumerable unknowns ahead.

Also, probably best that Perlah and Isa didn't join us. Best to keep the division of labor clear, as they are clearly a rung below Gavin and Flor, and clearly they understand that. How Gavin and Flor view one another is unclear.

Gavin sipped his club soda with lime and scanned the tree line along the fence. He pointed. I followed his finger and saw a large deer emerging from a stand of trees.

"Ten, maybe a twelve-point buck," he said.

Flor saw the animal too. She sat up.

"What do you mean with twelve points?" she said.

"Number of points on its antlers. Guessing he's three or four years old."

"That's it?" I said.

"In the wild, they don't live more than five or six years."

We watched as the beautiful creature took a few more steps, then dropped its head to eat something at the base of a tree.

"Want me to take him?" Gavin said.

He glanced over at me. I'd shared with him how the 250-acre compound had been seeded with 100 whitetail deer, 50 hogs, and 200 pheasants. Immediately, his concern was that without predators, the deer and pig populations would grow too quickly and, given a limited range to forage, would decimate our fruit trees and vegetable crops.

Gavin was already reaching for his rifle when I said, "Sure."

He'd told me I'd have to get used to the idea of him always having a firearm on or near him. I was, but knew this was going to be a problem once Zora and Natasha arrived.

He stood up, brought the rifle to his shoulder and his right eye to the scope. He set his legs, released the safety, exhaled. His shoulders settled.

Flor set her drink on the table and leaned forward, all focus. Perlah and Isa stood stock-still behind her.

The valley was quiet.

The buck began to lift its head from whatever it was eating just as the shot rang out. With its head still rising, the bullet pierced its chest. It took a step forward. Another. And then collapsed in a heap. The shot's echo circled back and was gone.

"Hope you like venison." Gavin smiled back at us. "Because

right there we got burgers, steak, pasta sauce, could even make sausage. All that and still probably freeze at least a hundred pounds."

"I never tried it," said Flor.

"Better than beef," he said. "And way better for you."

Gavin nodded at us, turned, and headed off in the direction of the electric quad parked by the shed. I wasn't sure how long gutting and cleaning would take, but was sure he'd get it done with the same efficiency and skill as everything else. Flor watched him, clearly impressed. Were it not for the power of the purse, I'd have no chance. He's younger, stronger, more handsome, and far better equipped to protect and provide in an uncertain future. Hegemony will have to be maintained through means other than money once their contracts are up, and once they realize that money as we know it today will be obsolete. The gold and silver reserves I have on site may be of value, but the dollars specified in their contracts will be useless.

I reach for my phone. Still no replies. So I text again:

> I'm here. Everything is set. Pls confirm that
> you received my last text, and that when I give
> you the go-ahead, you'll make your way here
> ASAP. I have transport standing by. xox

44

ELIJAH THOMAS

"I know you're feelin' me on this. Because it's just real simple and real clean this way."He made a good point, Troy.

Sitting there with the Beretta in my hands did focus the mind. Two options: one crystal clear, with a defined beginning, middle and end; the other a continuation of this mental churn of unknowns, second guesses, ad nauseam debates with myself and Troy.

He was sitting there in the passenger seat again, body angled my way, leaning against the door, observing me holding the gun in my lap. I didn't need to look over to know he was wearing the tank top and shorts, Auburn baseball cap on backwards, and that he was presenting with the right side of his cranium blown out, one eye basically dangling from its socket. He does this when he's trying to make a point or persuade me of something. And he's definitely been laying it on thick this morning, his perspective on our current situation. Even argued against me driving back here and parking across the street from Liza's house. He thought the beginning, middle and end of this particular scene would have been much more elegant if it had started at 9am at the counter of Southside Guns, with me exchanging $432.57 for the Beretta APX A1 and ammo, and ended at 9:09 a.m. in the gun store parking lot with a single bullet entering my left temple and blasting out my right. Twinsies.

The saleswoman told me the pistol weighs less than two pounds but it feels much heavier, maybe because of the bullets. She showed me how to load the magazine and went on about how this is the perfect gun for concealed carry because of its "slender profile" and "snub nose". She explained how Beretta is the oldest firearm company in the world. Told me this model, at this price point, was the very best option and would definitely get the job done. The job, in her mind, meant protecting myself and my loved ones wherever and whenever we might be in need.

I popped out the magazine. Six bullets loaded and ready. Check.

There *was* an elegance to this. A simplicity. A defined end.

As I was sliding the magazine back into the gun, there was a knock on the passenger window. I jumped, almost dropped the gun, and glanced over — through the space that had just been occupied by Troy's massive form — and saw two familiar faces staring in at me: Dr. Ira Salzman and Nina Salzman. Dr. Salzman smiled and motioned I should roll down the window. I set the gun on the floor between my legs and did.

"That you, Elijah?" he said.

I registered concern in his eyes. He was probably worried by my appearance, or maybe he'd seen the gun in my hands. Or both.

"Of course it's him," Nina said in a hiss-whisper, like she didn't want me to hear or thought maybe I'd lost my mind and couldn't decode simple sentences.

Dr. Salzman raised a hand, a gentle hand, indicating she should remain calm. Judging by her expression, I must look pretty bad, or at least very different than when they saw me last, which I guess was graduation four or five months ago.

I glanced in the rearview. My facial hair was growing in and my cheeks had more definition, like I was sucking on a straw. I looked hungry and, now that I was thinking about it, felt hungry. I hadn't eaten in at least 24 hours. Probably smelled pretty ripe too.

"If it's okay with you, Elijah, what I'd like to do now is open the passenger door and sit in the car with you for a moment. Would that be okay? To just sit together and talk?"

Dr. Salzman's face was framed by the open window, his demeanor calm, his eyes so open and accepting. I remembered that now. It's why I'd driven all this way, to see this face and feel the calm he exudes, and also maybe ask him some questions that I was still working to formulate, but that I thought he might be receptive to, or even might be able to coax from me. I was here because of how he engaged with me in the living room that one night, after the Seder dinner, in a way that was so different than my own father.

I must have nodded because he opened the door, motioned for Nina to give us space, and sat in the passenger seat where Troy had just been. Nina moved off down the street and stood there with Pavlov, pretending to check his ears for something, maybe ticks or burrs. I could tell she was just biding time, concerned for her husband's safety, maybe concerned for me too.

Without even saying anything, Dr. Salzman reached over and picked up the Beretta from beside my right foot. I watched him do it as if I was paralyzed. I could have stopped him, grabbed the gun, lifted it to my temple and ended this. Or shot him first and then shot myself. But by allowing him into the car, opening the door to other actors beyond only Troy, I'd relinquished control. There were more variables now, even though I could still feel Troy's presence. He was sitting right behind me, hands clutching either side of my headrest, and he was pissed.

Dr. Salzman popped the magazine out of the gun and placed it in his jacket pocket, on the far side of his body, then set the impotent pistol on the floor at his feet.

Troy slammed a hand against my headrest and cursed. I closed my eyes.

"We really weren't sure it was even you, Elijah. Nina saw a car parked here last night and for a moment thought it might be you because of your hair. But she talked herself out of it, because of course we thought you were in New Haven. That's what Liza had told us, that you were settling in at school."

I nodded, eyes closed.

"Anyhow, it doesn't matter. Doesn't matter at all. I'm happy it is you, and that we have a chance to talk about whatever it is that's going on."

I opened my eyes. Checked the rearview.

Troy stared right back at me with his one functioning eye, enraged.

My two choices had shrunk to one. Dr. Salzman was in charge now. I'd lost the focus and clarity I'd experienced only minutes before.

"Does anyone know you're here, Elijah? Your parents? Liza?"

I shook my head.

And just thinking about them, my girlfriend who was no longer really my girlfriend, her fearlessness, her ability to navigate the world with confidence, partly because she had this father supporting her, and then also my parents, or really my mom, it hit me hard. Like a punch to the solar plexus.

I couldn't breathe right. Couldn't get a full and satisfying breath. Maybe it was the lack of sleep, but all of a sudden I was emotional in a way I'm not usually. I felt Dr. Salzman's hand on my shoulder.

"It's okay, Elijah," he said. "I'm right here with you. You're not alone."

The following psychological assessment report is intended as a communication between professionals. This report includes sensitive information that is likely to be misinterpreted by those without the necessary training. Authorization for use of this report is limited to the examinee and their designated consultants. Any further use requires the authorization of the examinee or their legal guardian. Use or disclosure outside these parameters constitutes a violation of Section 5328 of the Welfare and Institutions Code.

Dr. Ira Salzman
Licenced Clinical Psychologist
Dept. of Psychology & Brain Science
Washington University of St. Louis
1 Brookings Dr.
St. Louis, MO 63130

RE: INITIAL PSYCHOLOGICAL EVALUATION REPORT FOR ELIJAH THOMAS-ENGEL

I conducted an initial psychological evaluation of patient in response to concerns about his mental health and safety. The evaluation was conducted at my home office. The purpose of this evaluation was to assess his current mental state, risk factors, and provide preliminary recommendations for intervention.

1. PATIENT INFORMATION:

- Patient's Name: Elijah Thomas-Engel
- Age: 19

- Gender: Male
- Contact Info: TBD
- Referring Clinician: Patient self-referred

2. Presenting Concerns

- Elijah was found sitting in a rental car in an agitated state, displaying clear signs of sleep deprivation and dehydration.
- He was also found in possession of a loaded handgun, raising concerns about his safety and the safety of others. He allowed me to remove the gun and ammunition from his possession without resistance. At no time did he exhibit violent behavior.
- Elijah has reported suffering from delusions, and there are concerns about his potential suicidality.

3. Background Information

- It should be noted that I have had prior contact with Elijah, as he is the ex-boyfriend of my daughter. However, I have taken all necessary steps to ensure objectivity and professionalism in conducting this initial evaluation.
- My understanding is that Elijah is currently enrolled as a first-year student at Yale University in New Haven. His family resides in New York City.
- Patient reported that he is not taking any medication.
- When invited into my home office for the evaluation, Elijah accepted water and food.

4. Clinical Assessment

During the evaluation, I observed the following:

- Elijah appeared disheveled and sleep-deprived, with impaired attention and concentration.

- He exhibited disorganized thought processes and paranoid delusions, reporting that he believed he was being pursued or accompanied by unknown individuals.

- He was unable or unwilling to explain why he drove from New Haven to St. Louis. He seems aware that our daughter, his former girlfriend, is currently attending college in California.

- He had limited insight into the severity of his condition and the potential risks associated with his behavior.

- When asked a second time why he traveled to St. Louis, and was parked across the street from our residence, he described in great detail a conversation he and I had approximately eight months ago about my maternal relatives, several of whom were murdered in Buchenwald. Elijah became animated, mentioning historical injustice and intergenerational trauma, epigenetics, referencing both his family and mine. His speech at this point was rapid, with atypical volume modulation; at times loud, at times dropping to a whisper.

- Elijah referenced his mother's African-American family down South, and the legacy of slavery.

Specifically, a cousin or uncle serving a life sentence; and another who perhaps was lynched or murdered.

- He then described how he himself murdered a young man in Mobile, Alabama several months ago. He said I was the first and only person he's told, and that no evidence has been found on account of him using a "ghost gun". He gave the victim's name as Troy Shelton or Sheldon and, according to patient, the victim was the grandson of a KKK member who lynched patient's relative (possibly his mother's cousin?). He described motivation for committing this crime as a desire to bring closure to the original injustice.

- After approximately 45 minutes, Elijah was visibly fatigued. He accepted my offer to shower and take a rest, and has now been sleeping for several hours on the couch in my office.

5. Diagnostic Impressions:

Based on the assessment findings, there is a provisional diagnosis of a possible psychotic disorder, such as schizophrenia spectrum disorder, given the presence of delusions and disorganized thinking. Further assessment and evaluation are warranted to confirm this diagnosis.

6. Assessment Tools:

During this evaluation, standardized assessment tools were not administered due to the emergent nature of the situation.

7. Treatment Recommendations:

Immediate intervention is crucial for Elijah's safety and well-being. I recommend the following:

- Hospitalization in a secure psychiatric facility for a comprehensive psychiatric evaluation, risk assessment, and stabilization. To this end, I reached out to colleagues at Alton Memorial, who have agreed to admit patient.
- Medication evaluation and management by a psychiatrist to address acute symptoms.
- Ongoing monitoring and therapy to address the underlying psychological issues.
- Coordination with law enforcement regarding the possession of the handgun, as well as any crimes that may have been committed.

8. PROGNOSIS:

Elijah's prognosis will depend on his response to treatment, his willingness to engage in therapy, and the severity of his underlying condition. Early intervention and appropriate treatment are essential for improving his prognosis.

9. INFORMED CONSENT AND CONFIDENTIALITY:

Patient consented to the evaluation and was informed of the limits of confidentiality, especially regarding the possession of the handgun, concerns for his safety, and any crimes he may already have committed. His safety and the safety of others are paramount.

Additionally, patient consented that I contact his mother, Zora Thomas, and confirmed the number I have for her was correct.

ADDITIONAL NOTES:

In an initial search post-evaluation, as well as calls placed to the Police Dept. in Mobile, AL, I was unable to verify a homicide victim with the name of Troy Shelton or Troy Sheldon in the state of Alabama.

I did find several news articles relating to a Troy Shelton, who played football at Saraland High School. There is no record of his being deceased.

When reached, Elijah's mother, Zora Thomas, reported she had filed a missing persons report with the New Haven Police Dept. the prior afternoon. She is en route to St. Louis now.

———

Dr. Ira Salzman
Licenced Clinical Psychologist
Dept. of Psychology & Brain Science
Washington University of St. Louis
1 Brookings Dr.
St. Louis, MO 63130

45

FLOR AGUILAR

He didn't have to include her, which was confusing. Or, not confusing so much as presented a set of questions about the future. Namely, would it be their future, a shared future, the two of them living as a couple in some distant land, perhaps under assumed names, or would they part ways once they reached civilization, which might come in the form of a logging road or mountain village populated by locals skeptical of two hikers reporting they'd lost their way. As they pushed through the heavy underbrush, Gavin ahead, his machete swinging side to side, her mind kept circling back to that pivotal moment that lay ahead. What would he say? What should she say? Because the fact was he could have killed her too.

That would have been clean and simple. To kill her and Perlah and Isa after he'd killed and disposed of Neil. But he hadn't done that, and therefore must have other intentions or desires. That was the only conclusion she could draw.

The forest surrounding them was more dense than any jungle she'd encountered in Venezuela, even though the canopy above was leafless at this time of year. Flor imagined that moving through this same area in the spring or summer would be impossible. Too much life, growing too quickly. Or when there was snow on the ground, when it would be impassable too.

She trudged forward, finding Gavin's footprints when their strides synced up, aware of the weight in her backpack and grateful for the Zamberlan hiking boots Neil had ordered for her the week before they arrived at the compound. He'd ordered two pairs, reminding her that they didn't know what world they might emerge to in two years, or ten years, and that placing a back-up pair in the temperature-controlled storage room was the least he could do. She'd noticed he had five identical pairs for himself, as well as replacement sneakers, jeans, jackets, rain gear and row upon row, shelf upon shelf of non-perishable food.

In hindsight, what happened over the past eight hours held a certain logic. It made more sense than the sum of the factors that led her to this remote place in the first place and, only yesterday, seemed to foretell she'd be living in an underground apartment for the next two years with a man who was losing his grip on reality. Possibly with his wife and kids, who were very beautiful and apparently equally accomplished, but no doubt also aware that Neil was succumbing to paranoia. For the agreed to $500,000, she definitely would have held up her end of the bargain. She would have given him what he wanted. Which, based on her experience, in no way deviated from what every middle-aged man wants. Or, really, any man of any age. Neil simply wanted to see himself as attractive to somebody. And for that somebody to reflect back to him an image of relevance and virility. And of course to allow, even encourage, that virility to manifest through sex whenever and wherever he might desire. Again, this was in no way unique. Male Psychology 101. No different than what every client she'd serviced over the past four years desired, and the boyfriends along the way too. Neil was far better than most, which is why she'd agreed to his proposition in the first place. He wasn't physically repulsive. He didn't demean her. In fact, he was often charming and humorous. And he clearly cared about her, possibly loved her. But despite all that, the farther she and Gavin got from the bunker and Neil's decomposing body, which she was sure would never be found based on what she'd gathered about Gavin's military background, the more she appreciated the logic of the new direction her life was taking.

The rhythmic, efficient swings of Gavin's blade, the way he

paused to calculate their best route through the forest, it spoke to his ability to thrive in this particular environment, and no doubt many others. This was why Neil had hired him, and so clearly respected him, maybe even envied him. The fact that the man he'd hired to ensure his safety was the one who'd snuffed out his life, and this prior to the apocalypse he envisioned would snuff out human existence at large, was both ironic and also made complete sense to Flor. It reminded her of the untrustworthy architecture that framed the lives of friends, family and acquaintances in her birth country. Their lives and their deaths. If you could zoom way out and look at the big picture, she thought, you had to admit there was almost a humorous quality to it. Although she'd been an atheist for as long as she could remember, it was entertaining to think of a god or gods just fucking with the mortals. Moving pieces around on a giant game board, whimsically knocking them over to see what would happen; killing off one character in order to witness the repercussions for others. Or that Shakespeare play with the fairies in the forest who delighted in just messing with people, projecting their petty jealousies on others rather than dealing with their own issues. The nuns had made her read that play in 8th grade, even act out a few scenes, and now that she was walking through a forest, surrounded by danger but also the possibility of magic and lust and maybe even love, she couldn't help but think about it. Titania and Oberon. Puck and Bottom. She also wondered exactly how Gavin had ended Neil's life, whether he'd suffered, and where Gavin had hidden the body, or body parts.

Gavin reached the crest of a hill and stopped to take a rest. He pulled a water bottle from his pack and offered it to Flor.

"Doing alright?"

She nodded, unscrewed the bottle top, and drank.

"Backpack feel okay? Not too heavy?"

She nodded and returned the bottle.

"I thought it would weigh more," she said. "When you explain this to me, what is inside."

This was true. If she'd understood him correctly, combined they were carrying 110 pounds of gold bricks, worth about six million dollars, as well as banded and unmarked stacks of various currencies worth another million. He'd told her this while kneeling beside her bed that morning, several hours before sunrise. He'd awakened her with a gentle hand on her shoulder and his pointer finger touching his lips. This was a man in control, and she knew to remain silent as he told her Neil was dead and asked if she wanted to leave with him. He explained, in a measured voice, that he'd reached the conclusion that they were in far greater danger staying with Neil, in the bunker, than facing whatever apocalyptic future his model predicted. There was simply no way to know what Neil's paranoia might inflict upon them. He worried he might wake up with a gun in his face one morning. Or that Neil might demand behaviors of them that weren't outlined in the contract and overstepped what he was willing to do for money. He explained he'd been prepared to cut his losses and walk away from the promised $700,000 payday until Neil chose to show him the safe with the gold, silver and currency. As head of security, Neil had insisted Gavin know what was on site and what he was actually protecting, in addition to the human life.

By this point, Flor had been sitting up on her bed. They were side-by-side, and she'd noticed Gavin was already dressed in boots and tactical gear. She also noticed there were two large backpacks on the floor.

"Way I see it, we're putting him out of his misery, his mental anguish, and we also have the opportunity to walk away with enough to set ourselves up for life," he'd said.

Flor had nodded, wondering what exactly he'd done to Neil, and how he'd done it.

"Thing is, it didn't seem fair to do this alone. For me to just walk away knowing you would lose what he'd promised you. So that's why I'm here. To see if you want to leave with me. Right now. Before Perlah and Isa wake up."

———

The way he'd looked at her then, in her predawn bedroom, was the same way he was looking at her now, as they stood taking a break in the middle of a forest so vast she wondered if they'd ever really make it out. He didn't seem to blink, and it was clear he'd thought through all the many potentialities, and was confident he'd made all the right choices so far. She decided now was as good a time as any, and probably better than waiting until they reached civilization.

"There would be more for you without me," she said. "Of course this is true. Much more money if you left me sleeping, or killed me too. Also, I think this would be safer for you, to go alone, because now maybe there is a small chance I say something to somebody, someday. So, because I am thinking about this, I think it is good for me to say this to you now, and for me to understand what you are wanting. In the future."

He smiled.

"Why do you smile?" she said.

"Because I like how direct you are. No B-S."

"Okay, yes. And so what is your answer?"

He nodded and smiled again. She didn't drop her gaze, something she'd always done when they interacted back at the compound while in the presence of Neil. She understood the fragility of the male ego, and hadn't wanted to fuel the fantasies she was sure Neil was already hatching about how she and Gavin were fucking behind his back. Gavin didn't drop the gaze either.

"Isa and Perlah will never know what happened," he said. "Other than the three of us just vanished. You, me and Neil.

They'll never see any of us again. And they also won't report anything to the authorities, because they don't want to get caught up in anything that might jeopardize their visa status."

"Okay," she said. "And so what does this mean for us?"

"From what I can tell, Neil's family won't come looking for him either. At least not anytime soon. I know for a fact they've been ignoring his texts and calls for the past week."

Flor continued to stare directly into his eyes. There was no backing down. She needed to know what he wanted. Whether it was merely what every other man wanted, or something more.

"Between us, in our bags, we're carrying between seven and eight million," he said. "My plan is to buy a ticket to South America, I'm thinking Colombia, and build the life I've been visualizing in my mind since I retired from the military five years ago."

Flor didn't move a muscle, didn't blink. She'd asked her question.

"You ever heard about radical honesty?" he said.

She shook her head.

"Yeah, well I've been doing some reading, and it's basically how I plan to live my life from here on out. Being honest with myself, brutally honest, and also being totally transparent with anyone else I interact with."

He pointed over Flor's shoulder, in the direction they'd come.

"That's hopefully the last life I'm ever gonna take, and the last person whose trust I'll have to betray. Even though, like I said, I'm pretty convinced I did him a favor." He nodded and took a deep breath. Flor could see tears forming in his eyes. He'd broken eye contact and was staring down at the ground.

"Okay, so this life in Colombia, how you imagine this life in your mind, what else do you see?" she said.

He was looking up and over her now, and she could tell the

tears weren't going to jump the banks of his eyelids. He'd controlled the emotion. Or maybe her question was the life raft he'd needed.

"Yeah, so a bunch of years ago, when I finished up a contract down there, I ended up on the north coast. Beautiful little fishing village near Santa Marta. Just a real simple life. I'd like to buy land somewhere in that area."

"Okay?"

"Yeah, so when I'm imagining that right now, and if I'm being a hundred percent honest with myself, what I'm seeing is that you're there with me. So I guess my question is if you'd even consider coming."

"Is this because you think I am attractive and want to fuck me?" she said.

He laughed.

"I'm not telling a joke," she said.

"Yeah, no, okay. Only laughing because... I mean, obviously, who wouldn't? You're like the most beautiful woman I've ever met. So I'd be lying if I said I haven't thought about it. Like, every day since I met you. And I'm done lying, so... yeah."

"Thank you. For not lying."

"Yeah. But... and clearly you know this, but you're obviously more than just the pretty package. I like your attitude. And I've watched you laugh, like the things that make you laugh, and I like your sense of humor."

She raised her eyebrow, shaking her head.

"What?" he said.

"So, maybe I am not clear, but I want you to tell me exactly what you want," she said. "So I can think about it and make a good decision for me. For both of us."

"I get it. Okay. Point is, what I'm really wanting is for you to come to Santa Marta with me, and for us to buy some land and live there and, yeah, see if we can build a happy life together.

Maybe even have kids someday, if that's something you'd even consider."

She nodded.

"What's that mean?" he said. "When you nod like that, is that a yes?"

"No. Definitely not. It means I will need to think about it as we are walking more through this big forest together." She gestured ahead, a smirk on her face. "So... we should keep going, yes?"

Gavin smiled, turned, and began swinging his machete again.

46

ZORA THOMAS

At some point the focus shifts from the desperate need to ascribe blame to questions directed inward, targeting oneself. What could I have done differently — nineteen years ago, six months ago, yesterday — to ensure this isn't our reality now? What were the factors I controlled and, instead of acknowledging the potential triggers and mitigating, I ignored because of self-involvement, laziness, denial, ignorance? Factors like the corrosive family culture I helped shape and then tolerated all these years. Or the knowledge of genetic predispositions on Neil's side of the family, and possibly mine. Or the stories shared and unshared, each with their own form of malignant power.

For me, the moment I knew blaming others was pointless came when I stepped out of the Uber and looked up at the psychiatric ward. It looks like a prison. In effect, it is a prison. Even though Elijah came here voluntarily, accompanied and encouraged by Dr. Salzman, and apparently signed himself in, the fact is he's now legally obligated to stay in a locked ward for an "evaluation period" lasting at minimum 72 hours. He agreed to this because, apparently, he agrees with the expert opinion that he poses a threat to himself and others. To me, however, the irrefutable fact is that he's behind these barred windows, monitored by all these security cameras, only and precisely because I'm his mother. He wouldn't be here, and wouldn't have suffered this "psychotic break", were it not for the fact that I made the choices I did over the past twenty-some years. Many thousands of choices, but chief among them that I agreed to marry Neil twenty-four years ago tomorrow.

———

Another irrefutable fact is that my beautiful boy no longer looks like himself. He sits opposite me on a single bed, back against the wall, legs drawn up before him, and his vibrancy is gone. He's pale. He's too skinny. He wears a hospital gown and has clearly lost all interest in how he looks; a lack of self-consciousness I haven't seen in him since he was a toddler. There's also a medicated lethargy to his movements and posture. Each time he blinks it's like he might not reopen his eyes.

"I'm sorry," he mumbles.

"No, there's nothing in the whole world you need to apologize for, Elijah." I reach over for his hand and he pulls it back.

"One in three," he says. "That's the stat." He nods and there's almost a smirk there, as he stares at the blank wall opposite. He hasn't once looked me in the eye since the attendant with all the keys tethered to his belt unlocked the door to let me in. And relocked it behind me.

"What are you talking about?" I say.

"At the Legacy Museum. That's the stat they're always reminding you about."

"Okay?"

"That one in three end up incarcerated. Black boys born today."

"Okay, not sure exactly what you're talking about, but you're not incarcerated. You know that, right?"

He shrugs.

"It was you that chose to be here," I say. "Because this place is going to help you get back on your feet. Dr. Salzman is pulling together an amazing team. Working together, we're all going to figure out a treatment plan to get you healthy again." My words fill the room but don't project any sense of confidence. I'm unconvinced. It's clear Elijah is too.

"They... they got me on some antipsychotic. Aripiprazole. Makes me tired."

"You should rest then. I'll be here when you wake up. Not going anywhere."

He nods and sinks down on the bed, rotating away, his back to me. I grab a blanket from the bottom of the bed and cover him. Sit back in the chair and scan the room. Nothing sharp. Nothing you could use to kill yourself, other than maybe a sheet. But even there, nowhere to hang it from. And then yourself.

I pull out my phone and find Neil's text from several days ago, the one he sent on the family thread:

> I'm here. Everything is set. Pls confirm that when I give you the go-ahead, you'll make your way here ASAP. I have transport standing by. xox

No one responded, and I'm sure no one will. Unless it's me.

What does Neil need to know about the current situation? Or, really, what would he want to know, given the choices he's already made and his new reality?

According to the doctors, Ira included, Elijah is presenting like many young men and women stricken by schizophrenia. Like Neil's brother, who's been in and out of psychiatric hospitals and halfway houses since he was in his early twenties. Maybe like my aunt, Willamita, who was never properly diagnosed but was known to hear voices and straddle the world we collectively agree is reality and some parallel world that included her dead son, various versions of Satan, and possibly also a merciful and forgiving Lord.

Elijah moans and pulls the blanket up and over his head, curling inward on himself. This is one of the possible outcomes and legacies we never discussed with him, or among ourselves. Did Neil consider the hereditary and environmental probabilities? I'm guessing he did, given the way his mind works. Maybe he was already churning through the various scenarios that first time he held Elijah in the maternity ward at Lennox Hill. Later, did he have his team run some numbers? Odds of bipolar disorder. Odds of schizophrenia. Odds of getting hit by a curb-jumping taxi or pushed in front of the A train by another tormented soul. Odds of being wrongly arrested and killed because some racist cop determined he wasn't pure of blood. If Neil did harness the predictive power of his algorithm for this, he never shared his findings. The sad truth is Elijah making the connection to incarceration is right. This is a form of prison and, within the multitude of possible outcomes, this is the one he's living, and may live for the rest of his life. Locked up, locked away, just like his father in his bunker.

I text Neil:

> I'm sure you've realized this by now, but we're not coming to join you. None of us. I do hope that somehow you're able to find peace, Zora

47

NATASHA THOMAS-ENGEL

So Amtrak isn't a glamorous way to travel. Not much of a news headline there. I mean there's like zero similarities to how it's depicted in Russian lit from a hundred and fifty years ago, or even what I've experienced in Europe and Japan in my own lifetime. Neither is riding the bus, at least if you're talking about the Greyhound from Montgomery to Mobile.

But just because it didn't match the way I'd built it up in my fantasy doesn't mean that you're not going to have the opportunity to witness young lovers making out in the far back row, tented under jackets, or bitchy tweens hissing at their parents, or lonely old men staring out the window for hours upon hours, probably just watching a lifetime of regrets play in a loop, all the heartache and broken promises and squandered opportunities unspooling before them like some vintage movie with a soundtrack that keeps hiccuping. It's like the subway that way, in that it's a mode of transportation that exposes you to all sorts of people and gives you little glimpses into their lives. Or maybe not really all sorts, because it's definitely the case that the passengers on these trains and buses are very poor, and on the NYC subway you'll always have some corporate or media or fashion types sprinkled in.

Also, because there's not a train station in Mobile, and the bus station has zero charm, I decided not to give Milton Riggs Jr. any advance warning I was coming. Like if he wasn't going to be standing there in his suit, shoes freshly shined, holding a handful of peonies so huge and white they'd blind us in the afternoon light, then it just seemed better this way. Even though this way brings with it all sorts of unknowables.

Take the fact that I'm standing here in front of his grandmother's house on Azalea Street. If you sort of pull back and look at it with some sort of omniscient eye, the whole scenario is almost like the most perfect definition of "teenage folly". Like it could explode in my naive face in so many different ways and directions and, because of that, probably will also provide some "teachable moments" that will be of benefit as I continue to stumble forward with whatever my life is and might be.

So I think it's important to remind myself that this is actually what I had in mind when we were texting that first time. Just like this, I imagined I'd be standing on the sidewalk with my feet mere inches from officially being on his grandmother's property, and the butterflies would be flying around like insane hornets in my belly, and my hands would be sweaty because it's Mobile and humid, but also sweaty because of my unfortunate condition, which I recently learned is called hyperhidrosis, and is probably something Milton will have to learn to love — or at least overlook — or it'll be a deal-breaker. And my hope, right now, is that Milton's grandmother is still at work, and his sister is still at daycare or some afterschool enrichment program, and maybe, if my visioning was and is correct, Milton recently returned home from band practice and has already showered and is now eating a snack or doing homework or reading some new manga he brought home from Books-A-Million.

Another thing I know is that I don't want to live a life of regrets. Books have shown me that and so have all the people on the trains and buses over the past few days. I don't want to stare out the window at a life that passes me by, or that I allow to pass me by because I'm paralyzed by the unpredictable and the unknown.

One thing I did get clarity on during the many hours of travel is that for sure I won't be living in some bunker with my father and his mistress, planning and hoping for the day when we can emerge to rule over some new and recently devastated world. Another thing I know is that I don't have the tools to heal my mother from the pain and regret and second-guessing that shackles her. And, although I love my brother, the Golden Boy around whom our family has always revolved, I'm pretty sure that if I can't comprehend and control the complexities that live within me, there's no way I'll be of any help to him. Plus it's never seemed like he's wanted or needed anything from me.

So I guess this is basically like the "two roads diverged" moment. Or maybe the fact that I'm standing here, and got on that train in New Haven in the first place, means I've already taken the road less traveled. And because I made that choice, either out of personal courage or maybe because I was able to access some preordained and otherworldly script, means that when I step onto this walkway, one foot before the next, and ring the doorbell, Milton will open the door with a wide smile and unquestioning eyes. His eyes will be unquestioning because he also knows this must be fated, and that of course he's been expecting me. And he'll step aside, gesturing with a confident hand that I should enter, and, as I do, at the far end of the hallway, on the kitchen table, I'll spot a generous pitcher of sweet tea and two glasses already filled with ice. Waiting for me and for us. Just like he promised. Just like it was promised.

ACKNOWLEDGMENTS

This book benefited from the insight and rigor of readers who engaged with the manuscript at different stages and asked difficult questions when it mattered most.

I'm grateful to Andra Miller for her editorial guidance, to Chonise Bass for her careful and precise copyediting, and to Sandra Rilova for the cover design.

Any remaining errors are my own.

———

Thank you for reading *Ghost Gun*. If you found something meaningful in these pages, please consider leaving a review. Even a brief note helps other readers discover the book. Reviews on Amazon or Goodreads are especially helpful.

ABOUT THE AUTHOR

cc ECK is a writer based between Brooklyn and the American South, whose work explores family inheritance, American violence, and the ways the past refuses to stay buried. *Ghost Gun* is a debut novel.

cceckauthor.com